AF231340

A PROMISE NEVER FORGOTTEN

NEVER FORGOTTEN TRILOGY, BOOK TWO

KALYN COOPER

A Promise Never Forgotten
KaLyn Cooper
Cover Artist: Drue Hoffman
Content Editor: Trenda Lundon
Published 2019
Copyright © 2019, KaLyn Cooper
Printed in the United States of America

ISBN-13: 978-1-970145-10-6

ISBN-10: 1-970145-10-2

All rights reserved. No part of this publication may be reproduced, stored in a retrieval system, or transmitted in any form or by any means, electronic, mechanical, recording or otherwise, without the prior written permission of the author.

This is a work of fiction. The characters, incidents and dialogues in this book are of the author's imagination and are not to be construed as real. Any resemblance to actual events or persons, living or dead, is completely coincidental.

A LETTER TO READERS

Dear Reader,

Thank you so much for purchasing *A Promise Never Forgotten*, the second book in the Never trilogy. This book has many genres including; contemporary, military, seasoned/mature romance, and romantic suspense, all tied together with a friends to lovers trope.

Although *A Love Promise Forgotten* is a complete romance novel with a happy ending for Logan and Teagan, it picks up at the end of A Love Never Forgotten. You may want to read that book first, so you get to meet the characters and understand the overarching suspense plot.

All the members of the failed mission in Syria ten years ago are included in *A Love Promise Forgotten.*

I hope this book makes you smile, cry, cheer, and shake your head as Teagan and Logan find their way to true love.

Don't worry, there's more to come. *A Moment Never Forgotten* will release late in 2019 where all mysteries will be discovered, as well as love for Micah.

I hope you enjoy *A Love Promise Forgotten.*

Always,

KaLyn Cooper

For the latest on works in progress and future releases, check out **KaLyn Cooper's website**

www.KaLynCooper.com https://kalyncooper.com/

Follow **KaLyn Cooper on Facebook** for promotions and giveaways https://www.facebook.com/KaLynCooper1Author/

Sign up for exclusive promotions and special offers only available in **KaLyn's newsletter** http://www.kalyncooper.com/newsletter.html

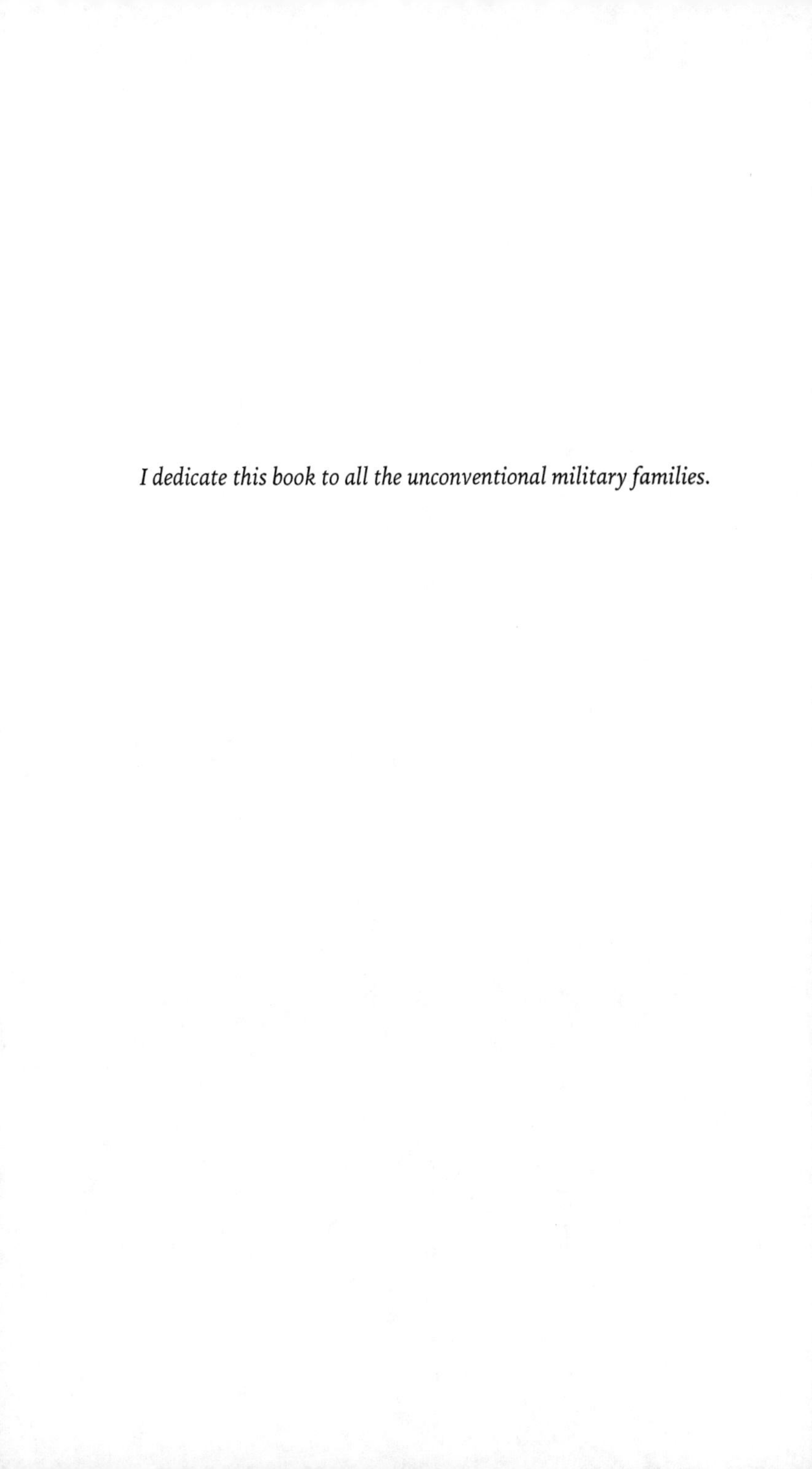

I dedicate this book to all the unconventional military families.

ACKNOWLEDGMENTS

A lot of people were involved in bringing you *A Love Promise Forgotten.*

I'd like to sincerely thank USA Bestselling Author, Maryann Jordan*, for "loaning" me Tony, a primary character from her popular Alvarez Security Agency series. I truly appreciate her friendship and advice, and the privilege to use of a book character.

As always, I'd like to thank the members of the Black Swan Book Club for all their valuable input. The following members assisted in the selection of trilogy character names; Denise Poteete, Melissa Marie, Michelle Lambert, Melissa Hultz, Sara Spence Conger, Jessica Whiteway, and Tamara Graham. Carol J. Thomas suggested Teagan's handle, used in this book.

Many thanks to Leigh Hale for naming the children.

I am a stickler for military accuracy and although I do a lot of research online, sometimes I need a hands-on expert. Thank you, Beth and Daniel O'Neill, for answering my helicopter questions and leading me to Teagan's job.

I can't thank my lunch bunch author friend, Kimberly

Grace, enough. As an attorney, she guided me through the legalities of child services so I could be as accurate as possible.

My sincere thanks to my wonderful content editor, Trenda London, who helped me think through everything from character motivation to conflict development.

Special thanks to my publicist, Drue Hoffman, for this awesome cover, formatting, and putting up with multiple changes.

Last, I thank my husband for showing me silver/seasoned romance and military romance every day.

* Check out all Maryann Jordan's romantic suspense books and series at www.MaryannJordanAuthor.com

PROLOGUE

"Teagan is going to meet us in the hotel room in ten minutes. Logan and Micah split a two-bedroom suite on the top floor so we should have plenty of room." Lizzie clasped her tense hands around her phone and bounced it nervously in her lap.

Out of the corner of his eye, Matthew Saint Clare watched his new wife grin in satisfaction before she added, "They've already swept the place for bugs."

"I hate like hell that they had to do that, but I guess they're as accustomed to it as I am," Matt admitted. Logan Jackson was the Marine lieutenant colonel currently in charge of 2nd Marine Raider Battalion. Their friend, U.S. Navy Captain Micah Reid, was the commanding officer of Naval Special Warfare Group Two.

As of two hours ago, Matt had been promoted from an assistant director to Director of Special Activities Division of the Central Intelligence Agency.

Although each of the organizations had a different mission, together, the three men controlled over three thousand special operators conducting covert activities around the globe. None of them took personal safety for granted. The American public could be so naïve believing they are safe simply because they live in the United States of America. These men knew the truth.

Thinking back to the meeting he and Lizzie had just left at Langley, Matt fought to tamp down the anger growing within him. When she touched his knee, he knew it was to soothe, not to arouse.

"We're doing the right thing," she reassured. "I don't give a shit if Noah Hennel is the Deputy Director of Operations for the whole damn CIA. I don't trust him. Besides, maybe the rest of our team can help us figure out what gold Gabe was talking about."

Matthew wished he could remember what happened during the failed mission ten years ago to blow up a munitions dump in Syria. He'd been left with a traumatic brain injury, a new face, and a rewritten past. But when he met Lizzie, the cap on all those memories started to fracture. The truth had been slowly seeping back into his brain, bits and bursts at a time.

Matt reached over and took Lizzie's left hand in his.

He could feel the wedding ring he had slid on her finger the first time over a decade ago, mere hours before they had been deployed on that disastrous op in Syria. He had recently met the son they had created that night, and a daughter she'd had since. He loved them both. As soon as the paperwork could be filed, they would legally be his children. Well, the children of Matthew Saint Clare, since technically, the CIA had officially buried Mason Sinclair, the man he'd been the first thirty-two years of his life.

Until they could figure out who was behind his brainwashing, and what gold Gabe had been talking about just before he tried to kill both of them, Matthew and Lizzie agreed not to reveal his past to anyone.

He pulled the SUV into a parking space in front of a brightly lit, high-end hotel mixed in with half a dozen others. As they walked toward the front door, he glanced over at the extended stay hotel where her mother was entertaining their children.

Since Gabe had been shot in Matt's living room, the CIA had immediately moved him out of his home as part of the cleanup. Closer to cover up, he speculated.

Grabbing Lizzie's hand, because he loved the fact he could touch her any time he wanted now that she was married to him once again, this time as Matthew Saint Clare, they strode across the parking lot. Ignoring the front desk as though they were guests returning from a long day of touring the DC area, they made their way to the top floor. Before they could knock, Logan opened the door.

"Come on in." He looked down the hall. "I was hoping Teagan would be with you."

Hugging him, Lizzie noted, "She's a few minutes behind us."

"I'm so sorry we have to meet under these circumstances. It seems like the only time we're together anymore is for a funeral." Micah stepped in for a hug from Lizzie. "I know you and Gabe were close."

When she stepped back, she punched her balled fists on her hips and scowled. "I take it you don't know how Gabe was killed?"

A chime filled the air.

"That'll be Teagan," Logan said with a smile as he checked the video on his phone. "I'll let her in, then, Lizzie, you'd better explain."

Teagan blew through the door like a tornado. "So, what

the hell was so fucking important that I needed to come here first before meeting Marsha and helping her get the kids ready for the funeral?"

"I think we should all sit down," Matthew suggested, taking Lizzie's hand and guiding her to the living room area.

When everyone was seated, Lizzie started, as they had agreed on the way over. "Gabriel Davis was not who we thought he was. He was a traitor."

"Whoa, what the hell are you talking about?" Micah jabbed.

"No fucking way," Logan spat.

"Why would you think that?" Teagan asked and she leaned forward.

Lizzie threw her hands up in the stop position. "Just hear me out." She took a deep breath. "I don't know what you've been told, but Matthew shot and killed Gabe."

That hadn't been the way they'd planned to tell their friends. Both Logan and Micah shot from their chairs. Matthew bolted to his feet. "He was going to kill Lizzie. He'd already tried several times."

Aghast, both men stared at her.

"Lizzie, what the fuck is he talking about?" Logan demanded, glaring down at her.

"Robert wasn't killed by accident," she said of her previous husband. "*I* was supposed to be in that car demolished by that big truck. *I* was the intended victim in the mall stabbing."

"Why?" Teagan asked as she put her arm around Lizzie.

"Everything seems to go back to our mission in Syria." Lizzie glanced from one face to the next. "And I think we're all in danger."

Matthew didn't miss the exchanged looked between

Logan and Micah. He knew both men received death threats on a regular basis and laughed it off. They were highly trained special operators. It would take a lot for someone to get the drop on them.

"Sit down," Teagan ordered the men. "I don't have a lot of time right now and I want to hear this." She turned her attention to Lizzie. "Start from the beginning."

Logan checked his watch. "We don't have time for the entire story. Why did Gabe want to kill you, Lizzie?"

She turned those piercing silver eyes toward Matt. They had talked about this, as well, but had agreed his true identity needed to remain a secret. Their greatest fear was that they, whoever the hell *they* were, would try to use the children against them. With a barely perceptible shake of his head, she returned her attention to the others.

"You're right, Logan. We don't have time to explain everything." She glanced, once again, at Matt. "Besides, I'm not sure we can." She took a deep breath and let it out. Then, as though clarifying an after-action report, she began. "Three days ago, while I was at Matthew's house, Gabe showed up and pointed a gun at me. He had Matt's house wired for audio and visual and had heard us talking about the Syrian mission. He kept asking us about gold."

Matthew carefully watched the faces of Logan, Micah, and Teagan. He wanted to see if there was the slightest recognition when the gold was mentioned.

Nothing. Not even a flicker in their eyes.

Lizzie continued, "From what Gabe said, there were gold bars under that building."

Given the shock on all their faces, they didn't know anything about hidden gold bars either. Damn.

"By blowing up the building, we were supposed to bury the gold bars." The corners of Lizzie's mouth turned up a fraction of an inch. "That part worked. The only problem is; the gold is now missing. Gabe ranted about someone double-crossing him and moving the gold."

Lizzie sidled next to Matt and put her arm around his waist. "When Gabe tried to shoot me, Matthew threw me on the floor." She looked up at him with those loving crystalline eyes. "Thank you for saving my life," she said, just above a whisper.

Matt lowered his head and kissed her gently before sliding his lips to her ear. "I had just found you, again. I wasn't going to let anybody take you away from me."

Glancing at the others, Matthew picked up the story. "I grabbed my gun and double-tapped the fucker. Two to the head. At the same time I shot, someone with a high-powered rifle shot him through the heart. They must've been hiding in my backyard."

"He's surrounded by woods," Lizzie interjected.

Matt shook his head. "I thought he was my friend. For the last ten years, I've worked with him, and for him. He's been my mentor at the agency for a decade." Hugging Lizzie to him, he placed a kiss on her head. "He showed up at my house, started talking crazy, and tried to kill the woman I love. I had no choice."

Teagan nodded her head once. "Okay. Matthew, thank you for protecting Elizabeth. I have no idea what came over Gabe, or anything about any damn gold, but if you two think we may be in danger, I'll be more vigilant." She looked at her watch. "Now, if that's all, I really have to go." She stood as though to leave.

"There's more," Lizzie announced, and stared up at Matt.

"We just came from a meeting with Noah Hennel, Deputy Director of Operations." Matt wrapped his arm around Lizzie's shoulders in a half-hug. It was support for both of them. "The agency is declaring this a terrorist attack on a senior agent. As far as they're concerned, Gabe died in the line of duty and will be buried as a hero. His years as Director of Special Activities Division, the innumerable lives he saved, and the threats to the United States government he eliminated in that role, overshadow this one indiscretion. Supposedly, he was influenced by pain medicine he was taking for past injuries."

"The good news is, they have cleared Matthew of any wrongdoing." Lizzie smiled up at him. "Deputy Director Hennel feels that I am no longer in danger. Matt and I are still on administrative leave for the next two days, standard operating procedure for any agent involved in a shooting. Then we are taking a much-needed vacation as we honeymoon in the Caribbean."

Matt gave her lips a quick peck before he added, "We're taking the children with us."

Lizzie smiled. "Thank God it's a two-bedroom condo… with kid activities all day long."

"Given the circumstances, will I see you at the funeral?" Teagan asked as she started toward the door.

"Yes." Lizzie walked beside her. "Director Hennel asked us to put everything that happened that night aside and remember what a good friend he had been to us for so many years."

"Can you do that?" Teagan looked over her shoulder at Lizzie.

"Although Deputy Director Hennel is not in my chain of command," Lizzie glanced at Matt. "He's Matthew's boss, which makes this a command performance. I still haven't reconciled the man we knew with the one who tried to kill me just days ago. I'm going today to bury the man I once thought I knew and be there in support of Marsha. By the way, how's she doing?"

Teagan shrugged. "She and Gabe had been separated for almost a year, so in a way, he was already gone from her life. She's much more concerned about the kids, but between us, he wasn't involved in their lives very much. That's part of the reason she was divorcing him."

Although Matthew would never say anything, least of all to Teagan, he knew that Gabe had stepped out on Marsha most of their married life. The man had an unusual way of looking at relationships. Gabriel believed that sex was separate from love. A wife was for love and children. But if you were offered sex—as Matthew and Gabe often were since they trolled the bars together on a regular basis—it was perfectly okay to accept the proposition, as long as there was no emotional attachment.

Matt looked at the love of his life, overjoyed that they had found their way to each other once again. The Mason Sinclair part of him regretted all those other women he'd been with, but Matthew Saint Clare had been single. Now, he could never be with another woman other than Lizzie. He loved her to the depths of his heart and soul.

After hugging Teagan goodbye, Lizzie announced. "We need to go get ready." Walking over to Logan and Micah, she held out her arms. "This is far from over. Promise me you'll watch your back."

Micah took her in his big strong arms. "Anything you need, just call." He glanced over to Matthew before returning his attention to Elizabeth. "Congratulations. I already have a good feeling about this guy."

Matt caught the little twitch at the corners of her mouth. Yeah. Maybe, on some cellular level, Micah remembered his friendship with Mason Sinclair. Their whole team had become very tight, extremely quickly.

"Hey, my turn." Logan reached for Lizzie as soon as Micah released her. "Same goes for me. Anything you need. Anytime. I'm just a phone call away. And as for the big guy over there, I think you got yourself a good one, this time." When he released her, he followed her over to Matt and offered his hand. "Thank you for saving Elizabeth. She's very special to us. Take care of her."

"Always," Matt confirmed as he took her hand and left the suite. The day he could tell them all the truth couldn't come soon enough. He missed their friendship. But there was so much yet to be uncovered before that could happen.

CHAPTER ONE

Marine Lieutenant Colonel Logan Jackson sat in the front row of St. Paul's Catholic Church and stared at the unsmiling picture of Gabriel Davis. Official photographs usually sucked, but this one was extremely unsettling.

Or perhaps it was the brightly gleaming silver urn that sat next to the large framed photograph.

Maybe Logan was just irritated that he had considered this man his friend for the past ten years. Obviously, he hadn't known him at all if the top-secret report he and Micah received from their boss at USSOCOM could be believed.

Gazing at Gabe's likeness, Logan wanted to reach into the past and rip the prominently displayed flag off the lapel of the dark charcoal suit he'd worn for the photographer. Good men had died for that flag and everything it meant. Just yesterday, two of his men had to be flown out of northern Africa. One was fighting for his life and the other would have to learn a new normal without his left arm.

Logan tuned out the priest as he droned through the funeral Mass.

The overwhelming smell of lilies saturated the air and turned his stomach. He fucking hated funerals. In his twenty-two-year career as a Marine, he had buried far too many good men.

Gabriel Davis would not be counted among them. He was a deceitful liar according to the report.

He may have been born in Chicago and raised Catholic, but during college Gabe had denounced the United States of America to follow the teachings of Nassar al Jamil. The half-crazy extremist had been building an army for nearly twenty years, claiming to have been chosen by Allah to establish the New Islamic State. He seemed to have stayed off the Top Ten Most Wanted List of international terrorists. Maybe now they knew why.

Gabriel Davis was a traitor.

Yet, that fact had been hidden by the Central Intelligence Agency where Gabe had been running covert ops all over the world. Had he used his position to protect al-Jamil? Who else within the CIA knew about his relationship with the terrorist?

Both Logan and Micah had hoped the new information they received just before they left for the funeral would answer the many questions they had about their former friend. Instead, it had them asking more. Nothing was making sense. Especially the talk of gold. His thoughts were interrupted by footsteps in the aisle.

Deputy Director of Operations Hennel stood next to the picture less than ten feet away and hailed Gabe as a hero. Well, according to the official report approved by Hennel, Gabe had died in the line of duty from a terrorist's bullet.

It was all bullshit.

Maybe that's why Logan was so pissed off. He knew the truth. Or thought he did. He had spin-doctored enough after-action reports to read between the lines. Gabe may, or may not, have been working as a double agent. He may, or may not, have been recruited by the CIA while in college to spy on Nassar al-Jamil's organization.

What Logan did know, for sure, was that Matthew Saint Clare had shot Gabe a millisecond before he fired on Elizabeth Kamp, one of Logan's best female friends, and a former teammate. But there had been a second shooter. Maybe the so-called terrorist was behind the sniper scope. All three of those bullets were swept under the rug of operational security.

Elizabeth and Matthew thought everything pointed back to that failed Syrian mission ten years ago. It had been a clusterfuck. Losing their friend, Mason Sinclair, that night had been hard to take. Elizabeth had totally lost her shit when the building had exploded early, with Mason still inside. When Austin was born nine months later, everyone understood her reaction to his death.

Matthew Saint Clare popped into Logan's head. He seemed like a good man. He and Elizabeth had clicked almost instantly. For a brief second, Logan wondered what that would be like, to meet someone and immediately know that they were meant for you. He shrugged off the notion. It had never been that way with any of his relationships.

The newlyweds were sitting two rows behind Gabe's first wife, Janey, and their eighteen-year-old son, Bradley. Marsha's parents had chosen the opposite end of that row. Her father, a retired CEO, checked his watch every five minutes and looked inpatient with the Mass.

Logan glanced to the other end of the family seating at Teagan Williams, who had been on their five-person covert team. The joint task force idea had been to test the integration of men and women from different military services under extremely stressful circumstances. Unfortunately, their Syrian mission hadn't turned out as expected. As a team, they had trained and worked well together. Although they had achieved the mission of destroying the ammunitions dump, they had lost a team member.

Logan examined the small-framed former Seahawk pilot who seemed almost fragile holding the small child. He would kill anyone who tried to hurt her. He chuckled inwardly. Knowing Teagan, she would have the perpetrator dead on the ground at her feet before he even had his weapon pulled. She was one hell of a woman. He was proud to call her his friend.

Teagan held Gabe's four-year-old daughter in her lap. Anora rested her small head on her godmother's shoulder, the child's soft blonde curls blending perfectly with hers. Not really a surprise. Teagan had told him that during flight school, she and Marsha had often been mistaken as sisters. As he glanced between the two women, Logan could easily see the similarities in their classic facial structure, long hair, and pretty blue eyes.

Marsha Davis dabbed at those bright eyes as a nun held onto the last mournful notes of *Amazing Grace*. Logan was a little surprised that the former Navy pilot was displaying so much emotion given that she and Gabe had been in the process of a divorce, separated for eleven months. At least she could save some attorney fees now, Logan thought cynically.

His own divorce had cost him thousands, but it was worth every dime to rid himself of Kember. She had gotten what she wanted in the end. And later, what she deserved.

"All rise." The priest's words jerked Logan back to the present and away from the past he'd rather forget.

A small soft hand slid into his. Without moving his head, Logan glanced at the growing boy to his side. As clearly as though it were yesterday, Logan remembered holding a tiny Brann in that very church seven years ago as a different priest baptized him. Logan and Teagan had made promises to God, Gabe, and Marsha to be there for Brann. Three years later, they had repeated the ceremony for his little sister, Anora. The sweet child now stood holding hands with both her mother and Teagan.

As he looked up to Christ hanging on the cross, Logan vowed, once again, that he would be there for those children. Always.

When his gaze dropped to Gabriel's photograph, he worried how hard it would be to hide his true feelings for their father, the traitorous hero.

"This concludes our ceremony. The interment of Gabriel Davis will take place at a later time with a private family ceremony." The priest gestured toward the urn. "The family asks that you join them in the social meeting area for the bereavement meal."

A white-gloved usher came to the end of the pew and indicated they should leave. With Brann's hand locked in his, Logan strode down the aisle, slowing when he realized the young boy took two steps to every one of his. In the lobby, they were met by the funeral director who pulled Marsha, the children, Teagan, and Logan into a private room off to the side.

"Do you need a few minutes to surreptitiously gather yourselves before facing all of Gabriel's friends and coworkers?" The man's warm voice was soothing.

"No." Marsha assessed her two children. "No. I believe we're fine. I'd like to get this over as soon as possible."

The man in the black suit and gray tie simply nodded. "I'll do what I can to hurry this along."

"I'd appreciate that." Marsha took a hand from each child. "We're ready." When he opened the door, she slowly inhaled a deep breath, squared her shoulders, and walked to the church's social area.

Logan touched Teagan's arm as she passed by him. "How's she doing?"

"Better than I expected." His friend shrugged. "They'd been separated for nearly a year and he hadn't been very active in their lives for the past two years. In reality, her life isn't going to change very much. She's concerned about the children. Brann is at that hero worship stage where he should be attached to his father, but he isn't. Anora barely knows the man." She corrected herself. "Knew the man."

It was clear what Logan needed to do. "I can take a few additional days' leave and spend some time with Brann while I'm here. Maybe he can come down and hang out with me for a week or two at Camp Lejeune before school starts." It might be kind of cool to share his world with the young boy.

Sorrow sliced through Logan once again for the son, or daughter, he never had. Kember, that fucking bitch, had lied to him about trying to get pregnant after their decision to grow their family. Pregnancy is nearly impossible when you have an intrauterine device. Teagan's voice jolted him back to the present.

"For a kick ass Marine, you have such a soft heart." She laid her palm over his heart and it kicked hard. No woman had touched him with such tenderness in years.

"Not really. I'm just trying to help out, like a good

godfather should." He held her gaze. "Sorry, but I'm not comfortable taking on Anora." He wasn't sure he was happy being responsible for a seven-year-old round-the-clock. Logan reached up and gripped her shoulder. "I'll leave her to her godmother."

"I'm more than happy to take on that child. I love that little girl. I love them both." Teagan's grin warmed his entire body. "Come on," she insisted. "Let's go help Marsha get through the next hour, then let's get the hell out of here. After everything we've been through today, I'm in serious need of a drink."

"Right there with you." Logan held open the door and walked beside her down the hall toward low, reverent voices and the tinkling of silverware on plates.

Marsha's parents were the first ones finished with their meal.

"We hate to eat and run, but your dad wants to get to the RV rally as soon as possible so we get a good space in the park." Her mother gently ran a hand over Marsha's hair and rested it on her shoulder. "Call us if you need anything. We'll get there as soon as we can." She stepped between the two children and hugged them. "Maybe next time you can come and spend a few days with Meme and Pops in the coach."

At the grunt from Marsha's father, Logan looked at the man's scowl. When he realized people were looking at him, he forced a smile. "That would be fun, right kids?"

"Sure." Brann's noncommittal tone spoke volumes.

Anora threw both arms around her grandmother. "Could we? Really?"

Marsha took over the awkward moment. "We'll see, sweetie. You've never been camping and I'm not sure you would enjoy it. Maybe when Meme and Pops are camping closer to DC, we can go visit them and try out camping."

With wide eyes, the little girl excitedly turned her attention to her grandparents. "How soon are you going to camp near us?"

"Not sure there, little darling." Her grandfather's smile was not for her as he threw his arm around his wife. "We've got big plans for the rest of this summer. We're headed to the RV rally over on the Eastern shore right now, then we're going to drive up the coast. I feel like eating lobster in Maine." He looked down at his wife. "We really need to get going, dear."

Marsha stood and hugged her parents. "Have fun at the beach."

For the next hour as Gabe's coworkers, family friends, acquaintances through church, and several social organizations Marsha was involved in, paid their condolences, their former team, plus Matthew, stayed close to Marsha. Both children clung to her side. Anora often hid behind her mother's flowing dress, obviously overwhelmed by all the adults.

Logan had never developed a close relationship with the little girl, like he had with Brann, but watching her cower behind her mother made him want to swoop in and protect her. He felt this insatiable need to make her feel safe.

Gabriel's first wife, Janie, and their only child, Bradley, stood a few feet away. Logan found it interesting that she had remarried a much older man and never had more children. He had passed away a year ago from a heart attack. A few people had approached them and exchanged words of sorrow, but most were congratulating Bradley and inquiring about his first few weeks at West Point.

"Oh, fuck." Teagan spoke under her breath.

Logan followed her gaze to the redhead in the tight green dress making a beeline for Marsha.

"I've got this," Matthew announced as he stepped away from the group to intersect the diva's progress.

Gabe's brief and tumultuous marriage to Lacey had ended relatively quickly. While they were both going through divorce at the same time, he and Logan had spoken often. Each had married shortly after returning from the failed Syrian mission. Sometimes, Logan wondered if the death of Mason, and the realization that life was too short, had anything to do with their hasty decisions to marry.

Smiling diplomatically, Matthew guided Lacey away from the other ex-wives.

"I have every right to be standing there with *them*." Her loud voice carried across the room.

Janie and Marsha exchanged a nervous glance.

Logan couldn't hear what Matthew was saying, but he seemed to be calming Gabe's second wife.

"Dodged that bullet," Teagan said, leaning into Logan. "At least Marsha's crazy ass sister, Ashley, isn't here."

"Yeah, I'm surprised she missed an opportunity for her over-the-top style drama." Logan scanned the room, checking each door, half expecting to see the drugged-out bitch make a grand entrance.

"Thank Christ, she's in rehab...again." Teagan glanced over at him. "That's one less thing for Marsha to worry about."

Silently, Logan agreed.

As the line exiting the bereavement dinner dwindled for a moment, Marsha turned to Teagan. "Could you watch the kids for a couple hours tomorrow? I need to clean out Gabe's apartment. When I called to cancel his lease, they only gave me three days." She then turned her attention to Micah and Logan. "If either of you are going to be around, would you mind helping me with boxes? Everything is either going to go to the dumpster or charity."

"I'll be more than happy to help you," Logan offered.

Micah looked worried. "Let me see if I can rearrange a few things at work. I'll let you know by the time we get back to your house."

"I don't want to take you away from something important, Micah," Marsha protested. "I just need someone to carry the heavier boxes and Logan will be there."

"How about I come up and help you this weekend?" Micah sounded hopeful. "You said earlier that you needed to clean out his office. I can help you with that."

"That would be wonderful." Marsha smile was genuine and thankful. "I don't want to sound like a bitch, but I'd like to get him out of our lives and move on." She gave her children one-armed hugs. "We deserve a fresh clean start."

"You're not thinking about moving, are you?" Teagan interjected.

"Actually, I am." Marsha glanced down at her son. "Brann will be entering a new school this year." She shifted her gaze to her daughter. "And Anora's about to begin pre-kindergarten, so the timing is good. They would be making new friends anyway. My parents aren't getting any younger, so moving closer to their home in Asheville, North Carolina is a serious consideration. There are several military bases in North Carolina and plenty of open federal jobs. Hopefully, I could just transfer."

"I thought you liked your job at Homeland Security," Teagan protested.

"I do." Marsha gave a small smile and a nod to three

men in suits across the room. "But with Gabe gone, there's really no reason for me to stay in the DC area."

With Matthew clasping her elbow, Lacey sashayed past Janie and Bradley without a word. She stopped abruptly in front of Marsha. "I'll be in contact with you to see what Gabriel left me in his will," Lacey announced.

Marsha raised her eyebrow. "Don't bother. As the executor, I can tell you that you weren't even mentioned."

"But Gabriel and I were—" she pleaded with crocodile tears.

"Divorced. A decade ago." Teagan stepped between the two women. "Matthew, would you be so kind as to escort this woman out of here?"

"Time to go, Lacey." Matthew tugged at her elbow. Quietly he added, "If you know what's good for you, don't ever try to contact Marsha."

"Gabriel promised he'd take care of me," Lacey protested.

"He also couldn't divorce you fast enough." Matthew exited the building, practically dragging Lacey the entire way.

Logan liked the way Matthew handled that situation. Elizabeth's new husband was growing on him, but he would always miss Mason Sinclair. Now, there was a good man.

When Matthew returned, he went directly to Marsha. "She won't be bothering you again."

"Thank you, Matthew." Marsha glanced at the three men making their way toward her. "Do you still work in the same department?"

"Yes." He looked sheepish for a second before he announced, "I'll be taking over for Gabe."

Marsha looked relieved. "Would it be possible…could I

bother you…to return anything personal that he may have had in his office at work?"

"Certainly." Matthew gave her a reassuring smile. "I have to stop in the office tomorrow anyway. May I bring the things I find to your home tomorrow afternoon?" At her hesitation, he added, "I'm sure Lizzie and the children would also enjoy a visit."

Marsha smiled brightly. "Yes. That would be wonderful."

"Thank you for handling that, Senior Special Agent Saint Clare." Deputy Director of Operations Noah Hennel stepped next to Matthew and held out his hand to Marsha. "Gabriel was one of our best agents and will truly be missed. I considered him a friend as well and I will miss him even more in that capacity."

Marsha momentarily seemed surprised but covered it quickly. "Thank you for allowing Matthew to clean out Gabe's office at work. I can honestly tell you I'm not looking forward to going through his office at home."

Director Hennel raised an eyebrow. "Forgive me, but I was under the impression that Gabriel had moved out."

Logan's senses piqued. Why would Gabriel's boss care?

Covering her slight embarrassment, Marsha said, "He did, but he still used his office at our house." She shrugged. "I guess he didn't have a safe in his apartment."

If Logan hadn't been watching, he would have missed the slight widening of the operations director's eyes. Was he worried that Gabe had brought classified information home and kept it in his safe?

Logan thought about the contents of his own home safe which contained a few guns, a couple thousand in cash, his personal passport as well as his red jacketed diplomatic passport, and, yes, a few classified documents that he needed to review before he returned to work.

Matthew must've been thinking along the same lines. "How about I help you sort through the contents tomorrow when I bring you the personal items from Gabe's office."

Hennel didn't exactly look relieved, more resigned. That was strange. He should have complete trust and confidence in Matthew, yet he didn't look pleased at the suggestion of his new Special Activities Division Director who had one of the highest security clearances of anyone in the U.S. government.

Logan stored that tidbit of information.

Giving Matthew a perfunctory smile, Hennel nodded. "I'm sure anything you find work-related will be immediately returned to Langley."

That was an order if Logan had ever heard one, and as a career Marine, he'd personally been given orders for over twenty-two years. Perhaps Hennel didn't trust anyone.

During the previous conversation, Marsha's eyes had darted back and forth between the two men until the next man in line cleared his throat. She extended her hand. "Thank you for coming. Did you work with Gabriel?"

"Yes, ma'am, I'm Deputy Director Stephen Boyer." He took her hand and held it. "On behalf of Director Mueller, we wish to extend our condolences. Senior Special Agent Davis has been an integral asset to the Central Intelligence Agency for over twenty years. The agency is doing everything within its power to track down your husband's killer."

Matthew's wince wasn't missed by Logan, or anyone else on their former team.

Lies.

The CIA was known for them.

If anyone was ever accused of murdering Gabe, he would be merely a sacrificial lamb, probably guilty of something equal or worse than murder. He hoped the clandestine organization wouldn't hang Matthew out to dry. Logan was beginning to like the guy.

The word *killer* spoken by the number two man in the Central Intelligence Agency seemed to stun Marsha. She visibly gathered herself before she spoke. "Thank you. Gabe worked hard to eliminate every threat to the U.S. government, but he always knew he could be in someone's crosshairs." She swallowed hard. "He would've preferred going in the line of duty over the slow death of suffering from cancer like his father."

"He died a hero, Mrs. Davis." When the second highest ranking man within the CIA laid a hand on Brann's shoulder, Logan wanted to rip it off. He wondered if this man even knew the truth.

The third man shuffled in front of Marsha. With his dark brown skin, Middle Eastern facial features, and nearly black hair, he and Hennel could be cousins. Their body language spoke volumes about their dislike for one another. Logan wondered if they were both practicing Muslims. Perhaps it went even deeper and one was Shiite and the other Sunni.

"Mrs. Davis, I am Joseph Lambert, Deputy Director for Support." At her confused look, the man with nearly black eyes added, "That's what we call our human resources. I have been assured that my assistant director has been in touch with you, assisting you through this difficult time."

"Yes, Berit Barker has been wonderful." Marsha threw a glance toward the brunette woman in her mid-forties speaking in low tones with the funeral director and his staff. "I'm grateful for all her help. She's been invaluable to me over the last few days."

"Excellent." He gave her a toothy grin. "She will continue to be your liaison for the next year. If we at the Central Intelligence Agency can do anything for you, don't hesitate to contact Ms. Barker."

Logan knew better than most that the weirdest shit could pop up over the next year. He lost his mother twelve years ago to a heart attack and was not at all involved in the decisions for her funeral. It wasn't until his father passed away just over a year ago that he realized everything involved in the business of death. He'd never been a Casualty Assistance Officer, although he'd assigned plenty as a commanding officer.

There were so many important decisions to be made quickly when all you wanted to do was grieve. He had never discussed his father's final wishes, and as an only child, everything fell on his shoulders. He alone had to decide on everything from viewing hours to the songs during the funeral Mass. The biggest surprise was mail that still arrived a year later, asking to renew his annual donations, or reminding him that an investment rolled over once again.

Pulling himself from the past, Logan's gaze swept the room. There were always a few stragglers, but the ladies of the church were already cleaning tables and packaging left over food.

"You ready to leave?" Teagan asked Marsha.

Nodding, she hugged her children to her sides. "I think we need some alone time." She glanced down at her droopy-eyed daughter. "And a nap. We're all rather exhausted."

Micah, whose phone had buzzed several times during

the past hour, swept in first. "I'm sorry, but I really do need to get back to Dam Neck." He kissed Marsha on the cheek. "I'll see you this weekend."

When Matthew and Elizabeth moved in to say goodbye, Logan caught up with Micah.

"Problems?" He asked his longtime friend.

"Some of my boys are in trouble in northeastern Iraq. I really need to get to the ops center," Micah gave him a considering look. "They are actually near Urmia, Iran gathering intel on Nassar al-Jamil. Rumor has it he's establishing his New Islamic State on the shores of Lake Urmia. Do you have anybody even close to that area?"

"Not that I can think of off the top of my head, but I can call General Lyon." Logan whipped out his phone.

"Thanks for the offer." Micah opened the exterior door. "As soon as I get in my car, I have a conference call with the general."

"Stay in touch." Logan called to his friend then turned to go back inside and came face-to-face with Teagan. "You're leaving?"

"Yes. We're done for today." She gave him a weary smile. "I wouldn't turn down a drink, if you're interested."

Oh, he was interested.

CHAPTER TWO

"Thanks for coming with me this afternoon." Teagan touched Logan's rock-hard bicep and gave it a little squeeze. Damn, the man was ripped. Impressive for someone pushing forty-five. She mentally shrugged. Of course he was. He was an active duty Marine, required to take a Personal Fitness Test twice a year. Plus, he was still a special operator and lead by example. She wondered if he got up before dawn to run and swim with his men.

"No problem, I enjoy spending time with the kids. How long do you think Marsha needs us to keep the children away from the house?" Logan asked Teagan as they followed Brann and Anora around the Great Cats exhibit at the Smithsonian National Zoo in Washington DC.

"Gabe didn't have that much clothing left at the house." Teagan noted quietly, wondering if Logan needed to leave, or if he was just bored. "But Marsha told me she hadn't even started on his office." She glanced over her shoulder at him. "It didn't take you long to go through his apartment this morning."

"Can you see the mama lion and her cubs?" Brann

asked Anora as he pointed down over the edge of the concrete wall. He tried to lift his sister, but Logan grabbed her and planted the little girl on his hip.

As the children watched the clumsy cubs try to crawl up the large rocks to the upper level, Logan leaned toward Teagan. "It was a completely furnished two-bedroom apartment so not much of the contents were his. All the clothes were donated to a charity that showed up just as we were finishing. There was surprisingly little in the office. He had a small laptop that Marsha took thinking Brann might like to use it for playing games. The desk drawer was full of thumb drives that at some point, someone needs to go through."

"She may need to give those to Matthew," Teagan suggested. Glancing toward Logan, she noticed how casually he held the little girl and wondered why he had never remarried. He'd make a great dad. He was wonderful with Brann.

"Good idea." Logan let Anora down as she chased her brother around the circle of big cats to check out the tigers. "There was a small container with more than a dozen microSD drives that Matthew should check out, too. All he had in the file drawers were a few personal bills; the lease for his rarely-used sports car, and a copy of the divorce papers, unsigned by the way. On the desk, he had a few pictures of the kids–all three of them."

Teagan purposely walked slower, allowing the children to get a few steps ahead. "Marsha said she didn't care about losing his deposit and was going to let the leasing agency deal with cleaning the apartment. I think she was afraid of finding remnants of other women left behind. She was relatively sure he didn't have the next Mrs. Gabriel

Davis already selected, but she didn't want to know who had been sleeping in his bed."

"I didn't see any indication of women." Logan grinned sarcastically. "That's probably why Marsha asked me to clean out his drawers while she tackled the closets. She only took a small box home with her."

"Are there tigers?" Anora asked excitedly.

"I don't see any," Brann replied. He turned toward his sister. "It's pretty hot out here. Maybe they're staying cool inside their cave."

Teagan saw the slightest movement in the far corner, deep in the shadows. She picked up Anora and pointed. "See how their stripes hide them? And their brown color blends in with the dead grass."

When the little girl wrapped her arms around Teagan's neck, she almost melted with love. If she had one true regret in life, it was not having children. For the longest time, she didn't think she wanted kids. Now, she couldn't have them.

She had loved the fast-paced life as a Navy helicopter pilot. Unlike so many other female pilots, she enjoyed being deployed. She lived for the adrenaline rush every time she donned her helmet and strapped into the ugly leather seat. She loved the way her heartbeat increased when she grabbed the stick and lifted off the earth, challenging gravity, focused on getting her passengers to the landing zone, or picking them up safely and getting them back to the ship or base. But that life was over. She now worked on helicopters on paper, only getting to fly during testing.

"They should mow the lawn so we can see the animals," Anora suggested, bringing Teagan out of her thoughts of the past. She hugged her goddaughter and inhaled that little girl scent.

Back in her twenties, had she known how much love she had for a child, she might have made different decisions. At forty-two, , she knew things about herself that made her both sad and relieved that she'd never had children. So, she would live vicariously through her best friend, Marsha, loving on her godchildren as often as possible.

As they continued around the circle, Teagan saw the sign for the bathrooms. "Let's make a pit stop and hit the restrooms. You two have been so good, maybe we'll be able to get some ice cream, or at least a cold soda, over at the grill."

"I don't have to go potty, but I want ice cream," Anora announced.

"Tell you what," Teagan kneeled down so they were eye to eye. "Why don't you give it a try. Let the air hit it and see what happens. It's a long way back to the car."

Begrudgingly, the little girl agreed.

Logan methodically scanned the area constantly as they walked down the wooded path. Nervously, Teagan grabbed Anora's hand. Did he actually believe they were in danger? Had they put the children in peril by bringing them out in this public place?

Over drinks last night, she and Logan had discussed the events of the day. He had shared with her the basics of the report from USSOCOM. Not for the first time, Teagan regretted introducing her former roommate to Gabe. They had seemed so happy, especially in the beginning. He had been a beaming father when both children were born.

Although Teagan and Marsha had always been close, her friend had never indicated why they had separated.

Maybe now that he was gone, Marsha would feel more comfortable talking about what happened, or didn't happen, between them.

By the time Teagan and Anora had waited through the long line to use the restroom, Logan and Brann were waiting for them, ice cream and sodas in hand.

"What took so long?" Logan asked while handing her a Coke.

She sniggered. "You haven't spent much time with women in public places, have you?"

He looked sheepish. "Well, not really."

Pointing to the long line that extended outside the restroom, Teagan commented, "That's what took so long. Obviously, public restrooms were designed by men. A woman would have made the ladies' restroom twice as big with three times as many stalls. On more than one occasion, I've seriously considered announcing that I was gender identifying as a male just so I could use the men's room."

Logan tried to fight a grin…and failed. Damn, he had a great smile. Too bad she didn't get to see it more often. He was the ultimate in serious warrior. "You might be shocked at what you see with a group of men lined up at urinals."

Glancing around to be sure the children were out of earshot, Teagan gave him a sassy grin. "It takes more than a line of men's dicks to shock me. If you've seen one, you seen them all." Then she corrected herself. "Okay, if you seen the two different kinds, circumcised and uncircumcised, then you've seen them all."

Logan leaned in close and whispered. "I wouldn't be so sure about that if I were you."

"Let's head for the fish," Brann said between bites.

"Sounds like a plan, but it's a long walk," Teagan warned.

The children finished off their snacks and headed down the paved trail.

"Listen, Logan, I wanted to apologize about last night. I'm sorry I had to bug out early. Mom's dementia is getting worse, seemingly every day." Teagan was so embarrassed. She'd gotten a phone call from the nursing home where her mother had been for the last five years. They wanted to sedate her because she was screaming for her daughter, Jessica. Their records indicated that Teagan was her only child. She'd left Logan at the bar and immediately driven to the nursing home. It'd taken nearly two hours, and a mild sedative, to calm her mother down.

"Not a problem. Did you get things straightened out?" Logan was such a nice guy.

"Yeah." Teagan was not going to discuss her mother's crazy rantings. Wanting to change the subject, she asked, "Did we put the kids in danger by bringing them here?"

"No," he said without hesitation. "Why would you think that?"

"Because you're constantly scanning our surroundings." She followed his gaze. "Do you think someone is after us?"

Logan shook his head. "It's just habit. A good one, by the way. I'm constantly aware of my surroundings, and you should be too." He shrugged. "Maybe after I've been out for six years, I won't be so hypervigilant."

She suddenly felt terrible for not being more aware of everything around them. She hadn't even thought about a secondary exit, or sniper hides. Damn. She'd been out of the game too long.

Sipping the last of her drink, she wished it had rum in it. She'd entertained the children in their home for three and a half hours that morning while Logan and Marsha cleaned out Gabe's apartment. After lunch, taking the kids to the zoo with Logan seemed like a good idea. As it was fast approaching four o'clock, Teagan was exhausted. She didn't know how Marsha kept up with two children and a full-time job.

"Walk faster Aunt Teagan." Anora grabbed her hand and pulled her along. "I want to see the otters and Brann said we only have an hour left."

Thank God. They could swoop through a fast food joint on the way home and grab enough supper for everyone, eating it once they got back to Marsha's house.

Matthew had tried to call Marsha's house a couple of times. He'd even tried her cell but got no answer. Box in hand with the personal items Gabe had at his desk at the office, Matthew tucked it under his arm to ring the doorbell.

The door was cracked open.

Alarm bells rang within his head.

Matt quietly set the box on the concrete porch and withdrew his weapon. With his free hand, he slowly opened the door. Listening carefully for any sound of movement, or voices. He stepped into the foyer.

The house was silent.

His gaze swept up the staircase to the left before sweeping the living room on his right.

He caught a whiff of urine and wondered if Marsha had bought the kids a dog since he had been there last with Gabe. That would be a smart move for a single mother with two small children. He hadn't heard any barking as he'd approached the house, though. Nor did a gangly puppy come tearing toward him. He negated the thought.

Although she said she was going to clean out his clothes from the bedroom, which was located upstairs, something urged him down the hallway. With the stealth of the trained special operator that he was, Matthew crept past the kitchen and family room, assuring each was empty.

Near the end of the hall, the smell grew stronger.

As he inhaled his next breath, Matthew knew the family didn't have a dog.

He also knew what he would find in the office.

Death.

The release of everything in the body always hit him hard. Regurgitation. The bowels and bladder. Blood. Death had its own unique combination of smells that always turned his stomach.

Mentally preparing himself, he took a single step into Gabe's home office.

The large leather executive chair facing the computer was rolled back from the desk.

His gaze traveled the room, but he couldn't see a body.

His stomach lurched.

Fuck. He could smell it, though.

Had Marsha killed someone and run away?

He slowed his gaze on the second pass around the room. The gun safe was wide open. Gabe liked guns and owned several. Butts resting on the bottom, his four rifles stood neatly in a row. Three of the four handgun slots were filled. The top cubbyhole was empty.

Where the hell was Gabe's 1911?

Was someone walking around the house with it? Aiming for him?

Matt forced his feet to move.

He stepped around the large oak desk and found Marsha's crumpled body folded between the stacks of drawers. The exit wound on the side of her head assured him he didn't need to call an ambulance.

He did need to call the local police, though.

His mind immediately went to his wife. Although Lizzie was not as close to Marsha as Teagan, they were friends. Their children were close enough in age and played together at least once a month.

Oh, fuck.

Reaching into his pocket, Matt withdrew his cell phone and speed dialed his wife. She and the kids were on their way to that very house. Lizzie was going to help Marsha while their children played.

Fuck. Fuck. Fuck.

Where the hell were Brann and Anora?

"We're about ten minutes out," Lizzie replied without a hello.

"Am I on speakerphone?" Matthew asked, but he already knew the answer. Everywhere around DC mandated hands-free telephones. "Lizzie, this isn't a good time for you and the children to be here."

"Is Marsha upset? Has it finally hit her that he's gone?" The compassion in her voice speared his heart as he looked at the body on the floor. He was so lucky to have such a wonderful, caring wife.

"No. We have a completely different situation here." Matt's gaze swept the room one more time, stopping on the computer screen centered in the middle of the desk.

I loved him so much. I just couldn't go on without him.

Matt looked between the screen and the woman on the floor. Although he would never say he knew Marsha well, he found it difficult to believe that she would commit suicide over Gabe's death. They had been in the middle of the divorce.

But, stranger things have happened.

"Matthew, we'll be there in just a few minutes and I'll help you straighten everything out." Lizzie's voice broke through the silence of the room.

"No," he snapped. He didn't want his wife or children anywhere near this scene. "Lizzie, please, take the children home and call me back. Do not, under any circumstances, come to this house. Promise me, you won't come here."

"Matthew." Lizzie had taken the phone off speaker. "What the heck is going on?"

He debated for a long moment before deciding to tell her the truth. "Pull over to the side and step out of the car."

He heard tires crunching on gravel, her door open and close.

"Matthew Saint Clare, you tell me right this minute what the hell is going on," she demanded.

He started to take a deep breath but the instant the vile smell entered his nose, he snorted it out. "Lizzie, Marsha is dead. Suicide." He glanced back at the note on the screen. "Maybe. But, listen, sweetheart, I haven't even called the cops yet. I just didn't want you or the children anywhere near this place. Please, take the children home and call me back."

"Marsha is…" Lizzie's voice cracked.

"I'm so sorry, sweetheart." He needed her to turn around and go home.

"Matthew, are you going to be all right?" There it was again. The concern in her voice, this time for him. Damn, he loved this woman. How did he ever get so lucky as to find her…twice? "It's only been a few days since…" She didn't need to finish that sentence. It had only been a few days since they had been up close and personal with another dead body…Gabe's.

"I need to handle this situation," he reminded her. "I've got to get ahold of Logan and Teagan before I call the cops. I don't want them walking into this blind. Now, I need you to take our children home."

"Headed home, right now." She sniffed back tears. He heard her crawl back into the car. "But we don't have a home. I guess that hotel is our home, for now. Let me call my mom and see if she can hang around a little while longer and watch the kids. Teagan may need help with Brann and Anora."

"Good thinking. I love you. Call me first before you head this way," he added before he hung up.

Matthew began to put his next moves into order.

First, he needed to call Logan and Teagan. He'd let them figure out what to do with the Davis children.

Second, he'd pick up the he'd box left on the porch.

Third, call Clarence, his computer guru at work. Local police may want that computer, but it just became part of a CIA investigation.

Fourth, take pictures of everything in the room the way he found it before dozens of uniformed cops destroyed the crime scene.

Last, call 911 and report the death.

Glancing at the computer screen one more time, he didn't believe this was a suicide.

But the cops would.

CHAPTER THREE

Logan didn't recognize the number but saw that it was a DC area code and decided to answer. "Lieutenant Colonel Jackson."

"Logan, are we on speaker?" Matthew Saint Clare asked, his tone serious.

"No." Since he was driving Teagan's car, he hadn't bothered to pair his phone. He dared anyone to try to arrest him for a hands-free violation. He'd taken several work-related calls since arriving in DC, two of them had to be scrambled and encrypted, an impossible function if using Bluetooth.

"Good. I need you to withhold any visible reaction to what I'm about to tell you." Matt's voice was very direct, as though he were speaking to a member of his Special Operations Group.

Fucking great. What the hell was the man going to say? Logan glanced over at Teagan who started a conversation with the kids in the backseat, distracting them. She seemed to recognize what he needed without even asking.

"Understood." Logan said as he glided off the Beltway.

"Logan, I want you to prepare yourself," Matt warned. "I don't want those kids to get even one vibe that there's a problem."

Holy fuck. Brann and Anora were in trouble. Had there been a direct threat on their lives? Was Teagan right to be worried about taking Gabe's kids out in public with them? Had they placed the children in danger?

Logan repeated the word, "Understood."

"Marsha is dead," Matthew said without inflection.

Marsha is dead. The words repeated over and over in Logan's head but didn't seem to make sense. No. He and Teagan were taking the children back to their mother. Marsha was moving Gabe's shit out of her house. She wasn't dead.

But she was.

Like a concrete block wall falling on him, Logan understood. He fought the urge to turn around and check the children in the backseat. Marsha's children.

Fuck. Damn. Hell. They had the funeral for these children's father the day before. How the fuck was he going to tell them that their mother was now dead?

Teagan's voice broke through his thoughts. She was talking and laughing with the children.

God. No. How was he going to tell Teagan that her best friend was gone, forever?

"Logan, you there?" Matt was still on the phone.

"Tell me everything you can," Logan ordered.

"About ten minutes ago, I was bringing Gabe's personal effects from the office. When I arrived, the front door was ajar. While clearing the main floor, I discovered Marsha's body in the office." Matthew's report was clear and concise, for which Logan was eternally grateful. "Gunshot wound to the head."

Logan wanted to close his eyes, but he couldn't. He needed to keep driving as casually as possible. "Fuck." The word escaped on a whisper.

"It gets worse," Matthew cautioned. "There's a suicide note on the computer."

"No," Logan snapped, then remembered he was supposed to stay cool, calm, and collected. Shit. He was fucking this up.

"I'm with you, I don't believe it," Matthew reassured him.

Logan heard sirens in the background.

"I've got to go. Local cops just arrived." It sounded as though Matthew was moving around. "Text me when you and Teagan have decided what to do with the children. If you bring them here, social services will take them away immediately. I've got to go. Remember, don't call, text." The line went dead.

A police car flew past them.

They were only about a mile from Marsha's home. Logan didn't know the area well, but Teagan did.

"How about we go to a park before we go home?" Logan suggested, his eyes pleading with Teagan's. He hoped she could read the mental messages he was trying to send to her.

She forced a smile. "That sounds like fun." She then gave him instructions to a park several blocks away. As soon as they pulled into a slot, the children hopped out and sprinted toward the playground equipment.

Before he could open his door, Teagan grabbed his arm. "What the fuck is going on?"

They could see both children while in the car, so he settled in behind the steering wheel. Just rip off the Band-Aid, he instructed himself.

"Marsha is dead."

The look of terror on Teagan's face grabbed his stone-cold heart and ripped it through his chest.

Fuck. He could've done that better. He'd treated her as though she were one of his male friends, not a woman with deep feelings for Marsha.

Logan reached for Teagan and pulled her close. "I'm so sorry. I know she was your friend."

Gasping in a breath, she asked, "Are you sure?"

She was being so diligent, trying to hold back the tears, but the dam was about to burst.

Logan nodded. "Yeah. Matthew found her."

Teagan looked confused. "Did she fall down the stairs carrying one of those damn boxes?"

Chastising himself for not thinking of that scenario, Logan shook his head. "Gunshot to the head. There's a note on the computer. It's meant to look like a suicide."

"No. No." Teagan shook her head side to side. "Marsha would never commit suicide." She pointed to the children on the swing set. "She loves those babies of hers. She would never leave them alone." The first tears leaked from her eyes. "I guess I should say 'she loved them'. Is she really…gone?"

He nodded as he pulled her in closer. "I'm so sorry. I should've found a better way to tell you."

She rolled her lips inside and closed her eyes as though to shut in the pain.

"Yes. You should have," she chastised him. As though she could no longer restrain her emotions, her entire body shook. She fell into him, her face buried in his chest.

Logan automatically wrapped his arms around Teagan's small body. He had held her as she'd wept several times before. Over a decade ago, in Syria, when they had lost

Mason, they had held each other, sharing the pain all the way back to base. A few weeks later, Logan had held Teagan once again as they buried an empty casket in the Virginia ground, pretending it was their friend and teammate, Mason Sinclair.

Each time it felt right to hold her. They were friends. They shared a bond that only those who faced bullets together could ever understand. Their friendship went deeper than most. She occupied a small section of his soul.

For the next several minutes, she alternated between quakes and quivers as she dealt with her grief. He did the only thing he could, he shared his strength. He admittedly didn't know Marsha very well. He thought he'd known Gabe but had come to realize he only knew what Gabe had wanted him to know. Always the CIA agent. Always playing the angles.

Teagan gasped in a breath.

Her head popped up and caught him in the chin.

"I'm sorry," she blurted as she rubbed the spot on her head. White surrounded her bright blue eyes as they met his. "The kids. We have to tell Brann and Anora. Oh my God. Those poor children. What's going to happen to them? They're orphans."

Okay. This was a question he could answer. "According to Matthew, when we take them back to the house, social services will come, and pick them up."

Anger instantly replaced grief. "They will do no such thing." She jabbed a finger toward the playground. "Those two sweet little children are not going into the system. I had a friend in elementary school who lived in one of those foster homes. They are not going there, if I have to kidnap them and take them to my house."

That was a brilliant idea. "Let's take the kids to your

place, now. I'll run back to Marsha's house and grab them some pajamas and clothes for tomorrow. While I'm there, I'll check out the situation. Overnight, we'll figure out how to tell them about their mother."

He pulled her back to him and kissed her forehead. "We'll figure this out." How hard could it be?

CHAPTER FOUR

Logan was pleased that Teagan had held back the tears as he drove everyone to her apartment. He knew her well enough to know that her quick smile was forced. Thankfully, the children never noticed her red, puffy eyes.

An hour later, Teagan was planted in the middle of her couch with Brann on one side and Anora on the other, a huge bowl of over-buttered, salty-as-hell popcorn held in her lap. An animated movie seized the children's attention.

"I'm just going to run over and get you two some pajamas," Logan announced on his way toward the door. No one looked at him.

As though capturing the scene with a mental camera, he inwardly smiled. That was exactly what he had always wanted—except in his dreams, he would be tucked into a corner of the couch, content to hold any one of three. Of course, the woman and children would be his. Finding the right wife had eluded him for far too long. Just another regret of choosing a military career over a normal, civilian life.

Starting a family at forty-four was a ridiculous idea.

Although he knew a few men his age expecting children, they were all part of the second family and a much younger wife. Logan didn't want an immature twentysomething girl, or a jaded woman in her thirties. He'd tried both with little satisfaction.

Teagan looked up at him and mouthed 'Go.' She tilted her head toward Anora whose heavy eyelids were nearly closed.

With a single nod, he left her small, two-bedroom apartment and drove to Marsha's suburban home. From the end of the tree-lined street, three blocks away, Logan could see the blue and white flashes of light from the local police department cars in front of Marsha's house. Two other cars, one black and one white, were obviously unmarked police vehicles.

Logan wondered if every law enforcement officer on the staff had shown up.

He pulled his rental vehicle to the curb at the end of the long line. As he approached Marsha's house, he was stopped by a uniformed policeman who looked fresh out of training.

"This is a crime scene, sir. I'll need you to cross the street and move along quickly, please." He was asking as much as ordering. Logan put the young man in his very early twenties. He instantly compared him to a Marine private first class, a year out of boot camp. There were so many differences, though. By the time a Marine earned his eagle, globe, and anchor, he was lethal in so many ways. He also had an air of confidence that this young man lacked.

Quickly analyzing the multiple ways he could handle the situation, he chose the most direct. "I am Marine Lieutenant Colonel Logan Jackson. That's Marsha Davis's home. I'm here to collect clothes for her children."

The uniformed officer peered around Logan toward the SUV he'd rented. "Are the kids in the car with you?" He almost sounded afraid.

"No. The children are with my friend." At the pinched look on the law enforcement officers face, Logan quickly added, "They're with their godmother. We haven't told them anything about the..." He wanted to call it murder but knew if he did, he'd be questioned for hours. In an investigation of this magnitude, he could only deal in facts. According to Matthew, Marsha was dead.

"Incident," the young policeman filled in for him.

"Yes. Now, if you will excuse me, I need to get the children's pajamas and something for them to wear tomorrow." Logan started to step around the much younger man.

"Hold it right there," he said brusquely, snapping his palm up in a stop position. "Let me call this in." He reached for the microphone on his shoulder and briefly relayed Logan's request. Within a minute, a man in his early thirties wearing khakis, a white button-down shirt, and a blue blazer walked toward him. He was joined by a woman in her mid-twenties in a dark blue pantsuit.

"Officer Strator, what's going on?" The man casually dropped his right hand to his hip, close to his holstered weapon. Up close, he was considerably shorter than Logan's six feet, one inch frame. If the man reached five feet, ten inches, he'd be surprised.

"Uhm, this is..."

Obviously intimidated by the new arrivals, Logan jumped in before the young man stumbled over himself. "I'm Marine Lieutenant Colonel Logan Jackson, godfather to the Davis children who are currently with their godmother. We have not yet informed them about the loss of their mother. I'm not sure if you are aware that their father's funeral was yesterday."

"We know," the woman said.

Logan continued, tired of repeating himself. "Look, I'm just here to pick up some pajamas for them to sleep in tonight and a change of clothes for tomorrow morning. May I proceed?"

"I'm Melissa Cook from Fairfax County Department of Family Services. Exactly where are the Davis children?" For such a young little thing, she was rather demanding.

If there was one thing Logan Jackson despised, it was repeating himself. "Brann and Anora Davis are curled up on their godmother's couch on the north east side of Falls Church."

"Why were the children not with their mother?" Her question was quick and crisp.

Okay, where to start? Before he answered, he needed to find out who the man was. "Who are you?" Logan asked bluntly. He purposely looked at the man's weapon. "Are things that bad around here that social services personnel carry G30s?" He said referring to the Glock subcompact .45 auto pistol in the man's holster.

The corner of the man's mouth kicked up. "You know your guns."

Logan raised one eyebrow. "United States Marine Lieutenant Colonel. Guns are the difference between life and death in my business. I'll only ask you this one more time, who the fuck are you?" If the pompous little shit didn't answer him this time, he would simply walk past them into the house.

The cocky little bastard seemed to roll the question around in his brain before he finally answered. "I'm

Detective Connor Russo, Major Crimes Investigation Division. This is my crime scene."

Logan wanted to roll his eyes. If this guy was in charge, he was going to write it off as a suicide.

"Now, U.S. Marine Corps Lieutenant Colonel Logan Jackson, answer Ms. Cook's question," the little prick demanded.

Answer only the question asked and tell the whole truth and nothing but the truth, as clearly and concisely as possible, Logan counseled himself. "At approximately 1400 hours, that's two o'clock in the afternoon civilian time," he sarcastically added for Detective Russo, "Teagan Williams and I took the children to the National Zoo so Marsha could remove all of their father's clothing from the house."

When Russo started to ask a question, Logan pushed on. "On our way to return the children here," he tilted his head toward the house completely lit up inside and out as darkness approached, "Matthew Saint Clare telephoned me asking me not to bring the children home. He said he had found their mother's body with a gunshot wound to the head. We took the children to a park approximately eight blocks from here so Teagan and I could discuss the situation alone in the car. We decided the best course of action would be to take them to her apartment, feed them and allow them to sleep there overnight."

He purposely focused his attention on Miss Cook. "As their godmother, they have spent several nights at her place."

The young woman seemed to be appeased by his answers. "I will allow them to spend the night with her tonight. You mentioned you had not yet told the children about the death of their mother. If you would like, I can be there tomorrow morning and break the news to them." She lifted her gaze to Logan's. "I'm trained on handling this exact situation, and to reassure you, this isn't my first, or my tenth."

"That sounds like an excellent idea," he instantly agreed.

Miss Cook giving the children the bad news could work out perfectly. They would never have to know that he and Teagan knew of their mother's death the evening before. He was sure Teagan would also appreciate someone else delivering that heartbreaking news.

"I will accompany you to the children's rooms." She turned on her low, sensible heels and headed toward the house.

Logan started to follow when Detective Russo reached out and grabbed Logan's elbow. He froze. He forced himself not to react. This man was a police officer. Breaking his hand, arm, or dislocating his shoulder would be a very bad idea.

Staring at the man's hand on his arm, Logan warned, "Are you that damn dumb? Don't you know any better than to touch an active duty military man, or woman? Do you have any idea how many ways I could...hurt you?" Thank Christ he caught himself before he said the word kill. "You have no idea who I am, so let me tell you. I command a battalion of the Marine Corps' most highly trained special operators. Our version of the Army Green Berets, Navy SEALs, but better. We start with the Marines. And I can guarantee you I got this job by being the best of the best. If you know what's good for you, remove your hand. Now."

Logan knew he didn't get through to the idiot when the younger man squared his shoulders and squeezed Logan's elbow, ever so slightly but he felt it, before he let go. "After you get the kids' clothes, I want to talk to you."

"I'll bet you do." Logan caught up to Miss Cook, who had turned and waited for him.

"His case of little-man syndrome got so much worse when he got promoted to detective three months ago," Ms. Cook said in a quiet voice. "He has no respect for the military. He's just a bitter little man because he didn't get into West Point, or the Naval Academy, or the Air Force Academy." She gave him a fake grin. "But he got into the police academy. Aren't we lucky?"

Logan grinned as she led the way into the house and up the stairs to Brann's bedroom. Knowing they were far away from Detective Russo, he asked, "You seem to know a lot about him."

She started opening drawers, but halted and turned to face him. "Every woman affiliated with the Fairfax County Police Department knows about the 'Con' man. He considers himself quite a lady's man. He chased me for weeks when I first started working in this area of the county. Then he found out that I was a Navy brat, and that I had been married to a SEAL, and his advances stopped cold. Trust me, I was ecstatic."

Logan glanced at her left hand. He was well aware of the divorce rate in special operations. "I'm sorry things didn't work out with your SEAL."

Her lips went into a straight line. "I loved Erik. And always will. We had three great years together." Her voice broke as she looked down at her feet. "Firefight in northern Africa. Two other men were lost at the same time." Her eyes met his. "I'm not supposed to know that, but Daddy knew, and he told me."

"Is that why you moved to Fairfax County? To get away from the military?" Logan snagged a pair of jeans, a couple pair of underpants, and two T-shirts. That should last Brann several days.

"No. Kind of. Maybe." It was as though she was trying to decide for herself as she spoke. "Daddy got transferred to the Pentagon and I just wanted to live closer to him and Mom. I had what they call a mortality check and realized my parents weren't always going to be there." She snickered. "They're not always going to be here, either. He's decided to retire. Now, he just has to figure out what slice of oceanside beach he wants to live on."

They moved across the hall to Anora's room. Logan wasn't sure he'd ever been in there. Llamas. There were fucking llamas everywhere. Llamas on the pillows, sheets, bedspread, curtains, walls. A stuffed llama stood in a chair. And pink. He hadn't known there were so many shades of pink. The drawers of her dresser started light pink and were nearly red by the bottom drawer.

Ms. Cook was laughing. "You're not used to little girls, are you?"

"It's that obvious?"

She had already selected several little outfits, some long pants, a couple of shorts, tops with guess what…llamas, all shades of pink and purple. The social services woman grabbed a small pink suitcase from the corner, decorated with Disney princesses.

"Do you want to throw the boy's clothes in here too?" She offered.

"Sure, what the hell." He handed her the clothes and she laid them neatly into the suitcase.

As she stood, she looked at the picture on the dresser. "Is this her mother?"

Logan moved closer. "Yes. And her Aunt Ashley."

Ms. Cook whipped around to look at him. "Are you directly related to the children?"

Logan shook his head. "No, I'm not a blood relative, and neither is Teagan. We are the children's godparents. Marsha and Teagan were roommates back in flight school. They both flew Navy Seahawks and roomed together for years. Teagan introduced Marsha to Gabriel, her husband."

She studied him for moment. "Are you and Teagan married?"

"No." Fuck. Logan could see where this was going.

"Is Teagan married? Or are you?" She pressed.

"No." He wouldn't lie about this. Ever.

Ms. Cook picked up the picture. "Does Marsha have any other siblings?"

"No. There's only Ashley." Before Logan let this get out of hand, he quickly added, "She's currently in rehab. Again." He shrugged. "I'm not even sure which one, or for what, this time."

Disappointment crossed the social services agent's pretty face. Holding his gaze, Ms. Cook asked, "What about Mrs. Davis's parents?"

The last thing Logan wanted to do was to turn those beautiful children over to Marsha's parents. Neither seemed interested in their grandchildren. "They're at an RV rally somewhere over on the Eastern Shore. They planned to drive north to Maine, taking the entire summer to get there."

"They may be a possibility, but we prefer siblings." she said as much to herself as to him. "Are you familiar with Mr. Davis's family?"

"I know his father died from cancer several years ago and I think his mother passed before that. Gabe never mentioned any close relatives," Logan admitted. He thought about it for a few minutes and couldn't remember a single conversation involving brothers or sisters. Reflecting back, that wasn't unusual. Logan rarely spoke of his family. "Perhaps Matt, that's Matthew Saint Clare, downstairs, maybe he can answer that question. He worked with Gabe for over a decade."

"I'll ask him." Her smile was sweet. "In the meantime, I'm satisfied leaving the children with you and…"

"Teagan," he filled in. "Teagan Williams. Their godmother," he added for reinforcement of their position.

Small pink suitcase in hand, Logan started down the hall. He peered into the open door of the master bedroom. Several cardboard boxes with folded tops sat next to the door, ready to be taken away. A stack of men's suits was carelessly tossed onto the bed as though Marsha had been interrupted in her task.

Had someone rung the bell? Or broken in and forced her to the office downstairs? He needed to talk with Matthew. And to see the office.

CHAPTER FIVE

Teagan picked up a sleeping Anora and placed her on one of the twin beds in the spare bedroom that she thought of as theirs. She quickly stripped the little girl out of her shorts and top and slid the nightie over her head.

"Come on, buddy, let's get those teeth brushed." Logan was so good with Brann, Teagan thought as she covered Anora with the pink polka dot sheets and princess comforter. She loved the nights her godchildren spent with her.

"I love you, Anora. Sweet dreams," The child was already asleep as Teagan bent and kissed her soft forehead.

She didn't bother to hide her smile as she watched Logan tuck Brann into bed. "Night, buddy."

"Good night, Uncle Logan," a sleepy Brann mumbled. "Love you."

Logan's entire body froze for several heartbeats before he raked his fingers through the boy's long bangs. "Sleep well." He'd spoken the words just above a whisper.

Teagan stepped over to Brann's bed and leaned in, kissing him on the forehead. "I love you, too." Halfway across the room she realized Logan was still standing there staring at the young boy, already breathing evenly in his sleep.

She crossed the room and wrapped her fingers around Logan's huge bicep, as much as she could. This man must work out every single day. He was in such good shape. She, on the other hand, hadn't bothered with regular physical fitness since she left the Navy.

His eyes sliced to her but immediately softened before he laid his big hand over hers. When he started to speak, she shook her head and tilted it toward the door. She tugged him out of the children's room and down the hall.

"I don't know about you, but I need a drink." Teagan said as she released his arm and turned into the kitchen. "I'm having red wine. Beer is in the fridge if you want one."

He'd already opened the door and was snagging a bottle. "Who knew kids were so exhausting?"

She snickered. "Me. Parents. Grandparents who take the kids for a day." She caught the fatigue in his eyes and knew it wasn't physical. "Today has been exceptionally hard."

"No shit," he said as he sat on one end of the couch.

She took the other end and curled her legs under her. "For Christ's sake, don't keep me waiting," she demanded.

He took a long swig of beer. "Be glad you didn't go. I thank Christ that Matt called us. I wouldn't want the children anywhere near there. The place was crawling with cops and the detective in charge was a snot-nosed, fucking little prick."

She gave him a sarcastic grin. "Were we not able to make friends and play nice?"

"I was in no mood to put up with his little-dick

syndrome." Logan took another sip. "He came charging out of the house with the social services lady before I even got to their walkway. At least she was nice. After a while." He looked up at Teagan and held her gaze. "Melissa Cook will be here tomorrow morning. She'll tell the children. She has training dealing with kids in this kind of situation."

Teagan closed her eyes and sent a prayer to God and all the angels in heaven, thanking them for relieving her of that burden. Heaven's newest angel popped into her head. Marsha. Fighting back the tears, she decided to take comfort in knowing that her friend was sending what she needed to take care of her children. She let out a long sigh. "Thank you for asking her to do that."

"She volunteered. She'll be checking us out at the same time." After a second, he amended, "Mostly you. She said they normally prefer the children to go to a family member, but once I told her about Ashley, she seemed to be okay with you taking care of them, at least for tonight."

"They don't have anyone else," Teagan pointed out. "And like I told you before, those two little kids are *not* going into the system." She would do everything within her power to keep them with her.

"What do you know about Gabriel's family?" His question didn't surprise her as much as her answer did.

"I don't know much about Gabe at all," she admitted. "I don't even know where he's from."

"Nobody seems to know." Logan took another sip. "Matthew didn't know about Gabe's past, either. He offered to try to use the resources at the CIA to see what he could find, but he didn't sound hopeful."

"Do you think social services will try to take them away from us tomorrow?" She really needed to know what to expect so she could prepare to counter anything they said.

Deep furrows appeared between Logan's eyebrows. "Teagan, I think what you really mean is; will Ms. Cook try to take the children away from *you*. You're the one who has been part of their lives. I'm just another fun uncle to Brann. Whenever I'm in town, I'll stop by to see him. I'll take him to a baseball game, go to the batting cage, or sometimes just take him out for burgers and a movie. I told you before, I really don't have a relationship with Anora." He leaned forward, elbows on his knees, and rolled the beer bottle between his palms. "I'm supposed to be back at Camp Lejeune within three days. I wish I could help, but I don't know how."

The severity of the situation hit her.

She was in this...alone.

Damn. I am such an idiot.

Logan was active duty. He had to go wherever Uncle Sam sent him and do whatever he was ordered. He didn't have time for a seven-year-old boy and a four-year-old girl. He lived three-hundred fifty miles away. If she needed him, it would take him at least six hours to drive.

Worse, he didn't seem to want to help.

Children were such a huge responsibility. Parenting wasn't a job she could leave at the end of the day. It was twenty-four seven. And kids weren't easy. They were little people. Teagan knew from experience that both children got tired and cranky. They could say things they really didn't mean, but the words still hurt. There were so many lessons they had to learn about life that parents taught every day.

For the first time, she wondered if she could handle it. In the past, she'd taken care of Anora and Brann for a day, here and there. Sometimes they would stay overnight. Once, she'd even had them all weekend. She was so exhausted by Monday, she called in sick and slept the entire day. She knew Marsha didn't do that. Her friend must have secretly been superwoman to work a full-time job, take care of two children alone, and maintain her sanity.

Teagan didn't think she could do it. Before she started into her own personal pity party, Logan's voice broke the silence of the room.

"On the desk computer was what could be considered a suicide note." He held up his hand before she could protest. "Matt had his computer guru already on it before the local PD arrived. It's possible that someone, not in the room, had typed the note. Since the computer was technically Gabe's, Matthew told the locals that it was CIA property and may contain classified information, so they were not allowed to even touch the keyboard. He was going to take everything back to Langley and have his lab test for fingerprints and outsiders using the mainframe remotely."

"So, Matt believes that she was…" Teagan's throat seized. She couldn't say the word. Murdered. "Why the hell would anyone want to hurt Marsha?"

"That's a two-million-dollar question." Logan downed the last of his beer and got up, heading toward the kitchen.

"Why *two* million?" Teagan took the first sip of her wine hoping to soothe the muscles in her throat.

"In the safe, which was open by the way, was Gabe's will. Each of his children, Bradley, Brann and Anora, automatically inherited one million dollars to be paid out from a five million life insurance policy." He took the same seat again but twisted so he faced her. "Even though none of us believed it, Detective Russo, in all his brilliant experience," he said faciciously, "has declared it a suicide."

"What the fuck?" Teagan realized her voice was a little too loud and glanced down the hallway toward the bedrooms. "So that's it? Case closed?"

"As far as the Fairfax Police Department is concerned, she was distraught over her husband's recent death and couldn't go on." He looked away and grimaced as though he were seeing something he didn't want to look at.

"You said Matthew found her in the office. Had she taken pills and gone in there and lay down on the couch? Why his office? Marsha never went in there except to get her gun." At the appalled look on Logan's face, she knew Marsha had been shot. "Oh, no." She shook her head but couldn't stop the tears that rolled uncontrolled down her cheeks.

The logical part of her brain knew that Marsha would never commit suicide, and certainly not with a gun. As a former naval officer, her friend knew the power of the small weapon. She was good with guns. She'd kept hers locked in the safe with Gabe's, on the bottom shelf underneath all of his.

She'd been killed with a bullet, and not one fired on the battlefield. She and Marsha both had a pilot's attitude, if they were going to die, they would go out in a blaze of glory, their bird shot out from underneath them by enemy fire.

Not murdered by only God knew who.

Hot tears ran steadily over her cheeks. She already missed her friend. Marsha would never get to see her children grow up. She would never hug Anora goodbye on her first day of real school. She'd never see Brann dressed in a suit with a pretty girl on his arm headed to prom. She'd never hold Anora as her daughter cried after getting her heart broken the first time. She'd never see her children walk down the aisle and commit their lives to someone they loved.

The back of Teagan's throat hurt but the pain was nowhere near what she felt in her heart.

"Go ahead and cry it all out." Logan whispered in her ear.

When had he moved? Teagan didn't remember Logan taking her into his arms, holding her as she cried. It had felt so right she hadn't questioned it until he spoke.

"You need to get this out of your system tonight, so you can be strong for the children in the morning." He patted her back.

Logan was right. She needed to mourn for her friend right then so she could help the children deal with their grief in the morning. She hated to cry. It made her feel so weak. But Marsha had been her best friend for years. They were closer than sisters. Marsha was the only person who knew her deepest, darkest secret...and she'd take it to her grave.

Once again, Teagan bore the weight of her secret alone. And she always would. Another wave of self-pity crashed over her, nearly drowning her in her own tears.

Teagan didn't know how long she'd cried. It could have been minutes, or it might've been hours, but she finally pulled herself together. She was shocked to find herself wrapped in strong, masculine arms.

"Are you sure you're done?" Logan's warm breath caressed the outer shell of her ear. He held her head against his chest, not allowing her to lift it to look at him. "I'll hold you all night, if that's what it takes."

Teagan couldn't remember the last time she'd been held all through the night by a man. She knew Logan would do it, though. He was one of the best men she'd ever known.

"Thank you." She leaned up and laid her lips on his scratchy cheek. She took a deep breath as she sat up. "There's so much to do. I was beside Marsha during most of the funeral arrangements for Gabriel." She closed her eyes to hold back the next swell of sorrow.

She whipped her head to catch Logan's gaze. "Her parents. Someone has to call her parents."

When she tried to stand, Logan caught her around the waist and pulled her down into his lap. "Whoa. That's not your job, or your place. You were her friend but not her next of kin. Notifying them is detective dickhead's job."

It was as though he had popped the balloon within her. Everything that had held her together, deflated. She wasn't responsible for any decisions concerning Marsha's funeral. Her parents could, and would, handle everything. Or so she hoped.

Her mind instantly went to Anora and Brann. They wouldn't handle the children. Hell, they had never even taken one of their grandchildren for a single night. They certainly wouldn't want to be strapped with both of them until they reached eighteen.

Teagan couldn't imagine growing up in that household. Marsha's father ran their home the same way he did his business; with very little personal compassion and almost no understanding of human frailties and failures.

Marsha, being the typical oldest child, had strived to make him proud. In her early teens, she had heard her father say, during the speech to the stockholders, that if he had a son, he would be so honored for his boy to join the military. Her first week in college, she had joined the Navy ROTC. Since the pilot program was one of the toughest to be selected for, that became Marsha's goal. She and Teagan had been assigned as roommates first day of flight school and had bonded instantly.

The day they pinned on their wings, there had been fewer than five hundred female pilots in the Navy. Teagan's mother had been ecstatic and so proud of her. Marsha's father had told her he was disappointed in her for not graduating the highest in the class. Maybe if she'd done better, she would have been selected to fly jets rather than helicopters. No matter what her friend did, it was never good enough for her father.

The mental picture Teagan had taken as she left the children's bedroom flashed into her mind. There was no way in hell she was going to let Anora and Brann grow up in that household. Marsha's father hadn't softened one iota since Marsha had left for college.

She was it. Anora and Brann had no one else.

Standing, Teagan announced, "I'm keeping the children. When the bitch from social services shows up tomorrow, I'll just set her straight."

"Melissa Cook isn't a bitch. She knows her job, which is to find the best place for the children." He stood. "You just need to prove to her that living with you is the best thing for Anora and Brann."

He glanced around the room, his eyes landing on the couch. "This doesn't pull out into a bed by any chance, does it?"

Teagan's gaze started with his boots and ran slowly up his long muscular legs. He had narrow straight hips and no indication of love handles. Through his tight T-shirt, she could see rows of defined abs before her gaze swept to his broad chest. She mentally measured his wide shoulders then slid a glance over her well-used couch.

It was small, like her apartment. Even when she fell

asleep on it, her feet and head touched the armrests. There was no way in hell Logan would ever fit. "You take the bed. I'll fit much better on this couch than you will."

"I'm not going to kick you out of your bed," he retorted. "I've slept on much worse."

"Don't argue with me. I've had a rough day. You are my guest and I'm not going to allow you to sleep on the couch. Go to your car and grab your bags while I change the sheets on the bed." She glared up at him. "We just have to make this work for a few hours."

"I'll get a hotel room close by, tomorrow," he promised.

CHAPTER SIX

The unusual sound brought the man wide-awake. The exclusive ring tone announced the caller before he even checked the ID.

Glancing at his bedside clock, he groaned. It was only three o'clock, the middle of the night in Washington DC. In Iran, though, it was eleven-thirty in the morning. As usual, his demanding uncle ignored the time difference.

He grabbed the encrypted satellite phone from the nightstand and turned on the light. "Uncle, how can I be of service to you?" He said in the unique Arabic dialect of his early childhood.

"Abd al Rashid." His uncle always called him by his Arabic name. He refused to use the name given to him by the Catholics who had brought him from the Middle Eastern refugee camp to the United States to be raised as a Christian. Both he and his uncle had come to accept this as Allah's will, especially during the man's surprising rise to one of the highest positions within the Central Intelligence Agency. "Reassure me you have secured the information Gabriel Davis stole from us."

He was not about to correct his uncle, the true caliphate and the founder of the New Islamic State, but Gabe hadn't stolen the information. He had been given it as a faithful follower of his uncle, Nassar al Jamil. The American had done much to further their cause, primarily by keeping the Muslim leader off the United States' most wanted terrorist list.

His uncle's following had grown significantly since Iran had granted them the promised land on Lake Urmia in the northwest corner that borders Iraq and Turkey, less than one hundred miles from Syria.

Their recruitment within the United States had tripled in just two weeks. His secret camps in Pennsylvania, Washington, and Kansas were thriving, bursting at the seams with young men anxious to follow the fundamentalist ways of Mohammed.

Money had poured in like Niagara Falls when he had gone against his uncle's advice and leaked the good news to the American press. Tens of thousands of displaced Middle Eastern Muslims, disillusioned and disgusted with the liberal United States and their lack of acceptance of Sharia law, had been willing to donate millions of dollars to the cause. He'd been able to hire the best mercenaries to train his secret armies, equip them with leading-edge weapons and ammunition, teach them modern-day tactics, and feed them well.

"Nephew, did you hear me?" His uncle's words brought him back to the conversation.

"Uncle, we searched his apartment immediately after his death and found nothing." He scrubbed his hand over his face and once again asked Allah to forgive him. "I went to the home he shared with his wife on occasion. While searching his office, his wife walked in." He quickly added,

"She wasn't supposed to be there. She saw me. Recognized me. I had to kill her."

"American women," the holy man said with disdain. "They are too interfering. Their husbands need to teach them better, keep them in line. It would not been a problem with any wife of mine. She would know enough to keep her mouth shut and walk away. His wife, she was nothing. A casualty of war."

His uncle was right. He was looking forward to joining his real family in the New Islamic State. He intended to take several wives, of various ages. He could afford them and all his children they would bear. He would arrive a hero and have his choice of the most beautiful women. Then he would fuck day and night, impregnating as many as possible. No more need for condoms, necessary to protect himself from dirty American women. He would have untouched virgins. His unsheathed cock would be the only one to ever enter those women.

He grew hard at the mere thought, proud that he had no problem getting it up at his age. Instead of watching his grandchildren grow, he'd be taking wives of that age to assure the continuation of his bloodline...and their virginity.

But he had much work left to do in the United States of America. Most importantly, to bring the country to its knees, bowing to Allah.

"Are you going to get in trouble with American laws?" The man sixty-five hundred miles away asked with concern.

He sat up in his bed and leaned against the headboard, grinning. "No. I made it look like a suicide and the detective in charge of the scene filed it as such. Nothing can be traced back to me."

"Excellent, my favorite nephew. I look forward to you joining us here in the promised land. Allah be with you and give you strength."

The line went dead.

The man smiled and ran his fingers through his curly dark hair, fisting his cock. Part of him hated to allow his seed to go unplantable, but his private doctor had told him an active sex life would keep him verile longer. He would be in Iran soon.

Everything was progressing as planned.

CHAPTER SEVEN

As Logan flipped the next pancake, he glanced into the living room where Teagan slept peacefully on the couch. One shapely leg lay on top of the sheet exposing her curves from her ankles all the way up to her rounded hip. She rolled onto her side, revealing one of the nicest asses he'd seen in years. As his cock started to stiffen, he chastised himself.

Teagan is a friend. A very distraught friend at the moment. Besides, she had relegated him to the friend zone last night. *Let her sleep. She needs it.*

A toilet flushed down the hall moments before Brann shuffled into the small dining area just off the living room. "Uncle Logan, are you cooking us breakfast?"

"Keep your voice down, please. Aunt Teagan is still asleep. Yes, I'm making pancakes." He said in a voice so low as not to wake her up. "I think I made too many."

Yawning, Brann slid onto a stool at the breakfast counter. "I'll start with five." He then looked up and added, "Please."

"That's better." Logan loaded a plate and set it on the

counter then pointed to the maple syrup. He turned and grabbed the milk from the refrigerator. "Do you have any idea where the glasses are?"

The boy immediately hopped off the tall seat and opened the cabinet next to the sink. "Would you like a glass, too?"

Well, the boy has manners, when he wants to use them. He looked at the contents remaining in the gallon jug. "Will Anora have milk with her breakfast?"

"Yeah. I'll get her cup." Brann opened the bottom drawer, which was filled with plastic plates, bowls, and covered cups. "This is Anora's stuff. Aunt Teagan makes her get her own." He lifted out a pink plate and a matching sippy cup. "I'll get hers. She's awake and will be out here in a few minutes."

Brann sat back down and drowned his pancakes in the sweet brown syrup.

The little pink whirlwind came running down the hallway. "Aunt Teagan, I smell food, like real food. Are you cooking?" She screamed at the top of her voice.

So much for letting Teagan sleep in.

"No, Uncle Logan is." Brann held out her plate. "Just one for her. You'll be lucky if she eats even that much." He cut through all five pancakes on his plate and stuffed the gooey mess into his mouth.

"Here you go, Anora." Logan set the plate on the breakfast bar.

She crawled onto a stool and looked at the single pancake on her plate. Big blue eyes then looked up at him, expectantly. She glanced down at the perfectly cooked pancake before returning her gaze to Logan's.

"Would you like me to pour the maple syrup on it?" He picked up the small jug and held it over her breakfast.

"Yes, please." Her voice was so quiet, especially compared to a moment ago.

He poured a circle in the middle. "Is that enough?"

The girl stared at her food. "What's maple syrup?"

Oh, fuck. Before Logan could answer, Brann took his sister's finger and stuck it into the pool of thick brown liquid.

"Taste it. You're going to love this." The boy moved his sister's hand to her mouth. "Stick out your tongue," he ordered.

She did as she was told, and he swiped her finger over her tongue. Her bright blue eyes went huge. "It tastes like honey," she said with amazement.

"Yeah, kinda, but better." Brann took another large bite.

Anora sat there with her hands in her lap, just staring at her plate.

I'm such an idiot when it comes to kids. She needed silverware. Brann had gotten some for himself but hadn't bothered getting any for his sister. Logan placed a knife and fork next to her plate.

The precious little girl with mussed up bed hair looked at the silverware as though they were going to bite her.

"What's wrong?" He asked. Fuck. He'd fucked up something else and had no idea.

"I'm too little to use a knife," she announced.

Logan tried to remember what age he'd been when he started using a knife. He couldn't remember a time when he hadn't carried at least a foldable pocketknife.

Brann leaned over and with the side of his fork, he started to cut her pancake into pieces.

Logan grabbed a knife. "I'll do that. You finish your pancakes and let me know if you want more." He looked at Anora and cut each piece in half again. Damn. She was tiny.

Logan was used to looking at full-grown men across the table.

"Why is Aunt Teagan sleeping on the couch?" Anora asked between bites.

"I'm too tall to fit on the couch so Teagan insisted that I sleep in her bed." Logan had always believed that honesty was the best policy. He took a sip of his coffee that was now lukewarm.

"Why didn't she sleep in the bed with you? Is she mad at you?" Her little blond eyebrows pinched together. "You should say you're sorry. Then she'd come back and sleep in the bed with you."

Logan swallowed hard before coffee went shooting through his nose. He wondered how many times the child had witnessed that scenario.

Teagan swung her legs over the side of the couch and stretched her arms over her head.

Holy, fuck. Teagan had a belly button piercing. Light reflected off the stone attached to her navel, throwing rainbows of color just above her flat stomach. He wondered if she had more piercings and if so, where. Or a tattoo.

He had never gotten a tattoo. When he'd first qualified for Force Recon, the predecessor to the Raiders, any identifying marks, like tattoos, were highly discouraged.

"Sweetie, Uncle Logan and I aren't married so we don't sleep in the same bed." Teagan stood up and squinted at him. "Please tell me you brewed an entire pot of coffee."

"I did." It had been a short night and was going to be a long day. He was going to need the additional caffeine. Obviously, Teagan would also.

"Good. Then I won't have to kill you." She padded barefoot over to the coffee pot. Reaching into the cabinet above, she extracted the biggest cup he'd ever seen. It was shaped like a coffee cup, but the size of a large soup bowl. When she filled it nearly to the brim, he was resigned to making another pot.

"Who wants more pancakes?" Logan asked all three of them when their plates were empty.

Ten minutes later, tummies full, the children wandered back to their bedrooms to change their clothes.

Teagan had finished her first cup and was on her second when someone knocked on the door.

He slid her a glance. This was it. Logan had no idea what to expect. He should have looked up information on his phone last night. It wasn't as though he slept much knowing Teagan was on the couch and he was in her bed. It smelled of her. Every time he rolled over, her pillow wafted her scent. It had been torture. Usually if he smelled a woman in the bed and couldn't sleep, he would roll over and slide into her, expending his excess energy until they were both exhausted. But he'd been alone in the bed.

Teagan took a deep breath and hopped off her stool. The torment continued. Her breasts rising and growing as she inhaled was bad enough, but he could see her soft nipples through the silky little peach-colored top and the shorts just barely covered the bottom of her perfect derrière.

"Teagan, you might want to reconsider answering the door." He ran his gaze over her toned body. "I'm enjoying your pajamas, but I don't think you want the woman from social services to see that much of you. She would definitely get the wrong impression."

She glanced down at the skimpy night clothes. "Fuck." Her eyes grew leery. It was as though she had just awakened to a nightmare, remembering why the woman was coming. Darting toward her bedroom, she called, "Logan, can you—"

"I've got it." He strode to the door and looked through the peephole. Ms. Cook stood next to detective dickhead. Both were once again dressed conservatively in navy blue suits.

Why the hell is he here?

Before Detective Russo could knock, Logan opened the door. He stepped out into the hall and left the door open a crack behind him.

"We haven't said anything to the children." Logan kept his good ear toward the opening, listening for the children. "All they know is that they had a sleepover with Aunt Teagan, and Uncle Logan made them breakfast. They're in their room changing out of their pajamas."

The door started to open, and he saw Teagan out of the corner of his eye.

She looked them up and down warily as she stepped into the hall. "I'm Teagan Williams, Anora and Brann's godmother. Thank you for agreeing to tell..." She swallowed hard. "Help the children learn about their..." She bravely fought back the tears. "About Marsha."

Logan just wanted to pull her to him and hold her as she once again cried. When she didn't move any closer, he took that as a sign and kept his hands to himself.

"Detective Connor Russo. Can we move this inside?" He reached up and shoved the door open, letting himself in.

"Yes, certainly." Teagan showed them into the living room. "Would anyone care for coffee?"

"No, thank you. This is not a social visit." The woman looked expectantly. "Could you please ask the children to come in here?" As an afterthought, she added, "Melissa

Cook, from Fairfax County Department of Family Services."

Teagan blanched.

Logan was afraid she was going to pass out. "Why don't you take a seat and I'll get the kids." Without waiting for consent, he walked down the hall to their bedroom.

Good. They were dressed for the day. "Brann, Anora, there's someone here to see you." He tried desperately to school his face but when his gaze met Brann's, he couldn't hold back the sorrow in his eyes.

"Who is it?" The boy asked quietly.

"Come on," he held out his hand. Brann immediately slid his hand into Logan's. He reached down and picked up Anora, planting her on his hip. The little girl wound her tiny arms around his neck. When he reached the living room, he sat in the empty chair and pulled her onto his lap. Brann chose to stand beside the chair, never letting go of Logan's hand.

"I'm Ms. Cook and you must be Brann and Anora." She smiled pleasantly and spoke to them in a soft voice.

Neither child said anything, simply nodded.

"I'm afraid I have some very bad news for you." She patted the seat next to her. "Would you like to come and sit next to me?"

"No," Brann said forcefully.

"I want Aunt Teagan." Anora leaped down and dashed across the living room, diving into Teagan's lap.

Logan could feel the young boy shaking so he pulled him around and parked him on his knee. "I'm here for you."

"Why don't you bring the children over here so they could sit next to me on the couch?" Ms. Cook suggested.

"They're fine right where they are." Teagan's voice was

stern. Anora had curled up into a small ball, peeking over her knees at the official-looking woman.

"I'm sorry I have to be the one to tell you this, but your mother passed away last night."

"No! No!" Brann screamed. "You're a liar." He looked around to face Logan. "Tell her, Uncle Logan. Mom's at home. She had to throw out Dad's clothes yesterday." Tears had started to streak down his face. "Dad's dead. Not Mom. It's not true."

Logan had never felt so helpless in his life. He pulled Brann to his chest and simply held him. "I'm sorry, buddy. I'm so sorry."

Across the room, Teagan was crying.

Anora twisted and stuck her face two inches from Teagan's. "What does that mean? Did Mommy have to go someplace? Like a hospital? Is she hurt?"

"No, sweetie, it means that your mommy is gone." Teagan's voice broke. "She's in heaven now."

Anora looked relieved. "Oh, she went to visit Daddy. When is she coming back?"

"I'm so sorry, sweetie. Your mommy isn't coming back." Teagan struggled to tell the child between her own sobs.

Tears began to flow from Anora's eyes. "Ever?"

Teagan simply shook her head side to side. "No, sweetie. She can't come back. But she'll always be right here in your heart." Teagan laid her fingertips in the middle of Anora's chest.

"Let go of me." Brann wiggled out of Logan's embrace and darted across the room. When he held out his arms to his sister, she instantly went to him. They slumped to the floor together.

"Mom's dead. Just like Dad." He cut straight to the point. "It's just you and me now."

Teagan slid next to them. "Oh, no. You're not alone." She embraced both children in her hug. "I'm here for you."

Logan shoved out of his chair and joined them. "I am, too." As he wrapped his arms around all three, he'd never felt so protective, and helpless, at the same time. He wasn't sure how the hell he was going to do it, but he would take care of these two wonderful children the rest of their lives. They had suffered enough grief and sorrow in one week to last a lifetime.

He vowed to bring them joy and happiness forever. He was their godfather. He needed to step up and figure out a way to keep these children together and safe.

"Ms. Cook and I need to ask the children a few questions." Detective Russo pushed off the far wall where he had been leaning, practically lurking in the shadows.

Teagan stood with Anora in her arms and sat back down on the chair. "What kind of questions?"

Logan took that as his cue. Throwing an arm around Brann's shoulders, they walked back to the seat they'd occupied before.

"Bradley, did your mother seemed depressed lately?" Detective Russo asked.

Brann stiffened. "I'm not Bradley. He's my older brother. Half-brother. He's at West Point. If you want to ask him questions, you'll have to go there. I'm Brann." The boy leaned back against Logan and crossed his arms over his chest defiantly. Logan had never been so proud in his life. The kid had guts to talk back to a police detective, correcting him on his assumption.

"Okay, Brann. Was your mother sad lately?" The idiot repeated the question.

Brann gave him a can-you-be-that-stupid look. "Yes, she was sad. My dad got murdered." His voice broke on the last word. "We had the funeral." When tears began to fall again, Brann turned his face into Logan's chest.

"Brann," Teagan called from across the room. "Would you please go to your bedroom and grab the box of tissues off your nightstand?" When the boy didn't move, she added, "Brann, I need to blow my nose, but I don't want to leave the room."

"Okay," he said between sniffs. He spun around, and trotted toward the hall, head down, not looking at anyone.

"Sweetie, would you help your brother find the tissues, please?" Teagan stood and Anora chased her brother out of the room.

"What the hell do you think you're doing?" Teagan punched her balled fists onto her rounded hips and got into the detective's face. "You're not allowed to question children without a parent present. Since I'm their godmother, I guess that makes me the closest thing to a parent, and as such, I'm telling you to get the fuck out of my house. You are not allowed to talk to either of these children."

When the detective took a step toward Teagan, Logan shot out of his chair to stand beside her.

"First of all, those two children are now orphans, and technically wards of the state." He pointed to Ms. Cook who stood. "She now represents the children in the eyes of the Commonwealth of Virginia, so I certainly can question them."

"As their godparents, we are designated to take care of them in the absence of their parents," Teagan volleyed back.

"Ms. Williams," Ms. Cook said with derision. "This is

the twenty-first century. In the United States we have a separation of church and state. Without anything in writing, we have nothing but your word that Mrs. Davis wanted you to care for the children. We spoke this morning with her parents, who didn't feel capable of raising the children, given their advanced age. Since you have no blood ties to any of them, we have to look at all resources available to us."

"Marsha made me promise if anything ever happened to her, that I would take care of Brann and Anora." As though she had just thought of something, her whole face brightened. "We talked about this just last week. She was going to write it into her will."

"Are her parents the executors of her will?" Logan asked hopefully.

"I don't know," Teagan admitted. "I could call her attorney and ask."

"Ms. Williams, if you're not specifically mentioned in the will as the designated caretaker of the children, I'm not sure if we will be able to assign them to you." Ms. Cook continued. "What is your marital status?"

Fuck. Logan knew where this was headed.

The children could end up in an orphanage or foster care.

Separated.

Alone.

And there was nothing he and Teagan could do about it.

Fuck!

CHAPTER EIGHT

"I'm single." Teagan admitted quietly. She could feel her custody battle slipping through her clenched fists.

Ms. Cook's face pinched. "Since there are two children, a boy and a girl, we prefer to place the children in a home with both a mother and a father."

"There are millions of single mothers out there raising a house full of kids by themselves," Teagan pointed out.

"Have you taken the training to be a foster parent?" Ms. Cook asked, ignoring Teagan's statement.

"No, but I could do that." Maybe they could give her custody of the children while she took the course. Perhaps it was online and would only take a few hours. She could squeeze that in between visits to her mother and work.

"I'm sorry, Ms. Williams, but you need to be approved for our program before we can place the children with you." Ms. Cook looked apologetic. "There's a lot more to it than you may think. You are required to have twenty-five hours of training to understand the needs of the children, CPR and first aid, group meetings, home inspections, medical information, and a criminal background check. The process can take months."

"Can they stay here in the meantime?" Teagan said hopefully.

"I'm sorry." The social services agent truly looked regretful. "I'm not allowed to do that unless it is stated in writing by the parents."

Logan put a comforting hand on her shoulder. "Why don't you call Marsha's attorney. It can't hurt."

She forced a grin. "Let me grab his number." She really wanted an excuse to check on the children. She also wanted to make a phone call from the privacy of her bedroom. It was obvious that Logan didn't like the detective. She hated the man. He seemed rude and arrogant.

"I want Mommy." Anora's plea almost broke Teagan's heart as she approached their bedroom. She was so young. Would she even remember her mother in ten years?

"I know. Me too." Brann held his sister and rocked her as they both cried.

"Did she go to heaven to be with Daddy, so he wasn't all alone?" The child tried to reason.

Teagan wasn't so sure that their father was in heaven, but her mother certainly was.

"I don't know," Brann admitted. "Something bad must've happened to her because she wouldn't leave us all alone. She loves us."

Tears streaked down Teagan's cheeks.

She stepped into the spare bedroom. "Your mommy loved you both, very much. Your Uncle Logan and I are going to do everything we can so that you can stay here with me. Are you okay with that?"

Anora ran over and threw her arms around Teagan's

legs. "I want to go home. Can you come live at our house? You can babysit us there."

The house. Somebody had to deal with the house. Teagan knew, from the many hours she spent with Marsha, that they had been able to build up an excellent equity in the house. Perhaps it was enough to start college funds for the kids.

Then she remembered that the children were already worth a million dollars each, thanks to their inheritance from Gabe. She needed to call Marsha's attorney.

"I have to make a very important phone call. Are you kids okay staying right here for a few more minutes? I don't want you to go back into the living room until I'm done with my call." She trusted Logan, but she felt like she had a better handle on the situation and dealing with the children.

Both nodded.

"Promise me you'll stay right here until I get back." She ran her hand over Anora's hair. "I'll be right across the hall, if you need me."

Brann took Anora's hand and led her to her bed. "We won't leave the room, I promise. I don't like those people. Uncle Logan needs to make them go away."

"We're working on that right now." She hoped her voice was reassuring.

After grabbing Ed Keller's card from her dresser, Teagan collapsed into the overstuffed chair in the corner of her bedroom. She took a minute to mentally practice what she was going to say. She didn't want to break down in tears. After taking a deep breath, she tapped in the number.

It took a few minutes to convince his secretary that this was urgent, but his guard dog finally put her through.

"Ms. Williams, I understand this is an emergency. How can I help you?" He genuinely sounded concerned.

"Mr. Keller, I don't know if you've been informed yet but," she blinked back the tears and tried to swallow the fist that was clenching her throat. "But Marsha Davis died last night." She squeezed her eyes shut for only a second then quickly added, "I have the children with me. Social services just told them of their mother's...death." Her voice broke on the last word. She wanted to say so badly the word murder, but that wasn't the ruling of the stupid detective in her living room.

There was a long silence before he replied. "I'm so sorry, Ms. Williams. I know you and Mrs. Davis were good friends."

She heard papers shuffling.

Teagan charged on. "Marsha had always said that she wanted me to take care of her children if anything happened to her. Just last week we talked about her putting it into her will."

"Hold on, Ms. Williams." More shuffling, before he called out to his secretary.

Needing him to understand the urgency of the situation, she went on to explain. "They're here, right now, trying to take the children away from me and put them into the foster care system," Teagan blurted as the first tears escaped her eyes.

"Don't let them leave," he demanded. "What's your address? I'll be right there."

If she wasn't already sitting down, she would have fallen to her knees in relief. "You can help?"

"Yes. Take a deep breath and let it out slowly. What's your address? I'll be there as soon as I can." His voice was calm and in control, exactly what she needed.

After giving him her address, and her phone number, he promised to be there within twenty minutes. Rejuvenated by the hopeful news, Teagan exited her bedroom, checked on the children who were coloring quietly, and strode down the hallway.

"Let me just clarify what you're saying." Logan glowered down at Detective Russo, their faces ten inches apart. "Because of a note on the computer screen, a ten-millimeter Colt 1911 on the floor near her right hand, and a hole in her head, you are declaring Marsha's death a suicide."

What-the-fuck? It took Teagan only a few seconds to process what Logan was describing.

"Yes." The detective punctuated the single word with a head nod.

"No." Teagan stepped into the room and repeated the word. "No." The second time she said it forcefully.

Both men turned to look at her.

"No. She didn't commit suicide." Teagan shot a quick glance down the hallway to be sure the children hadn't overheard her. Whew. Neither child emerged from the bedroom, nor did she hear crying.

"And you know that...how?" The detective defiantly cocked his head to the side.

"It's all wrong." Teagan ran the description of the scene through her mind one more time. "First. That Colt 1911 isn't her gun." She held out her hands and spread her fingers. "Marsha, like me, has...I mean had...small hands."

Her gaze found Logan's. "Didn't you tell me that her body was found in the office? Was the gun safe open?"

"Yes," he confirmed.

"Her gun sits on the bottom shelf for easier access and is a Smith & Wesson Shield. It's perfect for a woman with a small grip yet packs a powerful punch as a forty caliber. I helped her pick it out after Gabe left her." Teagan shifted her gaze to the detective. "Why the hell would she stand on her tiptoes and grab an unfamiliar gun that was too big to hold when she could slide her hand in comfortably and take her own weapon?"

"Maybe she wanted more firepower," the detective quipped.

"And maybe somebody else grabbed it," Teagan suggested.

There was something else Logan said that sent up a red flag. She suddenly remembered. "Did you say the gun was near her right hand?"

"Yeah." Logan stared at her intently.

Bingo. Marsha hadn't committed suicide. She was murdered.

Teagan refused to hide her smug smile. "Although Marsha was right-handed, she shot with her left-hand because she was left eye dominant. She also needed carpal tunnel surgery on her right hand. I doubt she could even grip that 1911 and hold it steady."

"Whoever killed her didn't know her well." Logan smiled down at her with pride. "You should be the one to check out the office to see if anything has been taken."

She shrugged. "I was in there a few weeks ago before Marsha and I went to the range, but I doubt I would recognize if anything was missing."

"I still think it would be a good idea," he reiterated.

Teagan wasn't sure she could walk into that room and hold it together. Someone had murdered her friend there. She wondered if they actually made chalk outlines around the body like they did in the movies. She couldn't bear to look at the bloodstain either. But if it would help find Marsha's killer, Teagan would do anything.

Logan slid an arm around her shoulders and leaned down to whisper in her ear. "I'll go with you after they leave."

Heat radiated from his arm, across her shoulders and down her spine. It seemed to float through her body, triggering every nerve ending. Teagan wasn't sure when she'd last been touched by a man, but it had never felt like this. Comforting and exciting all at once.

"Okay." She turned her head to whisper the word in his ear and brushed her nose across his. Their lips were a fraction of an inch apart.

She gasped in a breath.

He was so close.

It had been far too long since she'd been kissed. If she moved a few millimeters his lips would be on hers.

The doorbell rang shattering her thoughts.

Stepping back quickly, she forced herself to breathe in slowly. "Maybe that's Mr. Keller."

Her feet refused to move, and her gaze never left the heat in Logan's bourbon-colored eyes.

He blinked...and the cool Marine was back. "You should get that before he rings again."

She turned and walked toward the door. What the fuck was that all about? She laid her hand flat on her chest as though she could still feel the warmth that emanated throughout her entire body. Damn. She needed to get laid.

After checking through the peephole, Teagan opened the door to a tall, distinguished-looking man with white hair in a charcoal gray suit and white shirt. His tie was gray, adorned with small white, gray, and navy-blue chevrons.

"Mr. Keller, thank you for coming over so quickly." After shaking his hand, she introduced him to everyone in the room.

He stared a little bit longer than appropriate at Logan. His contemptuous glance toward Ms. Cook and Detective Russo spoke volumes. "Ms. Williams, Lieutenant Colonel Jackson, is there somewhere we can talk in private? I'll need at least fifteen minutes of your time."

Logan immediately took control of the situation. "Ms. Cook. Detective Russo. Why don't you go get a cup of coffee and come back here in thirty minutes? No one here is a flight risk. We're not going anywhere. And neither are the children." He punctuated each word in the last sentence as he stepped toward the door and opened it for them.

"I'm going to give you thirty minutes. That's all." Detective Russo said on the way out the door. "I need to speak to those children."

Ms. Cook gave Logan a small smile. "Please understand, I'm on the side of the children. I'm legally here to do what's best for them, in the short term and the long run."

"Enjoy your coffee." Logan closed and locked the door behind them, then took a seat in the chair Teagan was beginning to think of as his.

"We have a lot to cover, but I need you both to know that I'm here to represent you, and the children, in respect to Marsha Davis's wishes." Mr. Keller got straight down to business. "First, where are the children?"

"I have a room for them when they stay with me, down the hall." She pointed in the direction where the children were.

Mr. Keller nodded. "Second, I'm sorry for your loss. Over the past two years I'd gotten to know Marsha rather well. I was handling her legal separation and divorce. Can you tell me how she died?" His voice cracked on the last word.

Teagan swallowed hard and Logan reached over and patted her hand, giving it a little squeeze.

"Detective Russo filed it last night as a suicide." When Logan squeezed her hand once again, she realized he hadn't moved it. "New information came to light moments ago that has made Teagan and I doubt that she killed herself. To be honest, we've both believed from the beginning that it was murder."

Mr. Keller dropped his face into his hands. "Oh, Christ, no." He scrubbed his hands over his face before lifting it to look at them. "Ms. Williams—"

"Please, Mr. Keller, call me Teagan," she insisted. She had a feeling they were going to be working together a lot over the next several months.

He nodded. "Teagan. I know you and Marsha were close, but I'm not sure if she confided in you her fears about Gabe's work. She was protective of the children, fearing they could be kidnapped and used against Gabriel." He sighed. "She was also afraid he wouldn't do anything to rescue them."

"Jesus Christ." Logan sprung from his chair and paced the room. "Why didn't she tell us anything about this?" He looked accusingly at her. "Did you know?"

"Hell, no." She quickly thought back to several conversations she had about the way Marsha was so guarded of the children. Fuck. She could kick herself in the ass. Why hadn't she seen it. "I thought she was just a very cautious mother."

"She was," Mr. Keller noted. "And with good reason. When he lived there, Gabriel would get calls all times of the day and night, sometimes on their home phone, often on one of the many cell phones he carried. During the first part of their separation, she confessed to me that she thought he was leaving her and the children for their safety."

"I can see Gabe doing that." Logan nodded. "He'd want to draw the enemy away from them."

Enemy? Who the hell was the enemy?

The attorney glanced at his watch. "We need to get through this before they return." After opening the folder in front of him, he handed Logan and Teagan long legal sheets covered in thick blue paper. "Marsha signed these the day before Gabriel's funeral, and now, I'm so thankful she did. What you have in your hands are copies of her complete last will and testament."

"Anyone else want a bottle of water?" Logan asked.

"Yes, please." Teagan felt awful for not playing the good hostess. Thank God Logan was comfortable enough in her home to take over that role.

"I'd like one as well," Mr. Keller said as he flipped through the pages.

Teagan downed half of her bottle as soon as Logan handed it to her. She didn't realize how dry her mouth had become.

"Let's skip straight to page two. There's a lot of legalese here, and I'll have to explain to you your jobs, but to start, Teagan, you have been named the executor of the will. Lieutenant Colonel Jackson—"

"Logan, please. Given that my name is in this will, I'm sure we're going to be working together a lot over the next year."

"Actually," Mr. Keller smiled at him. "You and I both

have a fiduciary responsibility to the children until Anora turns eighteen. I'll explain more about that later."

Shifting his gaze back to her, Mr. Keller said, "As the executor, Teagan, your job is to liquidate all the assets and distribute them according to the will. Basically, you handle the business end of everything stated in these papers."

"Why did she put me in charge of that?" Teagan realized she'd said that out loud.

"Because Marsha didn't want her father to have anything to do with her money and the children." His gaze shifted between her and Logan. "And she sure as hell didn't want her sister to get a dime, or worse yet, custody of the children."

"We don't want Ashley anywhere around the kids." Teagan agreed.

Mr. Keller gave her a genuine smile. He'd been handsome in his day, she was quite sure. "And that's exactly why Marsha made you the executor. Now, briefly, Teagan, you will have to see to it that all benefits are collected which in this case, includes settling all of Gabe's estate which transferred to Marsha upon his death. All of this now falls on your shoulders."

He reached over and patted her back. "But I'm here to help you. Fortunately, Marsha's CPA works in the same offices I do. He's a specialist in estate taxes and preparation of all documents required for probate court, which is another one of your duties. We're going to help you through this but it's going to take time. At least a year."

"It looks like we're going to be seeing a lot of each other. When can I start calling you Ed?" She quipped.

The older man grinned. Yep. He'd been a panty-dropper in his day. "Right now."

"Well, then, Ed, if I have to do all this, what does Logan

get to do?" She looked up at her friend whose eyes narrowed.

"Page three, everyone." He flipped the long sheet to the next page. "Logan, I hope you have a good broker."

Logan laughed out loud, to her surprise. "That would mean I have money to invest. You must have missed the part where I said I was a lieutenant colonel in the United States Marine Corps. The government doesn't pay our servicemen very much money."

"Ah hem," Teagan interjected. "They don't pay their service*women* very much either, but it's one place where men and women of the same rank get paid exactly the same, which ain't shit. That's part of the reason I got out." Her mother's rapidly progressing Alzheimer's was the other.

"Well, in that case, you might want to find one because Marsha named Logan both the trustee and the guardian." Ed said.

What the fuck? "Wait." Teagan glared at the attorney. "Marsha said that I was supposed to get the children. She wanted me to raise them if anything ever happened to her."

"Hold your horses, Teagan." He held up one hand in the stop position. "Guardian in the legal term as to the last will and testament is different than guardianship of the children. Let me explain."

Mr. Keller leaned forward, his elbows resting on his knees and gestured with his left hand while holding the signed will in his right. "Technically, Logan isn't even the guardian until the court officially appoints him as such. The guardian also doesn't necessarily mean he has custody of the children. In this case," he shook the papers, "Marsha has recommended to the court that Logan be given the responsibility for the children's legal, financial, and healthcare decisions. She had me add a paragraph in there clarifying that she wants custody of the children to go to you, and for the two of you to work together for the good of Anora and Brann."

He rubbed his hand over his face. "It's just a legal way of assuring that there are checks and balances of the money inherited by the children."

Ed's gaze went to Logan. "You do realize, that the moment you are legally named guardian, you will be responsible for the investment and disbursement of approximately eight million dollars."

Teagan had no idea that their father left them so much money.

Logan collapsed into his chair. "Holy fuck."

CHAPTER NINE

Eight million dollars.

Logan was trying desperately to wrap his mind around that much money. Sure, as the commanding officer of a Raider Battalion, he oversaw a budget ten times that amount. Yes. He was responsible for that money, in a way, but it was mostly numbers on a spreadsheet, tangible only in the equipment his special operators used on missions.

Fuck me.

He would now be accountable for growing that money. He didn't know shit about investing. He vowed in that moment to learn everything he could and invest the children's money wisely. He would also see to it that they had a wonderful childhood, using the money so they could go to camps in the summer, travel and see the world— at least the good parts—and learn how to do whatever they wanted. Anora would learn ballet, or whatever the hell classes she desired. Brann could ride horses, sail boats, go to the best baseball camps available, if that's what he wanted.

Those kids would have a much better childhood than he did.

"I imagine you're going to want to sell the house as soon as possible," Ed announced. "You'll have to work together on that. Legally, Logan has the power of attorney to sell the property, but you, Teagan, are responsible for collecting those assets. Again, we're here to help you through everything."

"The house is still a crime scene as far as I'm concerned, no matter what Detective dickhead says. I'll go over his head if I have to." Logan chugged the last half of his water. "Somebody murdered Marsha and they may now be after the children...unless she gave them what they wanted."

"Oh my God, no." Teagan's voice was an octave higher than normal. "Do you really think someone may come after the kids?"

Logan put his hand over the back of hers and gave it a little squeeze. "Somebody murdered Marsha, and if the police aren't willing to look into this, I know some guys down in Richland. They're damn good detectives."

Ed glanced at his watch once again. "Speaking of detectives, the one I met, and the social services lady should be back any minute. We need to discuss the children. They're still here, right? They've been so quiet."

"Yeah, back in their bedroom." Teagan gestured toward the hallway. "They come and stay with me sometimes, so I've converted that room for them."

"Good." Mr. Keller grinned. "At this very moment, my clerk is filing with the probate court to give you, both of you, immediate custody of the children while their future is determined. We're also asking for an emergency hearing on their permanent custody." He waggled the papers once again. "Most often the judge will grant custody to whomever is named in the will, but that doesn't automatically mean you'll get them. The state is a bit old-fashioned in that it prefers children to go to a two-parent household. Also, given how much money these two children are worth, I wouldn't be surprised if long-lost relatives start crawling out of the woodwork."

He looked at Logan. "It's a damn good thing Marsha named you guardian. I don't think many people are stupid enough to argue with a Marine officer."

"They'll be sorely disappointed if they try." He grinned over at Teagan. "I'm going to do everything within my power to see to it that she gets the children."

There was a knock at the door. Their private time with Mr. Keller was done, but certainly not over.

Once everyone was reseated in the living room, Mr. Keller explained everything that was in Marsha's signed will.

"Mr. Keller, as you know, the state is concerned about placing two children, one of each sex, in the care and custody of a single parent," Melissa Cook explained. She looked at Logan with regret in her soft blue eyes. "We will be asking for placement in an established home with a husband and wife."

Teagan threw her hands up in the air. "What am I supposed to do? Run out and get married?"

Melissa, as she had instructed Logan to call her, gave Teagan a small smile. "I'm not sure that would help much. Again, the state prefers established families. In your favor, though, is that you have an established relationship with the children."

That sounded encouraging as far as Logan was concerned.

Standing, Melissa's gaze swept the room before landing on Teagan. "May I see the room you have prepared for the children?"

"Sure." Teagan showed the social services woman down the hall, as they talked in low voices.

When they returned, Melissa announced, "Given the wishes of Mrs. Davis as stated in her will, on behalf of the Commonwealth of Virginia I am going to grant temporary emergency custody of Anora and Brann Davis to Teagan Williams." She walked over and shook Mr. Keller's hand. "I'll see you in court."

As she headed for the door, Detective Russo stood and called out, "I still have questions for the children."

Melissa glanced over her shoulder. "You'll have to get that permission from the children's temporary guardian." Her gaze slid to Logan and she gave him a little wink.

Damn. Melissa Cook had been looking out for them the entire time. Logan only hoped she continued to keep the children's best interests in mind when they went to court. No matter what, though, he controlled the purse strings and would see to it that those two precious little children had the best childhood possible.

"Ms. Williams," Detective Russo approached Teagan.

Mr. Keller reached over and touched Teagan's forearm. "I've got this." The older man stood and quickly moved between her and the detective. "The children have just suffered two traumas in a row. At ages four and seven, I doubt they have any relevant information as to who murdered their mother."

"I haven't changed my assessment of the incident, yet." Detective Russo crossed his arms over his chest. "It's still filed as a suicide."

Incredulity washed over Ed's face followed quickly by

anger. "Marsha Davis didn't commit suicide. Detective, you need to do your job and prove that, then go find the son of a bitch who killed her. If you truly wish to waste your time interrogating the children, you'll need a court order to do so. I suggest you re-examine all of the facts in Mrs. Davis's murder so you can reopen the case."

Teagan was beaming when she stood. She looked at Ed with grateful admiration before she strode toward the door and opened it. "Detective Russo, I believe that concludes your business for today. You will not speak one word to the children, even if you see them on the street, without a court order which will be examined thoroughly by Mr. Keller. You will never speak to these children without me present."

"You have a good day, ma'am," Russo said through clenched teeth as he left the apartment.

Teagan shut and bolted the door closed. She practically skipped back to Mr. Keller and threw her arms around him. "Thank you. I'm so glad you were here to deal with him." She corrected herself. "Both of them."

Seeing Teagan in the other man's arms sent a rush of jealousy through Logan.

What the hell? He had no reason to be envious. It wasn't as though Teagan was his. True, Mr. Keller came charging in like a white knight and saved the damsel in distress, which was usually Logan's job, but that was no reason for him to be resentful. He and Teagan were just good friends. He was thankful Ed had shown up.

When Teagan placed her lips on the man's cheek, unexpected anger rose from deep inside Logan. He wanted to punch the man out.

She quickly released Ed, then launched herself at Logan.

"The kids are ours." Her huge smile was so full of joy just before she wrapped her arms around his neck. It was as though her touch forced her happiness into him. "I was so afraid Ms. Cook was going to take them away from us, then it might be weeks or even months before I could see them again." As he enveloped her small body, he felt her shaking.

Is she crying? Or were those happy tears? He could never tell the difference. Women always confused him. They were so emotional. He liked the feel of her body next to his.

She leaned back, grinning ear to ear. "I have children."

He could clearly see the excitement in her eyes. Deep down, she had wanted children in her life. He could see that now. He was happy for her. Teagan would make a good mother.

Logan had always thought he would make a good father, but that hadn't happened for him.

Her face fell. "Oh, fuck, I have kids. All the time. I can't send them back home when I get too exhausted. What the hell am I going to do with two kids?"

He couldn't stand that look of terror in her face.

"No, *we* have children." Saying the words out loud made them real.

Fuck. I have kids. What the hell am I going to do with two kids? Then he knew exactly what they would do with Anora and Brann. "We're going to do our best. We're going to love them every day and let them know how special they are."

When his eyes met Teagan's, a silent message passed between them.

They were in this…together…for at least fourteen more years.

"We *can* do this," she reassured them both.

"We're *going* to do this," he volleyed back.

"You'd better not walk out on me." Her warning made him wonder who had walked out on her before. Then she corrected herself, "I mean us. Me and the children."

He gave her a half grin. "Marsha already committed me until Anora turns eighteen. A judge is going to make it legal and binding." He squeezed her gently. "I'm not going anywhere. I'll be there for you and the children."

Her blue eyes darkened. "You're one of the best men I've ever known in my life." She laid her lips on his. The contact was all too brief, but he felt the shot of heat in his heart. His lips still tingled when she pulled back.

"You're going to make a great mother." Logan believed his words.

"I sure as hell hope so." She tilted her head. "You can put me down, now, big guy."

He grinned. "You're the one that jumped into my arms."

"Yeah, I was excited."

Loosening his hold on her, he gently slid her to the floor. "You have every right to be happy." Logan glanced over at the attorney who seemed to be taking in their reactions. "And Ed is going to make sure you keep those children."

Mr. Keller gave them a big smile. "It looks to me as though you two won't have any problem working together. It may take a few days before we can get in front of a judge, but I'll see what I can do to make that happen sooner rather than later." His phone buzzed and he checked the text. "Excuse me, please, I need to call my clerk. She's at the courthouse now."

Logan grabbed Teagan's hand. "Let's go check on *our* kids." They started down the hallway and didn't release their hands until the doorway. He wasn't sure why he'd done that, it just felt right.

Teagan sat on Anora's bed and grabbed each child around the waist, pulling them down next to her. "The social services lady and the detective are gone. I'm going to be taking care of you, now."

She looked up at Logan. He'd been content to stand back and let her take control of the situation. He wouldn't know what to do if they started crying.

"Your Uncle Logan is going to be helping too," she explained.

"What happens when he goes back to North Carolina?" Brann asked.

"Yes, that's a good question," Ed said from the door. "And one the judge may ask you…this afternoon." He grinned a bit nervously. "Judge Salter has a slot free this afternoon and since this is an emergency, he is willing to slide you in. What do you say?" His gaze bounced back and forth between Teagan and Logan.

"Hell, yeah. Let's get this thing settled." Logan looked at Teagan, Anora, and Brann for confirmation before returning his gaze to Mr. Keller. "Unless there some reason that we should delay it?"

"I have a great deal of paperwork I need to prepare. I'll see you all at the courthouse at three o'clock this afternoon." He turned to leave then spun back around. "Bring the children. Judge Salter can be a bit of an odd duck. He may want to speak to the children himself, possibly in chambers. Call if you have any questions. I'll see myself out." He glanced at his watch and disappeared through the door.

"The children are going to need nicer clothes," Teagan

announced. "One of us needs to go to the house and pick up enough clothing for them for the next week or two."

"I'll go." He sat them on the bed and pulled Brann onto his lap. "Do you have a suitcase in your bedroom?"

"No. All the suitcases are kept in the closet in the spare bedroom." Brann said without looking at him.

He lifted the boy's chin until their eyes met. "What's up? You know you can talk to me."

"What's going to happen?" Brann asked quietly.

Logan ran his hand up and down the boy's spine. "I'm going to go over to your house and pack up a whole bunch of clothes for you and Anora. This afternoon, we're going to go to the courthouse where Judge Salter will officially let your Aunt Teagan and me take care of you."

The boy sniffed back a tear. He was trying so hard to be brave. "Do we...will there be a..." A tear escaped his eye and trickled over his rounded cheek before he swiped it away with the back of his hand. "Will Mom have a funeral?" The tears now flowed freely as his shoulders shook.

Logan gathered the child into his arms. He was so small compared to Teagan who he had just held moments before. He wanted to surround this child and protect him from everything bad the world could throw at him. "Yes. I'm sure there will be a funeral, in a few days. In the meantime, you're going to hang out here, safe and sound with Aunt Teagan and me. Is that okay, buddy?"

Brann simply nodded. He waited until the boy calmed before he left the apartment.

When Logan pulled up outside the Davis home, he was surprised to see an unmarked police car sitting in the driveway. Using the key Teagan gave him, he unlocked the front door and walked in.

Fuck. It still smelled of death, but he knew the body had been taken away hours ago. Logan's stomach rebelled anyway.

Suck it up, Marine.

Detective Russo stepped out of the office into the hall. "What the hell are you doing here? How the fuck did you get in?"

Logan held up the keys Teagan had given him, thankful she and Marsha had been such good friends. "The kids need clothes." Disappointed that he couldn't spend some time in the office checking things out for himself, Logan headed up the stairs. In the guest bedroom, he pulled out the largest suitcases he could find and headed to the children's rooms.

More familiar with little boys, he decided to get Anora's bag packed first. He'd learned to get the bad shit out of the way before tackling more favorable tasks. After unzipping the suitcase on her bed, he opened all the drawers, assessing the spatial needs. Logan wasn't surprised when he heard footsteps in the hall.

"You seem to know your way around this house." Detective douchebag's tone was accusing.

"Brann and Anora are my godchildren. I've been here before." Not very often, but Logan wasn't going to give the detective that tidbit of information. He decided he had room to take everything in the little girl's room. Hopefully that would make her feel more at home in Teagan's apartment.

"To see Marsha Davis or the children?" The dickhead stepped into the room.

Logan wanted to deck the asshole for even suggesting that he had something going on with Marsha, but hours before going to court was not the time to get arrested for assaulting an officer of the law. Without looking at the man, he continued to pack small little pink and purple outfits.

"Marsha was the wife of my good friend." At least Logan had thought of him as such until his funeral a few days ago. "Gabe and I had worked together years ago and remained friends. That's why I'm his children's godfather. Even though he and Marsha were separated, I had promised both of them, and God, that I would take care of the kids." He looked over his shoulder at the young man and wondered if he understood responsibility. "I take all my obligations seriously."

"You were with Mrs. Davis yesterday morning."

Logan gathered everything from the next drawer and dumped it into the suitcase. "I was. We were cleaning out Gabriel's apartment and returning the keys to management." He shrugged. He'd give the detective what he wanted, his whereabouts all day. "We returned to the house where Teagan had prepared lunch for all of us, then Teagan and I took the children to the zoo. On our way home, Matthew Saint Clare called me and informed us what he had found when he had arrived."

Placing the last of the items from the dresser into the suitcase, Logan finally turned and looked at the man lounging against the doorjamb. "That gives you my alibi, and Teagan's. What else do you need to know, detective?"

Standing upright, the detective held his gaze for a long moment. "Why do you think this was murder and not suicide?"

Logan was surprised that Detective Dunce would even reconsider his immediate decision. "Marsha would never commit suicide. First, she loved those kids with all her heart and would never leave them alone. Second, she wasn't distraught over Gabriel's death. If anything, she was relieved. Because of his job, she was afraid the children were targets for kidnap. Last week, with Gabe's death, that threat was gone. Third, it was Gabe's office. His domain. According to Teagan, she rarely went in there. Forth, that was Gabe's computer and she wouldn't touch it. Marsha was a former Navy lieutenant. She was well aware of the meaning of the words top-secret, confidential, and eyes only. Fifth, you heard what Teagan said. Marsha shot a gun left-handed. I'll be surprised if the coroner finds gunshot residue on her right hand."

The detective narrowed his eyes. "Suicides don't require an autopsy."

"Are you telling me that you didn't request an autopsy?" Logan was flabbergasted. How fucking dumb could this guy be? "If you haven't already, you had better order an autopsy right this minute, before I go over your head and speak with your lieutenant. I'm sure he'd be interested in hearing why my friends and I believe it was murder."

He looked like a chastised puppy. "No need. Someone already called the captain. That's why I'm walking the scene once again."

Inwardly, Logan gave a fist pump. He'd bet money that Matthew had placed the call.

The detective tilted his head toward the master bedroom down the hall. "It looks as though Mrs. Davis was removing her husband's clothes from the closet and was interrupted."

Hearing the word closet reminded Logan of his task. He had to get the kids packed up and their bags back to Teagan's, then run by his hotel room, grab a quick shower and change back into a suit, then get everybody to the courthouse by three.

"That was my interpretation, also," Logan admitted.

Upon opening the door, he stared at rows of pastel outfits.

Holy, Christ. How many changes of clothes did one little girl need? The bottom row looked too small for her. Glancing at the floor, he understood. Six dolls, approximately two-foot-tall, lay in boxes. He recognized them as the popular, and expensive, American Girl dolls. In another corner sat a Barbie doll house filled with the iconic dolls.

Fuck. He was going to need a suitcase just for toys.

Logan let out a deep breath. "Look, detective, I got a lot to do and very little time. Is there anything else you need from me?"

All pretense of cockiness gone, the detective asked, "If you have just a few minutes, would you please stop in the office downstairs before you leave?"

"I can do that." Logan really wanted to see the office and spend a few minutes there. He'd make time.

CHAPTER TEN

Teagan was accustomed to the security procedures when entering a federal building since she went through a checkpoint every day at the Navy Marine Corps Air Acquisition office. She didn't think anything of it when she plopped her purse into one of the big white bins, laying it flat so its contents could easily be seen on the x-ray machine. She carefully scanned the children to be sure there were no large metal buckles or anything that might set off the alarms. The children were nervous enough, and Teagan had to admit, she was a bit apprehensive about going to court. She'd never been there before.

She glanced back to the end of their little line to see Logan emptying change, keys, and his cell phone into a small bowl and placing it on the moving black belt. For a split second, she wondered if he had to go through the same protocol entering his building.

Teagan kneeled down in front of Anora so they were almost eye-to-eye. "I'm going to walk through the archway first and show you how it's done. You wait right here until I call you. Will you do that for me?"

When Anora nodded, Teagan stepped through the great arch. No bells or whistles went off. One down, three to go. She looked at the armed officer to her right. He gave her a nod.

"Come on through," she told the little girl in an adorable light blue dress, white socks with a blue ruffle and blue-and-white sparkly gym shoes. Anora's gaze slowly ran over the eight-foot tall detection device before she met Teagan's.

"Just walk through, sweetie, you can do it," she encouraged.

Anora scrunched her face in determination and took off like a bolt of lightning. One minute she was on the far side of the security arch, the next she was standing beside Teagan. Several people in line started to laugh.

Once again, Teagan kneeled down so she could be on the same level as Anora. "Sweetie, we need you to walk through slowly."

Anora looked at the large metal device and her eyes grew huge. "I have to go back?" Her chin started to quiver. "No. I don't want to do it again."

A heavyset woman with graying hair walked over with her wand in her hand. "Hey there, pretty girl. My name is Ms. Darlene. If you don't want to walk back through there, you don't have to." She showed Anora the handheld device. "I can coat you in magic instead. This is my magic wand. I can tell if anyone has money in their pocket, or any kind of metal on them, or even inside them, and exactly where it's located. Want to see how it works?"

Anora nodded. The woman rose slowly as though her knees hurt. She walked over to the uniformed man watching the x-ray device.

"This is Sam and I'll bet he has money in one of his

front pockets. What do you think?" The officer was so good with Anora that Teagan just wanted to hug her.

Darlene ran the wand up one leg and when it reached his pocket area, it started to beep. She got all happy in an exaggerated way that a preschool teacher would. "I found it. I found it."

Sam reached into his pocket and produced several coins.

Teagan was pleased to see Brann and Logan pass through the arch without an issue. They moved in next to her out of the main path.

Ms. Darlene walked over to another man. "This is Darren and he has a metal knee. Watch this." Darlene then ran the device from his ankle upward. Around the knee, it started to beep once again. She got a huge smile on her face. "See. I found the metal and it's on the inside of his body."

Kneeling in front of Anora, the security agent asked, "May I run the wand over you? Let's see if you have change in your pocket, or a metal knee. If it doesn't beep, then it coats you in magic."

"I want to be magic." Anora stepped closer.

Darlene quickly ran the wand up and down, a few inches away from the child.

No beeping.

Darlene's gaze met Teagan. "You have a beautiful little girl here." She faced Anora. "To keep your magic, you have to sit quietly on the bench and do exactly what the judge says. Can you do that?"

"Yes, ma'am." Anora smiled at her. "We have to sit quietly and keep our hands folded during Mass so I'm good at not fidgeting."

"I'll bet you are," Darlene said as she stood slowly.

"Thank you so much, Ms. Darlene." Teagan held her hand out to shake. "You're really good with little kids."

The female officer gave her a quick smile. "Not my first rodeo with little ones. She's adorable."

Teagan put her arm around Anora's shoulders. "We think so."

"Our courtroom is this way." Logan gestured toward the hall to the right.

They were met at the door by Mr. Keller. "We need to enter and sit quietly until our case is called. I'll do all the talking, but like I said, Judge Salter can be a bit quirky. He may ask you direct questions. If he does, answer the question as succinctly as possible. Don't give him any extra details. Use as few words as possible. He's running on time, so we shouldn't have to wait long. Are you ready?"

Teagan realized how damp her hands were. She hadn't been this nervous in years. She wiped them off on the front of her slacks as though she were smoothing out wrinkles.

"Let's get this done and over with." Logan grabbed Brann's hand and headed for the double doors.

Teagan took a deep breath and let it out slowly as she reached for Anora's hand and followed them in.

Logan had selected an empty row about one third of the way down. They automatically placed the children between them, as though they had been doing it for years.

Fortunately, they only had to sit through one case, but it was ugly. Grandma had passed away and given her house to her favorite granddaughter. A grandson, from a different set of parents, got her car. Her own children got nothing, and they were the ones challenging the will.

With time to kill, Teagan took in the room. Surprisingly, it looked just like courtrooms on TV. Everything was dark wood, the exact same color, from the paneling on the walls, to the solid railing separating the area where people sat from the attorneys and the judge. The tall desk centered at the very front was flanked by the flags of the United States of America and the Commonwealth of Virginia. About ten feet away were two tables facing the judge.

Teagan wondered if Ms. Cook, or whoever the state social services sent, would sit at one table and Mr. Keller at the other. A lectern stood centered in between, directly in front of the judge.

In the current case, attorneys for the parents were on the right, and those representing the children sat at the table on the left. They took turns standing in the middle talking to the judge.

"I've heard enough." Judge Salter interrupted the parents' attorney. "Take your seat." He leaned toward the shorter desk where a woman in her fifties typed away on a computer. They had a brief conversation before he sat upright in his large executive chair. "I've made my decision. It's obvious to me that Mrs. Walters clearly stated her wishes in her last will and testament. You have not presented the court with any solid reason to alter her wishes." He then named the parents and mandated that they pay all court costs, in addition to attorney fees of the grandchildren. "Be sure to pay the clerk of courts before you leave the building." The grandchildren hugged each other as the parents mumbled, occasionally accusing each other more loudly.

For the first time, Judge Salter scanned the benches in the back of the room. He smiled when he looked their way.

The bailiff announced the next case. Theirs.

"Move up to the front row, behind me," Mr. Keller ordered just above a whisper. They stood as a group and once they hit the aisle, Teagan and Anora reached for each other's hand as they followed Mr. Keller to the front. He let himself through the gate and sat down at the table on the left, extracting his laptop from his briefcase.

Anora stopped five feet from the wooden wall separating the benches from the attorney's area. "I can't take communion, yet. I haven't had my Catholic-chism classes. We don't get those until second grade."

Teagan was stunned and confused for several seconds. All she could do was stare at Anora. Then she had to bite back a laugh. She kneeled.

"Sweetie, this isn't church, so there's no communion for anyone." Teagan hoped that satisfied the curious child.

Anora pointed at the judge. "But he's wearing a robe and that's an altar, even though it doesn't have candles."

Teagan had to roll her lips between her teeth to hold in the laugh. She looked away and caught the judge chuckling. That just made it worse. Returning her gaze to Anora, she tried to explain once again. "You'll see in just a minute. He's not a priest. He's a judge. And right now, sweetie, he's waiting for us to take our seats. Let's go sit down, now." She stood and took Anora's hand, leading her far enough down the front bench so there was plenty of room for Brann and Logan.

Ms. Cook and an older woman in a navy-blue pantsuit marched up the aisle and through the gate, sitting down at the table on the right.

After the legal preliminaries, the judge announced, "I've read the emergency petition for personal guardianship of Anora Davis and Brann Davis. I have a copy of their mother's last will and testament which has named Ms. Teagan Williams and Lieutenant Colonel Logan Jackson to have physical custody of the children." He looked over at the other table. "Ms. Cook, why does the state social services have a problem with this arrangement?"

Ms. Cook stood and walked to the lectern, her back straight, her shoulders squared.

"The Commonwealth of Virginia believes that it is in the best interest of all children, in the long-term, that they be placed in an established two-parent home. Neither Ms. Williams nor Mr. Jackson is married. There are only two blood relatives who could be considered possibilities. Mrs. Davis's parents have been offered the care of their grandchildren, but they have indicated that in their advanced years they would not be able to give the children the necessary physical support long-term. Mrs. Davis has a sister who is currently in rehabilitation for addictions and thus is considered unsuitable."

"Lieutenant Colonel Jackson, I would first like to thank you for your service." The judge glanced down at the papers on his desk. "Are you still active duty?"

Mr. Keller turned around and motioned for Logan to stand.

Logan came to attention, his back straight, shoulders squared, arms to his side, fingers slightly curled under. He looked directly into the judge's eyes.

Damn. He was imposing. All man. Testosterone charged. Virile. Fucking hot.

"Yes, sir." Logan's voice was deep and crisp.

"Where are you stationed, Colonel Jackson?"

Oh, damn. This could really hurt their chances.

"Camp Lejeune, North Carolina, sir." Logan slid her an apologetic glance.

"Ms. Williams, are you still employed at the Navy Marine Corps Air Acquisition office?"

Teagan stood on shaky legs. She could see where this was going. "Yes, sir."

"Ms. Williams, isn't that office located down near the Pentagon?"

"Yes, sir." She couldn't lie to a judge.

"I also see that your mother is in a local nursing home specializing in memory care." The judge held her gaze.

How the hell did he know that? And how did her mother's condition affect his decision? Was that legal? Inwardly, she laughed at herself. He was a judge. He would know.

"Yes, sir." It was the only answer she could give him. It was as though the children had slipped from her grasp another inch. She wanted to collapse on the bench and cry. But she couldn't. She had to fight for custody.

The judge studied each of them, including the children. He then picked up the papers in front of him and seemed to spend a great deal of time reading.

Mr. Keller motioned for them to go ahead and sit back down. When she did, Anora crawled into her lap, curled up in a tight little ball. Teagan wondered how much the little girl understood about what was happening.

Logan glanced her way, concerned, an apology in his eyes.

Judge Salter looked up and gazed at the four of them. "Lieutenant Colonel Jackson, are you planning to retire anytime soon?"

Logan stood. "No, sir, I am not. I was selected for Colonel six months ago and will be able to pin it on within the next few months. I have agreed to stay in the Marine Corps another three years."

Teagan felt her heart drop into her stomach which immediately protested. She was going to be sick. Why the fuck hadn't he told her about his promotion? She felt the children slip away from her a bit more.

"Congratulations on your promotion. Is there any chance you'll be transferred to Virginia? Or better yet, at the Pentagon?" It seemed as though the judge was trying very hard to find a solution.

Logan shook his head side to side in short jerky motions. "No, sir, I have a very unique and special military occupation. I'm slated for a position on the Marine Raiders Regiment staff at Camp Lejeune."

The judge nodded. "I understand." He picked up the papers on his desk once again.

The silence in the courtroom was deafening.

"Okay, let's get the assignment part of the will settled first." The judge looked at his clerk and nodded. "I hereby appoint Lieutenant Colonel Logan Jackson as the guardian for all beneficiaries as set forth in the will of Marsha Davis. His per the same last will and testament, I do hereby appoint Lieutenant Colonel Logan Jackson as the trustee. Colonel Jackson, has Mr. Keller explained to you the meaning and responsibilities of trustee and guardian as set forth in a last will and testament?"

Logan stood. "Mr. Keller has explained to me the duties and responsibilities I will have as both trustee and guardian. I am willing and able to take on those duties."

"Very well. Ms. Williams. You are not appointed by court but I want to be sure you understand your responsibilities as executor of the will. In one year, I want you in this court so we can probate the entire will. By that time you will have liquidated all assets, paid all outstanding bills, or you'll explain to the court why you haven't. You understand your obligations as executor?"

This part Teagan could handle. She sat up straight and

tall. "I understand, and will see you in one year on this matter."

"Good. Now let's move on to the matter of custody of Anora Davis and Brann Davis." Judge Salter laid the documents down and looked directly at her. "Ms. Williams, how badly do you want these children?"

She didn't care what Mr. Keller had said. She was going to lay it out for the judge. Standing, she set Anora on the floor and moved between the two kids, putting an arm around each. "I was there when each of these beautiful children were born. I was one of the first to hold them, change their diapers, pace the floor with them as they got their first teeth. They've stayed many nights in my home after spending long days together. I've been with and around these children all of their lives. That has to count for something. I would do anything for these children." She glanced first down at Brann and then at Anora. "I love them and would do anything to be able to keep them and raise them."

The children threw their small arms around her waist and Logan moved in to run his hand up and down her back.

"Good." The judge stated boldly. "Because you're going to have to be the one to make the sacrifices. As per the wishes in the last will and testament of Marsha Davis, I hereby grant joint custody of Anora and Brann Davis to Teagan Williams and Logan Jackson."

She couldn't hold in her squeal. She tried to pick up both children but couldn't. One look at Logan and she could see him grinning ear to ear. They won custody.

"Order in the court." A loud voice bellowed, then repeated the command.

"I'm not finished." The judge was very close to his

microphone, so his voice filled the room. "Ms. Williams, a few minutes ago you told me you were willing to do anything to keep custody of the children. If you lied to me, then I will accept the petition of social services and place the children into the foster care system here in Fairfax County."

Fuck. What the hell had she just gotten herself into? She then glanced down at the two children she loved more than anyone else in the world. No. She would do anything to keep them out of the system.

She squared her shoulders and held his gaze. "What do I have to do?"

He leaned forward, his forearms on his desk and stared at her. "In my opinion, the state of Virginia has it right. Children should grow up in a two-parent household. Truthfully, if I could, I would mandate that the two of you get married. Unfortunately, I can't do that, legally. But I can mandate you, Ms. Williams, and Lieutenant Colonel Jackson, live no more than thirty minutes apart. You are to share custody equally. Colonel, I expect you to be an active father figure to both children. I understand that you live in North Carolina, so I will allow the children to move there. Ms. Williams, since Jacksonville is a military town, I'm sure there are government jobs. As for your mother, I'm sure there are good facilities for her near Camp Lejeune. Colonel Jackson, Ms. Williams, do you accept the terms as I explained them to you?"

"I do." Teagan answered boldly. The two simple words rolled through her brain. I do. The same words one says during a wedding ceremony. Well, like a wedding where two people commit themselves to each other forever, she had just committed her life and love to the two children at her side.

She glanced up at Logan whose smile showed off two rows of bright white teeth. Damn. He was so handsome when he smiled. He should smile more often, especially now that she'd be around to see it.

Reality just smacked her in the face. Her *I do* extended to Logan, at least for the next fourteen years. Having him in her life wouldn't be bad at all.

CHAPTER ELEVEN

"We appreciate you guys having us over." Logan gave Matthew a chin lift as he herded Anora and Brann into the Saint Claire's beautiful new home.

Squeals erupted as Liza and Anora bounced while hugging each other. Logan hoped that once they moved to North Carolina that Anora would find good friends.

"Why don't you two girls go into Liza's room and play?" Elizabeth suggested.

Brann lifted his baseball glove and bumped it with Austin's. "Race you to the backyard."

Logan wondered where the nearest recreational department was in Topsail Island so he could get Brann signed up for Little League as soon as possible. He'd add that to his long list of things to do as soon as he got them all moved to North Carolina. Parenting was tough.

"Thanks so much for inviting us over, Elizabeth." Teagan hugged their friend and former teammate. "The kids needed some normal. It's been a long and stressful week for all of us."

"How are all of you doing?" Elizabeth pulled back and looked Teagan in the eyes.

"I'm over the initial shock." Teagan gave her friend a small grin. "I think the children are adjusting to the new situation well. They were both teary during the funeral this morning, but the child psychologist said we should expect that. She also said they may burst into tears at any given point."

Teagan shook her head. "Hell, I burst into tears at odd times, and over the dumbest things." She sniffed loudly. "The kids were running around the park yesterday, playing tag, laughing and squealing, just having fun. I grabbed my phone and started to video them, intending to show Marsha when I returned them." She swallowed hard and wiped tears from her eyes. "Then I remembered she was never going to see them again."

Elizabeth put her arms around Teagan and rocked her as they both cried.

"See what I mean? I cry over the weirdest things." Teagan took a deep breath and wiped away tears, regaining control once again. She stepped back and faced Matthew.

"I'm just glad we got to see you before you left." Matthew said as he gave her a friendly hug. If the man wasn't so in love with his new wife, Elizabeth, Logan would have been jealous. He hadn't been able to hug Teagan, or hold her, in over a week.

"You'd better get settled quickly, because I'm looking forward to bringing Austin and Liza down and spending some time on the beach before summer gets away from all of us." Elizabeth looked over at Logan. "How many years have you lived in that beach house and why have you never invited us before?"

Logan shrugged and suddenly felt guilty that he'd never invited his friend, Elizabeth, to bring her children down and enjoy a week at the beach. He decided to be honest. "You and the children could've come at any time, but you know how I felt about Robert." Logan flat out disliked Elizabeth's second husband and couldn't stand to be around the douchebag. He was right about the man, too. After Robert was killed in a car accident, Elizabeth discovered his many affairs. He'd left her in financial trouble to boot.

Logan was so glad that she'd found Matthew. He and the CIA special operations man clicked from their first meeting. Now, it was as though they had been good friends for years.

As if Matthew could read his mind, he handed Logan a beer. "Let's go sit in the living room. Micah should be here anytime now. He wanted to go back to his hotel room and change out of the suit he wore to the funeral this morning."

Logan and the women followed their host into a large room with two full-size couches and several overstuffed chairs. They could see the street as well as the backyard where the boys were now playing catch.

"This is such a beautiful home," Teagan gushed. "And it's perfect for your family."

Elizabeth smiled over at Matthew. "I swear, we looked at houses for a week before they showed us this one. The minute we walked in we knew we were going to buy it." She jumped out of her chair. "It's going to be about another forty-five minutes before supper is ready. I have snacks while we're waiting." A minute later she returned with a tray laden with plates of cheese, fruit, a basket of crackers, a bowl of dip, and a bottle of wine. She distributed the food throughout the room and topped off Teagan's glass.

Logan watched the gorgeous blonde sip her wine and close her eyes. She was exhausted. He hoped once they got to his house at Topsail Island, and they got everyone settled, she'd be able to relax. His house was all about kicking back and chilling, watching the ocean waves, seeing nothing but blue water all the way to the horizon.

Before Micah could ring the bell, Elizabeth opened the door and gave the large Navy SEAL a hug. "Thanks for joining us."

"You had me at a home-cooked meal." He released their former teammate and shook hands with Matthew. "I usually hate to come to DC, but if I could con Elizabeth into cooking for me, you'd see me a lot more often."

Logan stood as his friend approached and gave him one of the half-hug, back pound male greetings.

"I'm so fucking glad you got the kids." Micah moved to Teagan for a hug. "You doing okay, Ice-T?" He called her by her pilot handle. Logan had forgotten the name they had called her all during their mission together.

She nodded. "I'm just glad the funeral is finally over. The moving truck left yesterday, and we pull out tomorrow morning."

"I can't believe the autopsy took so long," Elizabeth complained.

"I'm just glad they did one." Logan gave Matthew a chin lift. "Thanks for making that happen."

"I was so pissed that night. That little pin-dick detective took one look at Marsha, a glance at the gun, read the message on the screen, and in less than five minutes declared it a suicide." Matthew scowled then downed half his beer as though to wash away the bad taste in his mouth. "I never pull the Fed card, but I wasn't about to let detective dickhead get away with that. He needs to fucking do his job. We all know it was murder."

Everyone in the room nodded in agreement.

"I'm just glad her parents finally agreed to a closed casket." Teagan shook her head. "I had the damnedest time getting her mother to understand the condition of the body. I finally told her I didn't think it was a good idea for the children to see her in the casket." She took a gulp of her wine. "I hate what they do to the human body with all that embalming and makeup. No one ever looks like they did when they were alive." She changed her voice. "They look like they're sleeping." Returning to her normal tone, she added, "That's just bullshit."

Silently, Logan agreed.

"It was a nice funeral, though. Short and sweet." Elizabeth put a piece of cheese on a cracker and popped it into her mouth.

Teagan chuckled. "Her father told the priest he'd better keep it brief if he wanted a donation to the church. Did you notice how fast they rolled out of there in their RV?" She sighed. "At least they promised to stop on their way home from Maine and visit the children." She pasted on a smile. "Oh, joy."

Logan wasn't looking forward to that day, either. He truly didn't care for Marsha's parents' attitude toward the kids. Anora and Brann were their own grandchildren. They should fawn over them, but instead they seemed so self-consumed. Disappointed. That was the right word for how he felt.

He was also disappointed that his own father would never be able to teach Anora and Brann how to fish, the correct way to sharpen a knife, or get to know the wonderful children that Logan was beginning to consider his own.

"Are you ready to do this, Ice-T?" Micah asked, then shoved a slice of apple into his mouth.

"Yeah." Teagan smiled and Logan's heart jumped. He hadn't seen a genuine smile from her since immediately after the judge awarded them joint custody of the children just over a week ago. "Sometimes I love working for the government. The people in our human resources department were really great. They got me approved for FMLA, gave me ten days off plus moving expenses, and set me up with a new job at New River Air Station."

"What's FMLA?" Matthew asked.

"Family and Medical Leave Act," Elizabeth explained to her husband. "The men in your Special Operations Group probably have never asked for it, but pregnant women often use the program to take off the first three months after the baby's born."

"Parents can get it for adoption, too." Teagan prepared a mini cheese sandwich using crackers. "That's how they were able to give it to me."

Elizabeth's jaw dropped. "You have off twelve whole weeks?"

Teagan was chewing so all she did was nod her head and grin.

While he was thinking about the move, Logan wanted to be sure to thank his friends. "Matthew, Elizabeth, I really appreciate you both helping us clear out Marsha's house. No way in hell would Teagan and I have been able to do it on our own."

"I wish I could have helped even more," Matthew said. "While I sorted through everything in the office, I was looking for clues as to why someone would murder

Marsha. I still have the feeling that everything goes back to Gabe."

"That's highly possible, given what you told us before his funeral." Gabe's treason still bothered Logan. "Whoever owned that ten million in gold isn't going to just let it go." He didn't miss the look that passed between Elizabeth and Matthew. They knew more than they were telling the rest of the team.

"Teagan, were you able to collect everything from the safe deposit boxes?" Matthew deftly changed the subject.

"Gabe must've been extremely paranoid. He had three safe-deposit boxes, and that was in addition to one that Marsha owned, all at different banks." She shifted on the couch and her loose-fitting blouse pulled tight over her impressive breasts. Strange that Logan hadn't noticed them before.

"Anything interesting in there?" Matthew took another long drink of beer.

Teagan giggled. "I'm lucky I found time to empty them. I've been a little bit busy lately." As though she realized the seriousness of the situation, she added, "Once we get moved in, I plan to start on those boxes, one at a time."

Matthew looked relieved. "So, you shipped them to North Carolina?"

"Yeah." She gave him a halfhearted grin. "Those and about three hundred more."

Logan jumped in to rescue her. "We sent everything from the children's bedrooms and almost everything from the family room including the furniture. Marsha's couches are so much nicer than what I have in that side of the duplex and we thought the children would be more comfortable surrounded by familiar objects."

Teagan leaned forward and poured herself some more

wine. "I also shipped about half of Marsha's kitchen. Maybe her tools will make me a better cook."

"I wouldn't plan on that," Elizabeth giggled. "You might want to consider taking cooking classes or watch a bunch of videos." She looked over at Logan. "I hope you know how to cook."

"Hey," Teagan retorted. "I know how to make some stuff."

Elizabeth laughed. "Chocolate chip cookies from the pack where you just break off the pieces and arrange them on a cookie sheet."

"Don't pick on me. Those are damn good cookies. The kids love them." Teagan was smiling and finally relaxing. Logan was happy to see her interacting so casually with all their friends. He hoped that she would make friends with some of his neighbors. Maybe she would even join the Officers' Wives' Club.

But Teagan wasn't his wife, so he wasn't sure she'd be allowed in the exclusive group. Since she wasn't retired military, she couldn't even get onto the base, or shop at the exchange or commissary. She would have to buy groceries out in town. Shop at the mall. She wouldn't have any of the privileges of a military wife. The children couldn't be seen for medical reasons on base, either. Suddenly, he wondered about the local hospital. Was it as good as the one on base?

Fuck. There were more complications, just when he thought he had it all figured out.

"So, they're moving in with you?" Matthew's brow pinched. "I thought they were moving into a duplex on the beach."

"It's my duplex." He took a swig of his beer and decided to explain. "Teagan, Anora, and Brann will be living in the other half. For the past three years, a flight surgeon and his wife, a nurse at the same hospital, have lived there. He got orders to Pensacola and they moved out a week before I came up here for Gabe's funeral. I was having some painting done and the carpets cleaned while I've been gone, getting ready to put it back on the rental market when I got home." He grinned over at Teagan. "Now I don't have to deal with that headache."

She shot him a glare. "We're fighting over rent at the moment."

"I own the whole building," Logan tried to explain.

"On a Lieutenant Colonel's salary, how the hell did you manage that?" Micah said accusingly. "I'm very familiar with the cost of waterfront property. From the pictures I've seen, it looks like a half million-dollar home, per side."

Logan grinned. "I got one hell of a deal on it." He shrugged and decided to tell them the whole story. "You want the long version or the short version?"

"Oh, is the long version subversive and juicy?" Elizabeth sounded excited.

"Long version it is." He drained his beer and set it on the coffee table. "After Pentagon duty, I had orders to go back to Camp Lejeune. There was no way in hell I was going to live in the Bachelor Officers' Quarters ever again, so I started looking around with a real estate agent. I was about to give up and rent. I walked out of the commissary one afternoon and the bottom fell out of the paper bag the lady in front of me was carrying. She just collapsed onto the blacktop in the parking lot."

Logan looked around at his rapt audience. "When I got over to her, she was crying. Mumbling about her bad day. After we picked up her groceries, we stood and talked next to her car for nearly an hour. She had just come from seeing her attorney and filing divorce papers. Her husband, a bird colonel, had been transferred to Quantico. She had gotten a few days off and drove up to surprise him for his birthday."

"Oh, fuck." Micah rubbed his forehead. "I can see where this is going."

"Yep. Since she left so early in the morning, she decided to take a nap while waiting for him to get home from work." He grinned. "She woke up to the sound of voices and caught him banging a major on the dining room table of his rented apartment."

"Fraternization." Elizabeth shook her head. "That's a big no-no."

Logan chuckled. "I've got to give Sadie credit, she kept her head and thought fast. She pulled out her cell phone and videoed them."

"Oh my God," Teagan squealed and slapped her hands over her mouth.

"No fucking way," Micah said between laughs.

"Good for her," Elizabeth nodded. "I hope she turned that cheating bastard in to the Inspector General."

"Typical man." Teagan said the words so quietly that Logan almost missed them. He wondered what had happened to her in the past? He knew so little about her, yet he knew so much. She was one of the bravest women he'd ever met. So was Elizabeth. They had handled themselves so well under extreme combat situations. He vowed he would learn more about Teagan by the end of the week.

Ignoring her remark, Logan continued with the story. "Come to find out, Sadie ran the sales office for a contractor on Topsail Island. They had built a couple of duplexes on the beach, so she'd been able to buy the whole duplex at builder cost. That was about five years before I met her. They'd successfully rented out the other half and nearly paid off the loan. Knowing that her soon to be ex-husband would get half of the profits, she sold the duplex to me for one dollar over what they still owed."

Logan shrugged. "I now own the building, free and clear, thanks to high-priced weekly summer rentals. After I paid off the loan, I rented the other half year-round to other military officers for extra income."

"Maybe I need to start trolling for disgruntled wives living in beach houses." Micah scoffed. "That's going to be the only way I can afford to live on the water."

"You could live on a houseboat," Elizabeth suggested.

"No." Teagan dragged out the word. "Micah needs to buy a yacht. A big one with several bedrooms."

Elizabeth jumped on the conversation. "And we can all come visit and cruise around on the ocean. You know how to drive a boat, don't you, Micah?"

The big man raised one eyebrow. "I am a fucking captain in the Navy. I know how to drive big boats."

The back door slammed. "We're hungry, Mom." Austin flew into the living room, Brann on his heels.

"Go wash up, boys," Elizabeth ordered. She swept her gaze over the room. "I guess I'd better serve supper."

An hour later, the children were in their rooms playing quietly, the dishwasher was running, and the adults were back in the same seats in the living room.

The circumstances surrounding Marsha's death had been bothering Logan for days. Before he left, he wanted to run something by his friends. "What do you guys think about hiring a private detective to dig deeper into Marsha's death?"

"It took proof from my computer geek to get Detective Russo to change it from a suicide to a possible homicide, but I don't think he's even investigating anymore," Matthew announced. "Clarence confirmed that someone at a different location wrote the suicide note to that screen. Whoever did it, had some damn good hacking skills because he couldn't trace it back to its origin."

"If we hire someone, I'd like to do it right away, before the specialized crew comes in to clean the office. We need to put the house up for sale as soon as possible," Teagan reminded Logan.

He agreed.

"You have someone in mind?" Micah asked.

"I do." Logan was relieved that his friends sounded interested. "I have a friend who works for the Alvarez Agency down in Richlands. If we're all in agreement, I'd like to have him take a look at the scene right away." He looked over at Matthew. "Do you mind being point here in DC?"

"I'm happy to help in any way that I can." He took his wife's hand. "Marsha and Elizabeth were close. Our kids act like cousins. And I know Marsha was murdered. If the police aren't going to do anything to find her killer, we need to. I said it before, and I'll say it again, I believe her death is directly related to Gabe's."

Logan stood. "I'll give him a call tomorrow morning." He glanced at Teagan who was curled up in the corner of the couch, her eyelids drooping. "We need to get the kids home and into bed. Tomorrow is going to be a big day." He looked around and realized he had no idea where the children's bedrooms were.

"This way." Matthew stood and Logan followed him.

Down the hall, they could hear the boys talking.

"My dad died too, but it was before I was born. Then my mom got remarried. I hated Robert. He took away all the pictures of my real dad." Austin lowered his voice. "But I got them out of the trashcan and hid them from him." The nine-year-old smiled as he pointed to the prominently displayed pictures on top of his dresser. "That's my dad, the one who made me. Matthew's now my dad. He's pretty cool. He likes to play baseball."

The two men automatically stopped in the hallway before the boys could see them.

"Both my mom and dad are dead." Brann said. "I guess that's a good thing. Then I don't have to get a bad stepdad like Robert before my Mom could find somebody nice like Uncle Matthew."

"That's a good thing that you don't have to have a dad like Robert. He sucked. I hated it when he was around," Austin declared. "But you get to live with Uncle Logan and Aunt Teagan. They're cool. They swear."

Matthew slid Logan a glance.

Guess I'd better start watching my language.

"Yeah, but the judge said we have to move to North Carolina because Uncle Logan works there." Brann explained. "I'm going to miss you, Austin."

"I'm going to miss you, too, Brann."

At the sound of sniffles, Logan and Matthew stepped into the room.

CHAPTER TWELVE

Teagan had no idea what to expect as they crossed the tall bridge onto North Topsail Beach and turned left. At the moment, she had both children in the backseat of her Honda sedan. During their many stops, Brann would occasionally switch vehicles.

Traveling with a four-year-old meant stopping regularly for potty breaks. Teagan also noted, that seven-year-old boys could consume mass quantities of junk food and were bored most of the time. She made a mental note to herself that before they traveled together again, she would hit the local stores for travel games for both of them that were age appropriate…and not messy.

She wished Brann had told her that they got to watch movies in Marsha's SUV with its built-in video screens. Two hours into the trip, and still fighting bumper-to-bumper DC traffic, Teagan regretted suggesting that they sell Marsha's car. Maybe she could still buy it from the estate. She wondered if that would be a problem since she was the executor and responsible for liquidation of all assets and personal property.

She thought about everything left in Marsha's home. She and Logan had agreed it would be best to hire an auctioneer to sell off anything they hadn't moved to North Carolina. She would handle that in a few weeks, after Logan's friend finished examining the murder scene. She had an appointment with Mr. Keller later in the month, so she planned on a trip back to DC anyway. Perhaps by then, she would've found a local facility for her mother and be able to transport her down at the same time she returned to North Carolina.

"Are we really going to live on the beach?" Brann said with excitement.

"That's the plan." She thought about it for a moment before asking, "Have you two ever been to the ocean before?"

"Yeah, we went once with Aunt Elizabeth, but we didn't stay right on the beach," Brann explained. "We had to walk a couple blocks then on a wooden walkway overtop the dunes. Are we really right on the beach?"

"So I'm told, but we're going to see in just a few minutes. Anora, can you see the ocean?"

"Yes." Her reply was quiet. "Those waves are big."

Chancing a glance—as often as she could—to her right at the Atlantic Ocean, Teagan was eager to be near salty blue water once again. While she was in the Navy, she was always stationed on the water. She and Marsha had spent long weekends soaking in the sun on Virginia Beach. During flight school in Pensacola, they had often hit the beach right after a morning training flight.

They seemed to drive a long way down the beach. There were very few homes along the left side of the road. Mostly it was marsh and sand except for the places where the road nearly touched the beach. In those cases, tall condos populated the opposite side. She often caught glimpses of the intracoastal waterway and large boats cruising the protected waters.

As they traveled farther down New River Inlet Road, condos crammed together facing the ocean blocked their views. Just when it looked as though the paved road was about to end, Logan turned on his blinker and pulled onto a crunchy white driveway. As she'd been directed at their last stop, she pulled into the driveway for the adjoining condo.

Teagan sat in the car and looked at the three-story building. It was painted a light blue, the same color as the sky that day. The two halves were offset, giving each side a sense of privacy. Under each half was a parking garage, but since Logan hadn't driven into his, she remained outside as well.

This was her new home. She was anxious to see the inside, but she was more interested in the beach and the views from the deck Logan had told her about.

"Aunt Teagan, I have to pee," Anora announced for the sixth time since they had pulled out of her apartment parking lot. Thanks to DC traffic, and potty breaks, the trip that GPS said should take six hours, ended up being eight. Teagan was exhausted and could definitely use a drink.

Brann helped his little sister out of the car seat harness as Teagan got out to open her car door from the outside. She remembered the day Marsha had shown her the little switch for child safety locks. Her friend had even been afraid that someone would steal her children out of the backseat of her car. Thank goodness the two children, now in her care, could not be used against Gabe.

By the time she had both kids out of the car, Logan had his keys ready and was trotting up the wooden steps to their new home. His jeans pulled tight across his butt with each step. Damn, the man had one fine ass. In his tight gray T-shirt, she could see back muscles and well-defined biceps stretch and contract with every move. She suddenly wanted to trace every one of them with the tip of her finger.

"I'll give you these keys, now," he said as he opened the door wide for them to enter. He was so close as she stepped through, following the children.

"Uncle Logan, where's the bathroom?" Anora did her potty dance, one that was now very familiar to all of them.

"Right down the hall." He pointed the way and she dashed off.

"This is a really cool place, Uncle Logan." The boy's head moved in every direction including upward toward the vaulted ceilings. His gaze held on the stairs. "Is my bedroom up there?"

"All the bedrooms are upstairs." When he grinned down at Brann, Teagan could see the growing love he had in his eyes. "The master is for your Aunt Teagan, but you can pick either one of the others. They both have beds in them right now, but they will be moved out tomorrow morning so we can put your own bed in there. I'll show you your bedroom for tonight when we go next door to my place."

Brann dashed up the steps. "This place is so cool."

Logan stuffed his hands in his front pockets and seemed to gaze around the room as though he'd never seen it before. "They'll be taking all the living room and dining room furniture tomorrow morning, too."

"I feel terrible that you're selling it all." She touched his forearm. This time she expected the heat that seemed to emanate from him through her.

He shrugged. "I'm not going to need it ever again.

Besides, it's getting kind of old and tattered. It's been here since I bought the place from Sadie." He smiled down at her and her heart swelled at what a good man he was. "You and the kids need to be surrounded by your own stuff. I want you to be comfortable here. As far as I'm concerned, this is your new home. Do anything you want to the place." He looked all around. "If you want it painted some other color, I'll get that done."

Anora came floating down the hall. He chuckled. "I'm pretty sure I have to contract a painter anyway." He held out his arms and the little girl jumped into them as though she'd been doing it all her life. He planted his goddaughter on his hip. "I'll bet this little girl wants her room painted pink."

She bounced up and down in his arms. "I want to see my room, please, Uncle Logan? Carry me up to my room." Realizing what she'd said, she quickly added, "Please."

Teagan looked longingly at the sliding glass doors at the far side of the living room that led out to a large deck. A patio table and three well-worn chairs were the only things occupying the large outdoor space. In her mind, she could picture an outdoor living room with a couch, loveseat, and a few chairs. A dining table, with a desperately needed umbrella, would fill one corner.

From halfway up the stairs, Logan called to her. "Ice-T, you coming?"

She smiled at him and trotted to catch up. "I'm right behind you." She actually was anxious to see the master bedroom.

"Let's start at the top and work our way down," Logan suggested. They bypassed the second floor and went straight to the iron spiral staircase.

"That room's mine," Brann declared as he dashed out of

one of the bedrooms and pounded up the metal steps. "This place is chill, Uncle Logan." A second later, he added, "And this is the most chill room here."

Logan grinned down at her. "I love my loft room." He set Anora on the second step up and followed her closely, so she didn't fall backward.

"These steps are fun," Anora announced. When she reached the top, she squealed.

Logan completely blocked her view as they wound around and around, so it wasn't until she reached the very top that she could see the wonderful space. Light poured through two huge windows, one facing the neighbors but the other had a magnificent view of whitecapped waves and green-blue ocean that touched the baby blue sky. Teagan could put a chair in that room and spend her day staring out the window. Gorgeous. Breathtaking. What a great place to sit during the winter, protected from all the outdoor elements, yet able to take in nature's beauty.

"Uncle Logan, can I move my bedroom up here? Please. Please. Please," Brann begged.

Logan chuckled. "I hate to break it to you, buddy, but it's a real bi—" he caught himself before swearing and Teagan had to bite back a laugh. "It's almost impossible to bring furniture up that spiral staircase. Lots of people use this for a play area."

"It's perfect for yoga." Oh, no. Did she say that out loud?

"You do yoga?" Logan asked.

Teagan could feel the blush travel up her chest into her cheeks. "When I have time." Which wasn't very often, nor on a regular schedule.

He kneeled down and wrapped an arm around each child. "How about we let Aunt Teagan have the space?" He looked up at her, his eyes filled with regret. "She gave up a lot to come here and be with us."

"No, no. Kids need a space of their own." She knelt down next to them. "I came here because I love you." She threw her arms around Brann and Anora. "You heard the judge, he said that all four of us have to live really close to each other."

At the worried look on the children's faces, she added, "I wasn't going to let Uncle Logan have all the fun with you two by himself. I want to have fun too." Then she started to tickle each of them.

Crisis averted, Teagan suggested, "I want to see the rest of the house. How about you?" She pasted on a serious look. "I haven't found my bedroom. Have you?"

"I know where it is." Brann darted down the spiral staircase. "Follow me."

Brann pointed out which room he wanted, then like a professional real estate agent, he showed Anora which room would be hers. Each room had the same large windows as in the loft. The rooms were about half the size of the ones in their DC home, but more than twice as big as the one they shared in her apartment. All their furniture should fit without making the room feel crowded.

Leaving the children in their new bedrooms, she found Logan waiting for her in the hall.

"Ready to see yours?" He asked nervously.

"Sure."

He dramatically opened the door to Teagan's version of heaven. She felt her jaw drop. The room was huge. A paddle fan that looked like something out of Casablanca with its huge blades of white rattan perched in the middle of the tray ceiling. There was plenty of space for her white provincial night tables on both sides of her king-sized bed, that thankfully would arrive tomorrow. She could lie in her bed and see the ocean through two sets of sliding glass doors. It was as though the entire wall was made of glass. She drew back the curtains, that would absolutely have to be replaced, and her breath caught.

Logan slid one of the doors open and stepped out onto the covered part of her private deck. She immediately envisioned a small loveseat and matching chair to sit in the shade, and a table to hold her coffee as she enjoyed the morning sunrise. Two chaise lounges, separated by a cocktail table, would sit in the sun.

And this was hers, now.

Thanks to the wonderful man standing behind her. Like a child, she twirled around and threw her arms around Logan's neck, hugging him tightly. "This really is chill," she said, mimicking Brann.

When his arms wrapped around her back, she gave him a quick peck on the lips then stepped out of his embrace. "Thank you doesn't seem anywhere near adequate, but they're the only two words I have." She held her arms out to her sides and slowly turned in a circle. "This is like a dream come true." She fought back tears...and lost.

Logan held his arms out wide. "Come here."

Without hesitation, she stepped back into his strong arms.

"Marsha and I always talked about pooling our money together and getting a place just like this," she managed to say even though her throat was tight. "We were always stationed near a beach while we were active duty. No matter how hard we tried, we couldn't come up with enough money between the two of us to rent a place right on the beach." She sniffed back sobs. "Now, I have a place of our dreams, and her children. What did I ever do to deserve all this? She was such a good person, and now she's gone."

She tried desperately to get her emotions under control. Logan simply held her and rubbed his large warm hand up and down her spine. Finally, she could breathe easily.

Stepping back, she looked into his eyes. "Thank you." She giggled. "There I go again. The only two words I seem to be able to say are *thank you*." She inhaled deeply and let it out slowly. "Let's go get the kids and get them settled in at your house. I vote for pizza delivery."

"Works for me." His voice was low and rough.

Teagan figured he was equally as stressed. They had both been through a lot in the past ten days. If he was anything like her, sleeping in his own bed would make all the difference in the world.

Ten minutes later, they had both children dragging suitcases, and a few toys, into Logan's side of the house. Since it was another image of the one that would be theirs, he instructed the children to take their toys up to their bedrooms. He grabbed all the suitcases, including hers, and followed the children up the steps. He'd insisted that she take his bed and he'd sleep on the couch.

She was too exhausted to argue with him.

An hour later, the kids kneeling on the floor across from them eating pizza off paper plates, Teagan took a minute to look around his half of the house. The furniture was a much higher quality, especially the soft leather couch with built-in electric recliners. On the wall facing them, was one of the largest television sets she had ever seen.

"Why don't you have a dining room table?" She asked, thinking it was an innocent enough question.

He shrugged. "I have this coffee table, and TV trays if I want to get them out and use them. It's just me here ninety-nine percent of the time. Besides, I can sit at the breakfast bar and eat leftovers."

"You're such a bachelor," Teagan accused.

"I guess I'm going to have to get one, aren't I?" He smiled down at the kids.

"Do you want to take the one from our side? It looks to be in okay shape," she suggested.

"No. I'll just go buy one on my way home from work." He stared at the empty space designated for the dining room. "I'm thinking dark wood, with some solid wood chairs.

Yes, she thought. That would fit in with the rest of his furniture which was very masculine, but so was Logan Jackson. His home was truly a reflection of the man.

Since it was still daylight when they finished the last of the pizza, they decided to go for a walk on the beach. The fresh air, long travel, and lack of sleep the night before made the children start to yawn as they turned around at the large condo complex. Teagan made the executive decision that the children could skip baths, just for that night, and head straight to bed. She wasn't surprised when neither argued.

When she returned to the kitchen, she found Logan opening a beer.

"Want one?" He started to hand it to her, but she waved him off. "Sorry, but I don't have any wine. We can pick some up tomorrow."

"I might just do that." She gave him a tired smile. "I'm going to take a shower and go to bed. The kids will be up early, they always are."

"I can handle them in the morning," he offered. "I eat a big breakfast, so scrambling a few more eggs is no big deal. You sleep in. The guys who bought the furniture from next door will be here around eight. The moving company said the van should arrive sometime around nine-thirty or ten o'clock. You're good until then."

Damn. That sounded really good. She worried for a few seconds about Logan handling the kids by himself, but he'd truly proven himself in the last few days. "I might just sleep in a little." Then she decided to give him an out. "Wake me if they become too much to handle with everything else you have going on tomorrow morning."

"Ice-T, I have over fifteen hundred Marines that report to me. I'm responsible for everything they do every day. Anora and Brann are good kids. Don't insult me again and get some rest." As he passed her, he kissed the top of her head, as he sometimes did Anora and Brann. She wasn't sure if she was flattered or insulted.

What she was, was tired.

She dragged her body up the stairs and into his bedroom. She quickly took a shower and changed into her favorite long T-shirt that hit her midthigh. She couldn't resist opening the doors to the ocean breeze. It called to her. She peeked through the slider to see if anyone in the houses next door could see her, which was ridiculous because people wore much less sunbathing. She walked to the railing and stared out at the horizon that couldn't be seen until sunrise.

The wind that constantly blew at the beach, lifted her long hair off her shoulders. She raked her fingers through her hair, allowing the breeze to kiss her scalp. She inhaled the moist air, forcing it all the way to the bottom of her lungs.

She had missed this. It felt like coming home.

Closing her eyes, she simply breathed. Calm washed over her, through her.

In her mind, she and Marsha were ten years younger, standing on the balcony of a Virginia Beach hotel, doing this exact same thing. Whether she conjured her friend in her mind, or Marsha spoke to her from beyond, she heard the words of encouragement they had given each other for years, *you've got this.*

She turned and walked back into Logan's room and crawled into his bed. She fell asleep, surrounded by his scent.

CHAPTER THIRTEEN

Logan took a long sip from the bottled beer and stretched out his legs. His beach chair was nowhere near as comfortable as the outdoor living furniture Teagan had purchased for their deck. Maybe he should step up his game and buy something similar for his place. He also liked the way she had decorated the deck outside her bedroom. He, of course, wouldn't put up the curtains that covered the unpainted posts, but he really liked the loveseat and chair arranged around the coffee table under the covered portion.

Although he'd only admit it to himself, his favorite part were the two lounge chairs. More than once in the past three weeks he'd come home from a long hard day at work and Teagan would be stretched out in nothing more than a bikini. For a forty-two-year-old woman, she had all the right curves.

The moon slowly rose to take its place among the constellations. Late night had always been his favorite time to spend on the deck. He loved to sit in his chair, sip his beer, watch the moon rise, and listen to the ocean before he stepped back into his bedroom, stripping out of his clothes and crawling into bed naked. Now that Teagan and the children lived next door, he enjoyed his bedtime ritual even more.

She was there and had established a similar habit.

Every night, Teagan would stroll from her bedroom to the railing on her personal deck and just stand there, absorbing the darkness.

The first night she'd spent in North Carolina, sleeping in his bed, she had walked out onto his deck, dressed in a white sleep shirt. From his viewpoint on the lower deck outside the living room, she was framed by the full moon and looked almost ethereal. Her light blonde hair lifted on the ocean breeze and when she ran her fingers through the tendrils, she looked like an angel about to take flight.

Logan knew he should say something to her, make his presence known, but he couldn't. In those few moments she took for just herself, she seemed to find peace. That's why he'd sat on the deck outside his bedroom since the first night he'd moved into the house, years ago. He would have cursed anyone who had dared to disturb him, so he gave Teagan the same quiet consideration. They could share the night, each alone in their private thoughts.

That night, his were centered around her and the children. In the past three weeks, they had fallen into a routine. His life hadn't changed much. He still rose every morning and ran several miles along the beach, then swam back to his home. As usual, he prepared a large breakfast, except now he shared it with Anora and Brann.

As he'd discovered, the children were early risers. Starting the first morning after they moved into their side, they met him as he climbed the beach to his house.

They were such good kids. They knew they were not

permitted on the beach alone, so they'd wait for him on the deck off what he'd come to think of as Teagan's living room. The first few times he'd invited them to breakfast, they'd met him at his door. Then it dawned on him, these were his children as much as they were hers. They should come and go from his home as comfortably as they did from Teagan's side.

Because she may also need access to his home at some point, he gave them the key which they kept on a small hook near the door. Now, they would let themselves in and wait patiently on his deck.

He'd grown to love his mornings with the kids. He would make sure they were safe back inside before he'd leave for work. Teagan was usually up and showered, meeting the children at the door where they all stood and waved goodbye to him.

On his way home, he often stopped and picked up something for supper, or they'd try out another restaurant in the area. Elizabeth hadn't been kidding when she said Teagan couldn't cook.

Often, Logan would take Brann to the batting cage or they would play catch on the beach until dark. Unfortunately, they had arrived too far into the season for the boy to join Little League that year, so they concentrated on skills improvement. After spending all day with Marines, he truly enjoyed his time with the young boy.

Downing the last of his beer, Logan sat quietly until Teagan had closed the sliding glass door to her bedroom. He took the beer bottle back to the kitchen and tossed it into the recycling. Chuckling to himself, he padded back to his bedroom. Before the children had moved in next door, everything had gone into the trashcan. Both children were little good-earth Nazis. Brann had lectured him on how it was necessary to recycle so that his generation was not left with a trashy world.

Logan had the hardest time not laughing. The faces Teagan had made while sitting in his line of sight during the chastising by the seven-year-old, tested his emotional control. Tomorrow, it would be tested once again. He had to work all day, then drive six hours, with everyone in the same vehicle, up to Washington DC.

When he rolled into home at five-thirty that night, he was shocked to see suitcases and backpacks lining the drive.

"Unlock all your doors and the back hatch," Teagan ordered. "Do you need to shower before we go?"

"Doors are unlocked," he announced.

"We have the green light to go. Load up." Teagan called out. The kids dropped their backpacks on the floor of the backseat then rolled their bags to the storage portion in the back of his SUV. They moved without complaint, as though they were on a mission, helping each other like a good team.

"Logan." Teagan peered around from the back of the vehicle. "Go shower and change. Are you packed?"

He looked down at his uniform and realized they were ready to roll, and he wasn't. "Of course. Give me five minutes to change."

Teagan looked at her watch. "Brann, would you please go with Uncle Logan and bring his suitcase down here? Anora, run in and go potty one more time."

When he slid behind the wheel, both children were already buckled into their seats. In the rearview mirror he could see his bag. He learned long ago to always double-check his own gear.

Teagan smiled at him. "Ready to roll with six minutes to spare." She looked so damn proud of herself.

"We needed somebody like you controlling the MEU loadout," he said referring to the Marine Expeditionary Unit which moved thousands of Marines and hundreds of tons of equipment into a combat zone.

"I didn't want you to have any reason to complain about the children or me." She reached forward and punched the *go* button on the GPS. "I knew it was important we try to leave on time."

She lightly touched his forearm. Over the past several weeks, she touched him more often. Casually. Never sexually, even though heat radiated from her body and shot straight to his cock every time.

"We'll get there, when we get there." He put the vehicle in reverse and backed out onto the road. "There should be less traffic since we're traveling on a Wednesday night. Coming home on Sunday is going to be a whole different story."

"Home." Teagan smiled as she craned her neck to look at their duplex.

Tilting the rearview mirror down, he saw the children were occupied. Both had on headphones plugged into tablets.

"When did they get those?"

"Brann already had one, but somehow it got shipped. I bought one for Anora, so she could watch her own movies," she explained. "We've spent hours deciding which movies to buy and most of the day yesterday downloading to their tablets." She twisted to check on them. "They should be good for at least two hours. They've snacked most of the afternoon."

"You're a fucking genius, and the headphones prove it."

He reached across the center console and gave her hand a little squeeze.

"No, I'm not."

"Fucking, or genius?" He teased.

"Neither. I haven't had a date in over six months," she confessed.

Good to know. He hadn't been out with a woman in eight weeks, and he kissed her goodnight on the cheek. Karen, his fuck-buddy, had shipped out almost four months ago for a fifteen-month Middle Eastern tour of duty. He'd been on the hunt for a new *special* friend when Gabriel died. Then his world turned upside down. He grinned as he once again looked at the two beautiful children in his backseat. His children.

"Elizabeth and Matthew know we won't get there until late. Even though both of them have to work tomorrow, they're going to wait up for us." Teagan talked as she texted.

"Let her know I'm willing to get a hotel room." He'd offered the moment he heard about Teagan and Elizabeth's plan.

"Oh, no." There was warning in her voice. "You're not getting out of kid duty. You've spoiled Anora and Brann by making them breakfast every morning. Remember, I can't cook."

"I think I'd better start giving you lessons." Then he remembered something that he saw in the base newspaper. "There's a gourmet shop out in Jacksonville that offers couples' cooking classes one night a week. Are you interested?"

Her face lit up…then suddenly collapsed. "What would we do with the kids?"

"The base has a childcare facility that comes highly

recommended by one of my captains. Now that the kids have military ID cards, we can drop them off. They can make new friends and play with somebody else's toys while we learn to cook." Logan had discovered that he had more in common with his married captains than he did with other lieutenant colonels on the base. Most of them had children in their teens, or they were working on a second family and had babies.

"That sounds wonderful. Do you want me to sign us up while you're driving?" She sounded excited about doing something with him that didn't involve the children.

That was encouraging. "Sure." He started to reach for his wallet in his back pocket.

"I've got this." She patted his forearm.

"Teagan. When you go out with me, I pay." He hoped his voice was insistent.

"Logan, let me make something perfectly clear." She twisted in her seat to first check on the children, probably to make sure they weren't listening, then to face his way. "This is not a date. This is me learning how to cook... something...so the whole burden of feeding us isn't on you. We're not dating."

"Why aren't we dating?" The idea of taking Teagan out, alone, somewhere nice, sounded like a good idea. Their joint custody of the children tied them together for at least fourteen more years, which was longer than any special operator's marriage he'd ever known. They were already acting like a family. The only thing obviously missing was the sex.

"I don't do relationships." She glanced back over at the children and lowered her voice. "I do men. They do me. Most often, that involves me putting on a little black dress, we go out to dinner someplace that has cloth napkins, and we talk. If I feel there's some chemistry, we have a repeat. If the man makes it through the third date, we'll get a hotel room on the way home. Sometimes, we'll have a repeat of date three."

She glanced out the window for several heartbeats before returning her gaze to him. "It's been a long time since anyone has made it to date number three. I go out on a lot of first dates." He saw the pain in her beautiful blue eyes.

She continued the self-deprecation. "There aren't a lot of men who want to date a forty-two-year-old woman who is set in her ways, tied down with a crazy mother, and would rather talk about engine performance than his boring job in politics. The good ones are all married. If they're divorced, there's usually a damn good reason. Same goes if they've never been married. There's a damn good reason."

He grabbed her hand and wove his fingers through hers, locking their palms together. "You're wrong. You've just been dating the wrong men." And he planned to prove it to her. "I'm divorced, and yes, there's a damn good reason for it. Kember had an affair with a married colonel. I was a major, several steps down that command chain. For me, adultery is an unforgivable sin. She broke up two marriages. Was I at fault? Maybe. I'd been up to my ass in alligators, running ops all over the Middle East. If I made a mistake, a good young man could die. I couldn't afford to make mistakes at work. But I guess I made a big one with her. My job meant more to me than she did." Logan had never admitted that out loud before.

She squeezed his hand. "I always wondered what happened to the two of you. But I have to be honest with you, I never liked her. She always seemed so fake. She was such a social climber. Did I ever tell you that I ran into her at a party one night about a year ago?"

Logan was surprised she hadn't mentioned it. "No. After Kember and the colonel were discovered, I asked to be reassigned to the West Coast during the divorce. With all the shit that went down here at Camp Lejeune, USSOCOM was more than happy to send me as far away from here as possible. I never kept up with her. I think most people saw me as a victim and never talked about her around me." It had been years since the divorce. The anger and humiliation had finally passed. "So, what words of enlightenment did she share with you?"

"First, I believe in karma, and as far as I'm concerned, that little bitch got what was coming to her." Teagan wasn't holding back. "You know that the Brigadier General was forced to retire because of his adultery with her."

"Yeah, it's nice to have low friends in high places." Logan went on to explain, "A good friend told me about that."

Teagan giggled. She fucking giggled. In all the years he'd known her, he'd never seen her quite like this. "Well, it seems that Kember made such an ass of herself blatantly flirting with the general's married friends, that he divorced her within months of them moving to DC. To her surprise, she had signed a prenup, leaving her with absolutely nothing. She's back to working civil service as an administrative aide somewhere inside the Beltway."

"Probably looking for her next victim. She cost me thousands to get rid of her, but as far as I was concerned, it was money well-spent." They had wandered off on a tangent so Logan brought the conversation back around. "So, Teagan, does my divorce shove me into that same box of divorced men?"

"Certainly not." When she squeezed his hand, he realized they were still connected. "Logan, it's no wonder the Marine Corps snatched you up so quickly. Even their motto says they are looking for a few good men. You are one of the best men I've ever known." She leaned in close to him and said in a very low tone. "You have taken in two orphaned children and promised to raise them to adulthood. Most men would run the other way. Hell, most men don't want their own biological children, say nothing about taking on someone else's."

He glanced in the rearview mirror to check on the kids. They were fine, totally absorbed in their videos.

"You took them on, too," he reminded her.

"Yes." She glanced over her shoulder at Anora and Brann, a warm loving smile on her pretty face. "But I loved both these children since the day they were born. Marsha shared them with me because she knew that I could never have children."

"What?" Teagan couldn't have kids? "Why?"

"Aunt Teagan, I'm thirsty." Anora took her headphones off and looked pleadingly at the woman beside him.

She slid her hand out of his and dug into the large cold bag that sat on the floor between the children's backpacks. "How about some apple juice?" She held up one of the little boxes.

"Yes, please." Anora was leaning very forward in her seat as though she was looking for something on the floor. "Is it too late to have a snack? When are we going to stop for supper?"

His question completely forgotten, or ignored, the next several hours involved conversations with one child or another. By nine thirty, though, their bellies filled with fast food, and snacks that they would sneak when they thought he and Teagan weren't looking, the children finally fell asleep.

About an hour later, after riding in silence, Teagan finally spoke. "Can I talk to you about something?"

"Sure, anything." Over the years, they have had some very bizarre conversations about everything from the attributes of baseball versus soccer, to international terrorism.

She glanced back, checking on the kids one more time before she shifted to face him. "I love that you spend so much time with Brann, but Anora also needs a father figure. Maybe even more than her older brother. I don't believe that Gabe ever spent much time at all with her."

"I spend a lot of time with her," he said defensively. "We have breakfast together every morning. Most evenings, if we're watching television together, she curls up in my lap."

"No, you spend breakfast with her and Brann. Like you admitted, when we're all watching television together, she likes to sit on your lap." Teagan shook her head as though in frustration. "I'm not explaining this very well. You spend time alone with Brann, but you never spend time alone with Anora."

He glanced in the rearview mirror at the two children he was coming to love. Teagan was right. He was comfortable spending time with Brann. He understood little boys. He used to be one. He had to admit the truth. "I don't know anything about little girls. What the hell am I supposed to do with her?"

"Play catch on the beach. She needs to learn the same hand-eye coordination that you're teaching Brann every night." She let out a long breath. "I've also seen you on the floor playing soldiers with Brann."

"He sees men in uniforms every time I take them on the base, of course he's interested." He loved taking the kids with him when he was just dashing to pick up something quick from his office. They always asked so many questions.

"And who was sitting in the car seat beside him?" Teagan's punch hit home.

Anora asked just as many questions as her brother, maybe even more. She'd been the first one to ask to see his office. Brann's questions dealt with things, objects that they used as special operators. Anora, on the other hand, wanted to know what the men did, what were their jobs? Both had an endearing curiosity, it was just different.

"All right, when we get back home, I promise to spend some alone time with Anora." Doing what, he had no fucking idea.

Teagan's hand on his arm registered. "Thank you. The fact that you'd even try, means a lot to me."

He moved his hand, capturing hers. "All three of you mean a lot to me."

CHAPTER FOURTEEN

Teagan stared at the two-story brick colonial that used to be the home of Gabriel and Marsha Davis. The yard was perfectly mowed and trimmed, as usual, but somehow it looked cleaner. Newer.

"The new landscaping certainly makes it look different." Logan pulled into the driveway. "The real estate agent was right about pressure washing off the bottom five feet of the house. The bushes had grown too large and created a green sheen. I think they did a good job."

"Yes, I have to agree." Teagan got out of the car and watched several more pull into the driveway and park out front on the street. All their friends were there, except Elizabeth, who had volunteered to stay home with the four children.

Teagan didn't recognize the man with short dark hair who stepped out of a black SUV. He walked with an air of authority, the same as Logan, Micah, and Matthew. She instantly pegged him as current or former military. All four men oozed power and confidence.

Logan left her side and moved to intercept the

newcomer. "Hey, Tony, how the hell have you been?" With big smiles, they did the bro-hug things—clasped hands and back-pounding.

"Busy." They started back toward her where she had been joined by Micah and Matthew. "I appreciate you hiring my company." He looked up at the house. "This has definitely been an interesting case."

When the two men joined them, Logan made the introductions. "Teagan, Micah, Matthew, I'd like you to meet an old friend of mine, Tony Alvarez. We worked together several years ago, when he wore a green beret." He gestured to each as he introduced them. "Teagan Williams, former Seahawk pilot. Navy Captain Micah Reid, he pushes around a bunch of SEALs down in Virginia Beach. Matthew Saint Clare, he runs the special operations group out of Langley."

"Damn. We're living proof the covert world truly is small." Tony's gaze swept the large lawn and well-established neighborhood. "Let's get started. I feel exposed standing out here. Let me walk you through what we think happened."

Everyone stood on the front porch. "I was able to hunt down and recapture some of the security video from the neighbors." He turned on his tablet and tapped to the correct file, then turned it around for everyone to see.

From three different angles, an average-sized man wearing dark slacks and a dark windbreaker walked down the sidewalk then turned toward the Davis's house. His hair was covered in a baseball cap, pulled low over his eyes which were covered by sunglasses. None of the videos showed the front door. The timestamp on all three was exactly the same.

"We know that this man approached the house, but we

have no idea if he knocked or simply walked in. I'm not sure if you're aware, or if Mrs. Davis even knew, but her entire security system had been compromised. For instance, the front door didn't lock all the time."

"What the hell?" Teagan shook her head. "No. Marsha and I had an arrangement. I'd wait at the door until I heard the three chirps which meant system was armed. It became second-nature to us after Gabe left. She was very afraid of being in the house alone."

"Oh, it beeps, but the locks don't always slide into place. Inside the house, it would have seemed as though she'd armed the system. When the code actually locked the doors, those times were recorded by the security company and the backup system inside the house. Then, as though by magic, certain doors would unlock. It happened while we were working in the house. We thought there was a fault within the system." He went on to explain, "Several of the men I work with are experts in installing and maintaining residential security systems and initially they were baffled. When they started tracing individual lines, they discovered the entire house could be unlocked remotely."

"Was that something Gabe set up so that he could come and go as he pleased?" Micah suggested.

"Doubtful." Tony took what looked like a key fob for an electronic start car and clicked it. Everyone heard the deadbolt slide. "Unlocking this door didn't record anywhere, not with the security company nor on the internal system."

This seemed to greatly interest Matthew. "What you're saying is that somebody with knowledge of the Davis' security system unlocked the door and simply walked in."

"Yes." He pointed toward the closed garage doors.

"With the big doors down, no one can see whether there's a car parked in there or not. Even if someone walked around to the main door on the far side, it's so dark in there, and Marsha's car is navy blue, the intruder may not have realized that she was in the house. "

"So, you're not thinking premeditated murder." Matthew crossed his powerful arms over his chest.

"No. I'm not. I don't believe the intruder came here to murder her." Alvarez manually opened the door. "Here's why."

They all stepped into the foyer.

Tony pointed up the steps. "Marsha is on the second floor all the way back in the master bedroom, in and out of the closet." He pulled a picture of the master bedroom out of his black backpack. "As you can see, several bags are already filled with men's clothes. It looked as though she was in the process of filling this one. Notice the haphazard way the suit is lying on the bed. We believe she tossed it there. I'm going to circle back to this in a minute."

"Our intruder had disabled the system. No code was entered according to the records. We think he believed he was alone in the house. The intruder has been here before and knows the layout." Tony headed down the hall and everyone followed him into the office. He pulled several large photographs from the backpack. "At some point, the safe gets opened. In our opinion, the intruder opened the safe."

"What makes you think the intruder didn't go find Marsha and force her to open it?" Logan asked.

"Two things jumped out. First, the keypad on the safe had been wiped down. Why wipe her fingerprints off the buttons? Law enforcement would expect to find them there. Second, the 1911 gun. Had she opened the safe, she would have instantly grabbed for her gun, which by the way, has a bullet in the chamber and her fingerprints on it, although it had been cleaned since it was last shot." He spread several photographs across the cherry cabinets that ran along the left-hand side under the bookshelves that reached to the ceiling. Other than the new carpet, it was the only flat surface left in the empty room.

Teagan quit breathing. All she could do was stare at the lifeless body that had once been her roommate, her best friend. She had been Marsha's maid of honor. She'd introduced Marsha to Gabriel.

"It's all my fault," Teagan mumbled as a ton of invisible bricks fell on her.

Logan whipped her around so she couldn't look at the pictures. He cupped her face with his large hands and forced her to look up into whiskey-colored eyes. "Breathe," he insisted.

She tried but could only manage small sips.

"Dig deep. Find that cold-blooded pilot called Ice-T." Logan didn't blink. "Where's that woman who flew into a hot zone, guns blazing to push back the enemy, allowing that SEAL team to drag two injured sailors into her chopper? Find that woman."

Yeah, that had been her and the greatest damn crew on the fucking planet. There was no way in hell she was going to let that radical cell continue to wound any more good men. She'd known exactly what her helicopter could do, if pushed. And that night she'd pushed it to its limits to save those seven men.

Logan held her gaze captive. "Breathe in."

She had already buried Marsha. She could do this. She managed half a lungful.

"Now out slowly." Logan's words were kind and tender.

Teagan obeyed. Without his command, she filled her lungs. And again. As her blood soaked with oxygen, she refilled her courage. Her determination grew proportionately. In a combat zone, she'd been fearless. She would do whatever it took to succeed, especially when it came to helping others. What she needed to do now, was help find Marsha's killer.

She saw her resolve reflected in Logan's eyes. She'd pulled her shit together and he knew it.

Logan smiled. "There's my girl."

Before she could protest that she wasn't his girl, he laid his lips on hers in a soft, sweet kiss.

What was I going to say? Her mind was suddenly blank.

Logan no longer filled her vision. "You can do this." His voice sounded so far away, as though it were just an echo in her mind.

"Would you feel better sitting in the car and waiting for me there?" Logan asked.

That was all it took. Anger and determination shot through her veins.

"I'm not some recalcitrant child to be sent to the car. I had a minor shock seeing my best friend for over two decades lying dead with a bullet hole in her head." She slammed her fists on her hips. "Forgive me. It took me a few minutes to wrap my head around the situation. Now, let's continue with the briefing."

"That's the Ice-T we all know and love." Micah stepped over and gave her a one-armed hug. "Nice to have you back."

"Ma'am, I'm terribly sorry for your loss." Tony looked embarrassed. "I thought…everyone else here had been to the murder scene."

Teagan absolutely hated being the center of attention.

The only thing that was worse, was being pitied. "Okay, Tony, let's just proceed. You left off where someone was in this office and had opened the safe."

"Yes." The owner of the Alvarez agency picked up a picture of the master bedroom. "It's our belief that Marsha heard something downstairs and went to check it out." He pointed to the ceiling. "Their bedroom is directly above this office. We believe she discovered someone in here. She must have recognized him, and that's why he killed her. He must not have known that she shot left-handed.

"That may have been his biggest mistake," Logan pointed out.

"No." Tony dragged out the word. "He may have made an even bigger mistake, but I'll come back to that one."

He tapped on his tablet for a minute then showed the video of the man exiting. "He was in this house for exactly twelve minutes, forty-two seconds."

"He didn't run," Micah noted. "I'd say he tried to look as casual as possible and succeeded."

"He's a pro," Matthew suggested.

"We agree." Tony ran the video again. "He was very careful to look away so none of the cameras got a good shot. We've enhanced this video several times, several different ways, and can't get any facial features. All I can tell you is that he is approximately five feet, eleven inches, and wears a size ten shoe."

"Okay, he did several things right." Logan cocked his head to one side. "What's the big mistake he made?"

Tony's gaze went directly to Teagan. "When was the last time Ashley Helms visited her sister?"

"Months." Then Teagan thought again. "Hell, it may have been over a year ago. Marsha and Gabe used to fight about Ashley. She'd show up here at the house with some very unsavory men claiming she owed them money. Marsha would give her money, then Ashley and the man, or men, would leave. Gabe didn't like the fact that these men knew they kept cash in the house."

Teagan tried to put dates to the occurrences. "The last straw came when Ashley showed up on their doorstep, beat to hell. They took her in and about two days later, while Marsha was taking the children to school, Gabe watched on his phone as Ashley took several expensive items and walked out. Gabriel was still living here then, so that had to be at least eleven months ago, probably even longer than that."

She looked at the private detective. "Why do you ask?"

He pulled a close-up picture of a handprint on the corner of the desk. "We found Ashley Helms' full handprint on the desk and several of her fingerprints inside the safe." He then picked up the tablet and five seconds later showed them the video of Ashley moving quickly up the walkway to the house, looking nervously side-to-side. The timestamp showed this was two minutes after the mystery man left.

"So, Ashley may have seen him?" Teagan was shocked. "And that little bitch didn't call the cops after she found her sister dead?"

"Given what I found, that might actually have been a good thing. I had plenty of time to take pictures on my own before the locals showed up." Matthew hit the button to show the next video. They watched her sprinting across the lawn toward the neighbor's house on the right, stop at the hedge separating the two homes, and throwing up.

"She actually got sick the first time off-camera. My team thought that perhaps one of the uniformed cops had thrown up in the bushes at the bottom of the steps, but upon further investigation, we're quite sure it was Ashley." He stopped the video. "She has something in her right hand as she left. She came in empty-handed."

"Any idea what it is?" Micah asked.

"We're working on that." Tony reassured everyone. "Fingerprints from her left hand were on the shelf below the stacks of money. Our best guess is that she took at least one stack of bills. Given that the others were in one thousand dollar packets of mixed denominations, we figure she walked away with at least a thousand dollars."

"I thought she was supposed to be in rehab?" Logan mentioned.

"She was," Teagan agreed. "Her parents even thought she was there. I guess she didn't care enough about her sister to show up for the funeral."

"According to the records at the rehabilitation center, she had checked herself out the morning of the murder." Tony looked intently at Teagan. "Do you think Ashley is capable of murder? Could she have shot her sister and stage it as a suicide?"

"I never met the woman," Teagan confessed. "Marsha talked about her quite often, but I personally never met her. I would say that's a question for her counselors at the rehab center."

"That's on our list of possible leads." Tony said. "Would Ashley have known that Marsha shot left-handed?"

"I doubt it." Teagan shook her head. "Marsha and I started shooting together while in flight school. It wasn't until we helped with a class for women at a local range about five years ago that she discovered she was left eye dominant. The instructor took some time after the class to give each of us some personal coaching."

"Do you know where Ashley is now?" Micah asked.

"Yes. She's back in the same rehabilitation center that she left the day of the murder. She checked herself back in about ten days ago." Tony looked chagrined. "We haven't been able to talk to her. We did, though, turn over all our findings to Defective, I mean, Detective Russo."

Everyone snickered.

"I'm sorry," Tony grimaced. "Freudian slip."

"No problems, brother, we feel the same way about him." Logan smacked Tony on the back. "Now you know why we hired you."

"Dickhead or not, he has the authority to get past the privacy bullshit and question her."

Teagan snorted. "Do you think he's going to do that?"

Tony grinned. "Yep." He looked directly at Matthew. "When someone as high up in the CIA as Gabriel Davis is murdered by a terrorist, then his wife is murdered days later, the local police department gets a lot of heat. Since you guys hired us, we've been providing Detective Russo with loads of information. Thankfully, he's agreed to share his findings with us."

Teagan's phone buzzed with the text. "The real estate agent will be here in five minutes."

"Do you have anything else for us?" Logan asked.

"No. I've given you everything we have so far. Be assured, we're still pulling on several threads." Tony slid his tablet into the backpack. "We're working this one hard. We'll all keep in touch."

"Could you forward those video clips to me, please?" Matthew grinned. "I'll have Clarence, my computer geek, run them through a few of our programs."

Tony gave him a knowing grin. "Check your email in ten minutes. I'm sure you'll share anything you discover."

"Of course." Matthew agreed.

Teagan, Micah, and Matthew shook Tony's hand on his way past and thanked him.

"I'll walk you out." Logan put a hand on his friend's shoulder. "When this is over, you'll have to bring Sherrie and that new baby boy down to Topsail Island and hang out on the beach with us for a few days."

"We'll be sure to do that." Their voices faded down the hallway.

"Do you think the sniper who shot Gabe did this?" Micah stared at the photographs.

"Possibly." Matthew said. "He came here looking for something. I think I agree with Tony—Marsha surprised him and recognized him. She was collateral damage." He looked at Teagan. "Have you had a chance to go through the contents of the office and the safe deposit boxes?"

"Yeah, and I didn't find anything that I would consider a clue." She took them one at a time. "The safe deposit box he had the longest time, contained coin collections. Several of the coins were from the eighteen hundreds, so I photographed them and sent them to a collector recommended by an old friend. He's still evaluating them. In the next one, I found a bag of diamonds. I took those to a local GIA-certified jeweler who appraised them right there in front of me. I wasn't going to let those diamonds out of my sight. He said they were all of the highest quality, FL grade, and natural diamonds. Wholesale they're worth $1.3 million."

She remembered the day that she and Logan had entered the bank in Jacksonville together to get a new safe deposit box. He had an account there since the first time he was assigned to Force Recon as a fresh-faced Marine second lieutenant. They'd received several side glances from the women who worked behind the tall counter, especially when Logan reaffirmed, twice, that he and Teagan were neither engaged, nor married. Just friends. They couldn't understand why they would want a joint safe deposit box. In truth, it wasn't any of their fucking business.

"Lots of covert operators prefer diamonds to cash or investments." Matthew continued to explain, "They're easily transportable, rarely ever in history have natural diamonds lost their value, and nobody keeps track of them, yet they can be quickly traded on the black market."

"You're just going to hold onto them for the kids?" Micah asked.

Teagan nodded. "For now." She continued with the inventory. "In Gabriel's third safe deposit box, were the passports that I have for you in the car, Matthew."

He didn't bother looking guilty. "We provide all of our agents several means of escaping countries." He grinned. "I've been a citizen of a dozen countries, according to my passport at that time."

She continued, "We're going to hang onto the cash from the various countries. As you said, Matt, you never know when it might come in handy. As for Marsha's safe deposit box, it contained her and the children's passports, their birth certificates, which were necessary for us to register them from school, vehicle titles, a copy of her previous will, and that's about it."

"What about the contents of the desk?" Micah asked.

Logan answered as he walked back into the room. "I checked through all of that. I forwarded a few things on to Matthew, but there wasn't much."

"Same with the computer that sat on the desk in this room," Matthew reported. "Clarence was never able to figure out where the suicide message originated, just that it wasn't typed on that keyboard but sent in from an outside source. Everything else on that computer was standard shit we all keep. He had nothing work-related."

The doorbell rang.

Logan quickly pulled up the security app on his phone and saw the person on the porch. "It's the realtor."

"I need to get back to work," Matthew said as he headed out the office door. "I'll see you two back at the house tonight."

"I need to check in with my office," Micah said as he followed Matthew. "I heard Elizabeth was cooking so I'll see you at supper."

CHAPTER FIFTEEN

Logan slid behind the wheel. "Well, that's good news. At least the house will be up for sale by this time next week."

"Good to know this is a highly sought-after neighborhood," Teagan added. "I hope it sells quickly. Her suggestion of painting and new carpet sounded like a great idea." She reached over and touched his forearm. "I'm so glad you were there. I had no idea about painting and carpet costs."

"She must have some serious connections with subcontractors." Logan sometimes had to wait months to get renovations done around his home. "I can't believe they'll have everything done, and the house cleaned, within a week. I figured covering the dark blue walls in Brann's room would take at least three coats, especially since they want to bring it to white. There's nothing quite like literally waiting for paint to dry."

"I can't believe the price she thinks we're going to get." Teagan tapped on her phone. "Oh. My. God. She's right. The average home in that neighborhood is on the market for less than twenty days. According to this app, sellers are getting what they ask. One house, only a block away, sold last week for more than what she suggested we list as market price." She laid the phone in her lap and dropped her head back.

"Are you okay?" He glanced over at her and quickly returned his eyes to the busy road.

"I've never lived in a house." Her statement shocked him.

"Never?" Logan couldn't imagine what that would be like. The house he grew up in was nothing to brag about, nowhere near the five-bedroom, four-and-a-half bath house they'd just left. He knew what it was like, though, to maintain a home. He'd mowed the lawn since he turned into a teenager, helped his mother weed the garden and landscape, learned how to fix a toilet, and anything else that needed to be repaired. It wasn't much, but it was theirs.

"Nope. We always lived in apartments. We moved quite often. It was just Momma and me." She scoffed. "I can't tell you how many schools I attended, but I can tell you I have either traveled through, or lived in, every state in the lower forty-eight."

"Sounds like your mother changed jobs quite often." Logan wondered what was up with that. He knew many military families who could make the same claim as Teagan. The Marine Corps had moved him coast-to-coast, twice. He'd seen much of the United States on those cross-country trips.

"This is the first time I will ever have sold a house, yet, I've never bought one." She glanced over at him. "Have you been through this before?"

"Yeah," he admitted. "I bought a condo the first time I got stationed at Camp Lejeune. It had two master bedrooms, so I rented the other one out. When I got orders, my renter bought it at the going price. I made a few thousand dollars, so the next time I bought a three-bedroom house."

Teagan giggled. "You were a house flipper."

"No, not exactly. I didn't bother fixing them up. Most of the time I bought new houses, so I didn't have to worry about anything breaking." He thought about it for a few minutes. "Over the years, I've made some damn good money on real estate. Back to your initial question, yes, I've been through this several times."

She let out a long breath. "Good. I was scared to death to sign that listing agreement."

He pulled into a parking space at Mr. Keller's office. "We're going to have a lot more papers to sign here. Are you ready for this?"

"I'll sign anything if it means we get to keep the kids." She was out of the car and headed toward the door to the office before he turned off the engine.

Two hours later they were back in his SUV. They'd had so many legal documents that the law agency ended up giving them leather cases to hold the copies of everything they'd signed.

It still hadn't sunk in that he was currently responsible for nine million dollars now, counting the diamonds in the safe deposit box in Jacksonville. Thankfully, Ed had asked everyone to come to them, so they didn't have to leave the private conference room. While Teagan met with the CPA, Logan endured the broker who currently handled Gabriel's investments. Their relationship would end very soon.

In the few hours of research Logan had done since he'd never needed a broker before, he knew the needs of the children were not the primary focus of that man. Logan would do a lot more research, then move all the accounts to someone else. After the man left, he found Mr. Keller in his office and they discussed the matter. Thank Christ, Ed didn't like the weasel either.

As they headed back to Elizabeth and Matthew's home, Teagan was very quiet.

"What's wrong?" He asked.

"This is just a strange arrangement." She flipped her hand back and forth between the two of them. "I'm supposed to ask you for every dime needed to spend on the children. The CPA suggested we set up a household bank account using the interest off the children's investments." She dug in her folio and pulled out a sheet of paper. "Here's a list of everything that we should buy using that account. He was upset that you're spending your own money to feed us."

"Fuck that shit." Talk like that pissed Logan off. "You're all now my family and I need to support you."

"Nope. The way the court sees it, you and I are caretakers of the children." Teagan went on to explain, "My money should support me, your money should support you, and their money should be used to support them."

"That's just bullshit."

"The CPA also said that the children's account should be paying you rent because before we moved in, it was a rental property." She read from her notes.

"No way in hell am I going to take money from those children." Logan would just have to call that CPA and have a talk with him. He thought of Anora and Brann as his children, ones he shared daily with Teagan.

Teagan. Children. The words triggered the memory of their previous conversation where Teagan told him she couldn't have children. He wondered why. Just as he was about to ask her what she meant, her phone rang.

Ending the call a few minutes later, she twisted in the seat to face him. "They have a bed for Mom in the memory care unit in Jacksonville." He could hear the enthusiasm in her voice. "I need to call the medical transport company and check on their availability, then I can contact the nursing home that she's currently in…Logan, I'll have Mom in a home twenty minutes away by the end of next week if all goes as planned."

She was so excited.

"That's great." He felt like such a selfish ass. He hadn't realized that having her mother so far away had been stressful for her. He'd been so consumed with his job and the children, he hadn't given any thought to Teagan and what the move had meant for her.

Their lives would become even more complicated when the children started school, got involved in activities, and oh, fuck, when Teagan went to work full-time on New River Air Station.

"Will you be able to parent next week while I deal with getting Mom settled?" She was making a list on her phone. Damn. This woman was so organized.

"Sure. I'll work something out so I can come home and babysit." He turned into Matthew and Elizabeth's neighborhood.

Teagan raised her perfectly arched eyebrows. "No, you won't babysit, you'll come home and parent. There's a big difference. These children are half yours. I certainly do appreciate everything you do for them—especially for making them breakfast, in case I haven't mentioned how much I truly appreciate that before—but we're now technically their parents. Babysitters are teenagers who will come into our homes and watch over the children, making sure they stay alive while we're gone. We'll need to hire babysitters soon."

"Does that mean you and I get to go out on dates?" He knew he'd said something wrong the minute he glanced at her.

Teagan's sun-kissed face blanched. "I'm sorry…I…I've been inconsiderate. Of course, you're dating." She turned her head and looked out the side window.

Well, he had been dating, up until Gabe's funeral.

When she faced him once again, she had pasted on a smile. "I apologize for occupying your every evening. I never meant to keep you from your friends."

Logan pulled into their friends' driveway.

Where the hell was she going with this?

Teagan babbled on. "I truly appreciate you taking us out to dinner, or bringing something home for all of us to eat, but you don't need to do that anymore."

Not have supper with them? Or did she mean not to have him spend his money on their supper?

He put the car in park.

Her fake smile grew wider. "How about we switch off? I can take care of supper and bedtime one night, and you can do it the next."

Logan turned off the vehicle and faced her.

"That way it's fair to both of us, and you can meet up with your…friends." She shrugged. "I need to get out and meet more people anyway."

Logan hated this entire line of thinking.

"I already told you that I don't have anyone special in my life, right now." He reached across the console and grabbed her hand, holding it between both of his. "I want to clarify. I want to go out on a date with you. Just you and me. Without the children. We can hire a babysitter to make sure the children don't kill each other or someone else."

"You don't need to thank me for taking care of the children by taking me out on a date. I'm parenting. Just like you." Thanking her for being such a good mother figure to the children was not what Logan had in mind for their date.

"Although I appreciate everything you do for the children, I have no intention of taking you out as a thank you." He leaned in and brushed his mouth over hers.

Leaning back, he held her gaze. "And I can assure you, if I didn't want to be on that couch watching television with you and the kids, I wouldn't be there." He laid soft kisses on each corner of her mouth.

"I want to be there with *you*...and the children." He wanted to show her just how serious he was about dating her. He leaned forward, slowly, giving her time to say something, hopefully not reject him.

The front door of the house flew open and four children, all yelling the same time, came running toward their vehicle.

Knowing he only had seconds before experiencing his first child-interruptus, he lifted her chin so that she met his eyes. "You and I are going on a date when we get back to North Carolina."

She blinked as though in a daze. "Yes. Date."

Knocking came from the window beside her.

"Come look what we made," Anora screamed through the glass.

"Cupcakes for dessert," Brann announced from Logan's side.

"We should go inside." Logan rolled down both

windows. "Step back, munchkins. Let Aunt Teagan and me get out of the car."

As though the children had awakened her from a trance, Teagan said, "We're going to talk about this some more."

"Guaranteed." He wanted to take her hand as they walked into the house, but he didn't think she was ready for that public display of affection. Instead, he placed his hand at the small of her back, guiding her into the house as the children bounced around them.

Three hours later, with the exhausted children asleep, Logan and Matthew sat on the back patio sipping eighteen-year-old scotch.

"How are things going with the kids?" Matthew asked. "They seem happy."

"They have their moments, but overall I think they're adjusting." He set his glass on the patio table. "I guess, I'm adjusting too. I had to stop at the grocery store the other night when Brann and I were coming back from batting practice. At the counter, getting ready to check out, he asked if he could have a pack of gum. Before I paid the bill, he'd added ten more items. He gave me the line, *my mom used to always buy this for me after baseball practice.* When I delivered him back to Teagan, she ripped me a new one for allowing him to have all that candy. Fuck, Matthew, every day I think I know less and less about raising kids."

The man with the almost-white hair and nearly black beard laughed. "And let me guess, the next time, when you told him *no,* he said you were being mean to him and that his real parents would have let him have it." The man shook his head with self-deprecation, a smile on his face. "You should see when Liza gets wound up. She'll turn on the tears and tell me that her real father would buy that piece of junk jewelry for her or take her to an adult movie or whatever sin I had committed."

"Thank Christ, it's not just me." An emotional weight lifted from Logan's chest and shoulders. "I'm just trying to be a good male role model to these children."

"No, you're not," Matt accused. "You're trying to be the father Gabriel never was."

He couldn't argue. Matthew was right. Logan wanted to be the best father possible to both those children. "I think coming back here this weekend might be good for them. I'd like them to see Washington DC as a fun place to visit. Your kids are helping a lot."

Matthew smiled and grinned into his glass. "They're good kids. Lizzie did an excellent job raising them so far. Don't get me wrong, they can be little shits. Liza is becoming a master at manipulating men. Last weekend, when Micah came up to join Austin and me for a Nationals baseball game, she had him feeling so guilty that he took her out for ice cream."

That opened the perfect opportunity for Logan. "Do you find yourself doing more stuff with Austin than Liza?"

Shaking his head, Matthew confessed, "I admit, I bonded with Austin right away. Everything seemed easy with him. He'd been ignored for so many years by his stepfather, and we both like baseball. Liza, I had no fucking idea what to do with a little girl." He chuckled. "Now, she has me wound around her little finger."

"So, how did you finally win Liza over?" Logan was really hoping for some serious tips.

"Elizabeth saw that video on YouTube where the man gets all dressed up in a suit and tie then takes his little girl out on a date. She got the brilliant idea that I should take

Liza out at least once every other week and do things with her that she wants to do."

"How's that working out for you?" Logan picked up his glass and sipped. The scotch was fucking smooth.

"Last week, Liza wanted to go to the mall. She got all dressed up and I stayed in my suit and tie after work." By this point, Matthew was grinning. "We ate at one of the chain restaurants in that area. She's gotten into ordering a virgin strawberry daiquiri when I order a drink from the bar." He was smiling. "She's so fucking cute trying to be a young lady."

Their gazes caught, and Matthew explained, "We practice our manners. And we have a no electronics rule. We're not allowed to sit anywhere I can be distracted by a television and my phone has to be on vibrate. I'm only allowed to answer if it's Elizabeth or a nine-one-one work emergency."

"Too bad more parents don't teach their children those rules. I swear, teenagers are becoming more and more rude. Their table manners are atrocious, and they never look up from their phones." Logan took another sip and set the glass back down.

"No argument here," Matt agreed.

"So, you take Liza out to dinner," Logan pressed. "Do you go to a kids' movie afterwards?"

"Sometimes." Matt burst out laughing. "I told you that last week she wanted to go to the mall. What I didn't tell you, was that I bribe her. If she acts like a little lady, and is very good during supper, I buy her something special. I bought her a purple fuzzy purse that she just couldn't live without. You should have seen the look on the clerk's face when I approached the counter. Liza had stopped to look at something on the other side of the display so the woman couldn't see her. I swear she thought I was some kind of child abductor."

Matthew thought about it for a moment before he added, "We don't always go out. Sometimes I just get on the floor and play with her for a few minutes. Little girls are amazing. Their imagination is so different from boys'."

"Thanks for the advice. I've never been around little girls before and to be honest, sometimes Anora scares the shit out of me. One minute she's walking around with a fluffy crown on her head, and the next minute she's wrestling with Brann." Logan chuckled. "I'd love for her to grow up and be a strong woman like Teagan and Elizabeth. In the next breath, though, I want her to stay this beautiful innocent child."

"I know exactly what you mean," Matthew agreed.

For a long time, the two men sat quietly, their faces lit only by flickering citronella candles. The clink of their glasses touching the patio table the only thing disturbing the creatures of the night.

As they both set their empty glasses down for the last time, Matt locked eyes with Logan. "I love both my kids, and would kill anyone who tried to harm them or Elizabeth. I've seen you with Brann and Anora. I think you feel the same way about them."

"I love those children more every day," Logan admitted. His feelings for Teagan, though, were nowhere near as easily defined.

CHAPTER SIXTEEN

The rain had shifted back to sheets of water dumping from a gray sky for the second day in a row. The kids were cranky and so was Teagan. She was having the period from hell. She felt as turbulent as the choppy ocean.

It was a damn good thing Logan had to work late for the last several nights. Very late. It was just her and the kids for supper the last few nights. That night, microwaving a container of frozen macaroni and cheese and a box of chicken nuggets was all she was capable of making. Everyone should be damn glad for Midol. At the moment, it was the only thing keeping her sane.

Teagan promised herself a better attitude...tomorrow. Bad weather or not, she would load up the kids and take them to visit their new grandmother. Nana, as they had decided to call her, had arrived the previous week. Teagan was pleased with the brand-new facility. It had many safety checks in place so her mother could no longer walk out of the building and go for a stroll by herself, clueless to the danger.

As the children watched an animated movie, and sang

along to all the well-known songs, Teagan decided she needed to do something constructive to take her mind off her cramps. When they had left DC two weeks ago, she had promised Matthew to meticulously go through each of the remaining office boxes.

She hiked all the way to the third floor and curled up in her favorite overstuffed chair, heating pad in place.

For a long moment she simply stared through the large windows at the shades of gray. Purplish clouds filled with water continued to empty into a green gray ocean. After looking at water all over the world during her years in the Navy, Teagan had come to know its moods. Today, just like yesterday, it was punishingly angry, nothing more than a reminder that humans had no control over mother nature.

As her uterus squeezed hard enough to take her breath away, she, and every other woman on the planet, understood what an uncaring bitch mother nature could truly be.

Leaning to her side, she opened the next box and started to empty its contents. When she pulled out the laptop from Gabriel's apartment office, she wondered if she could delete its contents and give it to Brann. Perhaps having something of his father's, and having a computer of his own, might brighten the boy's spirits. He, like everyone else in the house, was suffering from cabin fever. Perhaps something new could hold his interest.

Hitting the *on* button, she was surprised when it started up. She quickly checked the battery, then found the cord and plugged it in. At the white box demanding a password, she was ready to give up and say fuck it all. She started looking for the tiny hole for factory reset when the battery fell out.

Well, damn. Wasn't that just my fucking luck.

She slid the battery back in place and restarted the machine. It opened in admin mode and asked her to set a new passcode.

What-the-fuck. Why not?

She entered her favorite because she knew she could remember it. Gabriel's landing page automatically opened. Teagan had zero hacking skills, but she did know her way around a computer. She checked his history and clicked on a few files and found nothing interesting. She would send those to Matthew. Perhaps they meant something to the CIA.

The next file on the list opened.

Teagan sucked in a breath.

Nassar al-Jamil. She knew that name. As she read through the notes about his New Islamic State, its exact location in Iran, her blood began to boil. Why the hell had the U.S. government allowed this terrorist to continue to live?

Her friend, Mason Sinclair, had died because of this man. She had been there. Every time she thought about that night, she remembered the force of the explosion as it pushed her and Elizabeth to the ground. The scrape of coarse sand on her hands had hurt for days. Gabriel had helped them up and had practically carried both of them for nearly a quarter of a mile.

She clearly pictured in her mind Logan and Micah running toward the three of them, cursing that one of the bombs had gone off early, causing all of them to explode.

Elizabeth's screams had pierced through Teagan's ringing ears. The pain of her friend's loss still hurt. Mason had been such a great teammate and a wonderful friend to all of them. No one on the team knew for weeks that

Elizabeth and Mason had been married hours before they lifted off for Syria. To lose her new husband so brutally and right in front of her, disturbed her friend for years. Then she had married that fucking asshole, Robert. When he was killed, it was not a great loss to mankind.

Teagan was thrilled that Elizabeth had found another wonderful man like Mason. Everyone on that team from a decade ago seemed to have an instant connection with Matthew. He fit into their group seamlessly, as though he'd always belonged. His love for Elizabeth, and her two children, was evident every time Teagan saw them together.

Thoughts of her friends guided her mind back to the mission. She'd been planting her bombs in the designated places, just as they had practiced over and over again before leaving for Syria. Completely focused on the placement and arming of the deadly weapons, she'd ignored the chatter through her earbud. As a pilot who flew in and out of busy airports, she'd learned to tune out everything except keywords that pertained directly to her.

Poking her head out the door, weapon to her shoulder, she looked down the iron sights from one end of the hallway to the other. It was clear. Knees bent, she stepped quietly into the next room.

The first time, she remembered hearing voices coming from the room across the hall. The words weren't coming through her comm unit. Men were yelling at each other. At the time, she'd ignored it. Gabe and Mason could argue all they wanted. She had a job to do.

She dodged around boxes of rocket propelled grenades in her last assigned room. As she exited, she heard a noise and looked over her shoulder at the back door. One of the men stepped through to the outdoors. Since neither man was supposed to be there helping the women plant the bombs, she shrugged it off.

Even though the back door was closer, she was ordered to leave the building the same way they'd entered, what she thought of as the front door. She made her way down the short hall and through the open room where two guards lay dead. As they had practiced, Teagan followed Elizabeth into the dark of night. They hadn't made it fifty feet before the impact of the blast threw them on their knees.

Teagan had been yanked up by her backpack.

"Run." Gabe screamed into her ear as he grabbed Elizabeth around the waist. She was yelling and screaming something about Mason while trying to run back to the building. Gabe threw her over his shoulder and sprinted toward the rendezvous point.

So much had happened since that failed mission nearly eleven years ago.

Returning her attention to the al-Jamil file, she clicked on several links in the report. Some led to maps, infrared satellite photos, one led to a picture of the five on their team as they stood outside of the practice house. It had obviously been taken without their knowledge. It was just a random, casual shot.

Teagan stared at the picture. There was something in the way Mason stood that reminded her of Matthew. There were some similarities, same height, same build, but Matt, with his white hair and almost black mustache looked at least early fifties. She wondered if Elizabeth had been attracted to him because of those similarities.

After searching through several more files, Teagan

decided the best course of action would be to copy the entire hard drive and send it to Matthew. She didn't want to lose the operating system and programs currently installed, so she decided to use several of the microSD drives Gabriel had left in the desk drawer in his office at his apartment.

Checking each drive before she started to copy the files, she found a few more with information on them that she would just include with the package to Matthew.

Two hours later, she'd made backups, transferring all the files she felt were important onto one of her terabyte microSD drives, and deleted everything as she went. Brann would have plenty of hard drive space to download any games he wanted. Since she knew nothing about videogames—they'd never interested her—she'd ask Logan to help select age-appropriate games. This was also a great excuse for her to call Elizabeth, not that she needed a reason to call her friend.

Glancing at her watch, it had been over three hours since she'd checked on the children. They rarely went over an hour without checking in with her. The child psychologist had said that was not unusual behavior and once they become more comfortable with her and Logan, those time spans would naturally increase.

It had been far too long. She practically flew down the spiral iron staircase. Glancing into Brann's room, she found him on his bed, headphones over his ears, smiling at a video.

Relief started to wash through her. One down, one to go.

His smile broadened when he saw her standing in his doorway. "Hey, Aunt Teagan, are you feeling any better?"

Fuck. Had she been so obvious even a seven-year-old understood her bad mood? She took a second to analyze her body. The medication and heating pad had helped, as did the mental distraction.

"Yes. I'm feeling like soft-serve ice cream. How about you?" she suggested.

"Nah, not anymore. Uncle Logan took us out to that frozen yogurt place where we get to mix our own cup and put on whatever toppings we want." The boy swung his legs over the side of the bed and eagerly told her, "I had chocolate and peanut butter and birthday cake ice cream with ground up chocolate cookies and gummy bears on top. I put some strawberries on it too 'cuz you're always telling us that we need to eat healthy."

The sincerity in his youthful face almost made her laugh. Just to give him a hard time, she asked, "Why didn't anyone invite me?"

"Uncle Logan said we had to let you have some alone time since he'd been so busy at work and you had to take care of us day and night." Brann screwed up his face. "He said it was his turn to be the parent."

Teagan burst out laughing.

Brann looked as though he'd said something wrong and might cry at any minute. She rushed into the room and hugged him to her.

"Neither you, nor Uncle Logan, did anything wrong." She kissed the top of his head. "Matter-of-fact, you both did everything right." She gave him a mock scowl. "Except bring me home some chocolate yogurt with lots of awesome toppings."

The little boy beamed up at her. "Uncle Logan made a special yogurt just for you and we brought it home and put it in the freezer. Want me to go get it?"

Fuck, yes. If the boy wanted to wait on her hand and foot, she'd let him. At what age could she teach Brann to pour wine? "Thank you, I'd really like that."

As he tore down the hall, she wandered out of his bedroom and over to Anora's. The little girl was sitting on the floor next to Logan, one of his long legs stretched out, the other balancing a large tablet, their backs against the bed.

"What you think about this place?" They both stared intently at the screen.

"Let's look at the kids' menu." Anora seemed very interested.

"Oh, look, they have miniature hamburgers, grilled cheese sandwiches, shrimp poppers, and your favorite, chicken tenders and macaroni and cheese." Hope wound through Logan's voice.

"Uncle Logan, mac and cheese is what we eat at home. If you're taking me out for special dinner, I want to eat something special. I'll order the hamburger. Or the shrimp poppers." The little girl sounded so serious that Teagan had to step out in the hallway and giggle quietly.

"How about we make an on-the-spot decision?" Logan suggested. "Do you have a pretty dress to wear?"

As soon as Anora stood up, she spotted Teagan.

"Aunt Teagan, Uncle Logan is taking me out on a date tomorrow night. Just him and me. To a real adult restaurant. Want to help me pick out a pretty dress?" The joy in the child's eyes was more than Teagan had ever hoped for.

"Absolutely." She entered the room and Logan stood in one smooth movement.

As she walked past him, he brushed her arm with his hand. "Feeling better?"

Brann bounced into the room with a dish of chocolate ice cream covered in chocolate sauce and chocolate cookies. There was also a slice of strawberry. Just one.

"Here you go, Aunt Teagan. We all helped make it." He handed it to her with pride.

"I am now." After stuffing a big scoop of chocolate into her mouth, she kissed Logan's cheek as she headed for Anora's closet.

"Come on, Brann." Logan called as he headed for the door. "I'm sure we can find a baseball game or an action video to watch while the ladies deal with dresses." He turned back around and kneeled in front of Anora. "I'll pick you up at six o'clock. It's not nice to keep your date waiting, so you be ready, okay?"

Anora dramatically bobbed her head up and down. Then, to everyone's surprise, she threw herself into Logan's arms and gave him a tight hug. "Thank you, Uncle Logan. I'll be ready."

He kissed the little girl on the forehead before he stood and looked at Teagan. "We'll talk later."

"Okay," she managed around a mouthful of chocolate deliciousness. Her mood was improving by leaps and bounds.

Fifteen minutes later, the perfect dress hanging on the closet doorknob, white patent leather shoes and frilly socks set out, Teagan was living vicariously through her goddaughter. This is what she had always imagined having a daddy would be like. There had never been a father figure in her life. It had only ever been her and her mother.

When she'd suggested to Logan that he spend more time with Anora, she had no idea that he would choose to take her out and treat her like a princess. She'd hoped for batting lessons, playing catch with her, or letting her beat him at one of her board games. His choice went far beyond her expectations.

"It's perfect," Teagan declared as they left Anora's pink bedroom with the pink flamingo decal on the wall, the pink flamingo pillow, and the pink flamingo bedspread that covered the pink polka-dotted sheets. Anora was definitely a girly girl, and that was just fine with Teagan. She could be anything she wanted to be.

Taking her dirty dish to the sink, she rinsed it, and placed it in the dishwasher before throwing a bag of popcorn in the microwave. Joining the others, she snuggled under the blankets next to Logan. They'd turned down the lights in the living room to better see the large television, so when Logan found her bare arm and started stroking it, the children couldn't see anything.

Teagan could certainly feel it though. His warm hand sent heat rushing through her body. As he caressed up her bicep, he ran his thumb over the top curve of her breast. Swollen and tender as they were every month during that time, sex was the last thing in the world that interested her.

She closed the few inches between their heads and whispered in his ear. "This isn't a good time."

"I know." He dropped his hand over her uterus and massaged. His fingers kneading the area felt like heaven.

"Kember used to have bad cramps." He answered her question before she was able to ask.

Teagan wasn't sure how she felt about him using techniques on her that he learned with his ex-wife, then she thought about things she'd learned from former lovers that she'd consider using on him…if and when they finally got naked. But they needed to talk first.

The movie was only half-over, but it was bedtime.

Brann protested a little as Logan carried a sleepy Anora up the stairs. They had the children into bed within fifteen minutes and reconvened on the couch.

"Are you okay with me taking Anora on a date?" Logan asked as he handed her a glass of wine, a beer in his other hand.

She couldn't hold back her smile. "I think it's a wonderful idea. And I love the fact that you allowed her to pick the restaurant."

His sideways glance was filled with guilt. "I only showed her certain restaurants. I'd already narrowed down her options." He pulled her in close. "Put your feet up on the couch and lay back on me."

She did as he instructed and his hand immediately fell on her lower abdomen. Applying the perfect amount of pressure, he rubbed back and forth. Teagan wondered if this was something all husbands did for achy wives. She had no clue. Growing up without a father meant she'd never seen the interaction between her mother and a man who stayed around long enough to create that closeness.

"While Anora and I are out on our date, that gives you the perfect opportunity to spend one-on-one time with Brann." Logan's heat emanated through her back where it touched his chest and from his hand. She could fall asleep surrounded by him.

"No problem, I'll just let him beat me at video games." She thought for about another minute. "He loves shrimp and fish. Maybe I'll take him to a seafood restaurant down at Surf City."

"This weekend, you and I are going out to dinner." Logan brushed a kiss across her temple. "I've wanted to take you out since we were in DC."

"We need to talk about this date." She rolled to face

him. She needed to make sure they were thinking the same thing. If not, the next fourteen years could be a living hell for her. "You said you weren't seeing anyone special, and neither am I. I don't think it's a good idea for either of us to bring another person into the situation. Not for a while, anyway." She stared into his eyes, hoping he agreed.

When he didn't say anything, she continued, "I don't want to put any more stress on the children by introducing more people into their lives just when they're getting used to you and me."

Damn. Still no indication as to whether he agreed or not. "I think the idea of us dating is a good one. And if it leads to...more...I'm okay with that too. I don't know how long it's going to take for the four of us to be comfortable enough with each other that you and I could resume dating others. Hell, it could be years. But I can tell you that I don't want to go that long without a man."

Logan's grin was not exactly an answer.

She waited. When he said nothing, she marched on. "I want to make it perfectly clear, though, that I'm not looking for commitment. I'm not interested in getting married, and I don't want to have kids...well, except for Brann and Anora." Oh, hell. She was fucking this up. Time to shut her mouth.

"You done?" He finally asked.

"Yes." At least until he answered her.

"Let me get this straight. Because of the children, you don't want either of us dating anyone else, but you and I dating would be fine." Logan's grin widened. "And *more* is okay too."

Damn. He summed up everything into sentences. "Yes," she confirmed.

"Unmarried parents, with benefits," he clarified.

Now he condensed it into four words. "Exactly." She didn't want to tie Logan down forever, so she added, "For now." She wanted to leave him an out. Once they had established a routine, and the child psychologist thought the children could handle another change, then they could start dating others again.

"Monogamous, of course," he defined.

"Definitely." She understood why he needed to add that clause into their verbal agreement. She had no plans of seeing anyone else while *dating* Logan and she didn't want him fucking anybody else but her.

"Agreed. Let's seal the deal with a kiss." He wrapped his hand around the back of her head and pulled her to him. The kiss started out gentle, soft, tender, but soon took on a life of its own, filled with need.

When his hand grasped her breast and began kneading, she had to put a stop to him.

She broke the kiss.

"Not tonight." At her words, understanding filled his eyes. "Soon, though, I promise." Teagan couldn't wait to follow through on that vow.

"I'm not sure I'm very good company tonight, anyway." Logan settled her back into his arms. "I'm sorry things have been so crazy the past two weeks. I know it hasn't been easy for you, handling everything here. I haven't been around to parent as much as I should."

She rolled her head to look up at him. "You know who you're talking to, right? I spent ten years in that world. I know what you're going through. It's not as though you can just leave because the clock strikes five." She'd been so consumed with her own situations, she hadn't considered him in weeks. "Do you want to talk about it?"

He was quiet for a long moment. Just as she was about to tell him he didn't have to, his hands stilled. "I had two teams in trouble. One in North Africa and the other in Honduras. Both were deep in bad guy country. It seemed like every time we tried to extract them, the situation just got worse. We lost two good men in Chad. If we'd been able to get them out as soon as they'd been shot, even within twenty-four hours, they'd be alive right now."

She rolled over to face him, crawling up into his lap. "This is not your fault."

He glanced away.

She cupped his face and forced his gaze to meet hers. "Did you do everything you could to rescue them?"

"Of course."

"Were they trained as well as they could be?" She pushed.

"Absolutely. Our men are some of the best trained in the world. I'd put them up against any SpecOps team from any service in any country." His voice was filled with conviction.

"You did your job, and then some, I'm sure." At the questioning look in his eyes she added, "because I know you. That's why you worked so late the other night that you ended up sleeping at your office. I'm proud of you. Two teams made it out."

"But I couldn't be here to help you and be with the kids." His eyes were filled with regret. "I couldn't do my half of the parenting. On top of everything, you weren't feeling well. I promised to help you, and I failed."

"You didn't fail me, the children, or those men." She had to make him understand. "I've got this." She waved her hand in the air meaning to include the children. "Sure, the kids missed you, but they understood. I personally believe that Gabriel was gone more often than he was home. By the way, thanks for calling me and letting me know you're going to be gone."

"It was the least I could do." He rubbed his hands up and down her bare arms.

She grinned at him. "The kids weren't the only ones who missed you."

He ran his long fingers over her scalp, through her hair. "You missed me?"

She decided to tease him. "Yeah, that meant I was stuck dealing with dinner. Three nights in a row."

"I'll try not to let that happen again." He pulled her head toward him, and she let him. "You missed me."

She laid her hands on his chest then leaned in and kissed him. It started as a light touching of lips. He was so gentle as he kissed his way down her jaw then took little nips from her neck. He worked his way back up to her lips while caressing her breasts in both hands.

She reached between them and stroked his hard cock through his jeans. He rocked his hips into her hand and thrust his tongue into her mouth. He ran his thumbs over her nipples and they hardened even more.

When she reached for his belt, he pulled back from the kiss and clasped his hands over hers.

"I don't like having sex during my period, but I can take care of you." She purposely licked her lips and tried to free her hands. "You had a rough week. It'll help you relax and sleep better tonight."

Keeping her hands held captive, he leaned in and gave her a gentle kiss. "I truly appreciate the offer, but not tonight." He shook his head. "Someday I would love to have that talented mouth of yours wrapped around my cock, but the first time I come inside of you, it won't be in your mouth. I'll be buried deep inside your hot wet channel, after I've already made you come at least twice."

Two orgasms? She wasn't sure she was capable of two orgasms the same night anymore. It had been a long, long time since any of her dates even tried for the second. Hell, most of her dates shot off within five strokes, leaving her hungry for her own release. More than once, she'd arrived home disappointed, yet needy enough to drop the batteries into one of her favorite vibrators and get off to her fantasy man.

He grinned. "You don't believe I can do it. Mission set." He carefully rose with her in his arms. "We're going out to dinner on Saturday night. I've already arranged for a babysitter. We'll see how you're feeling then, but I want you to make me one promise. Will you do that?"

"Depends on the promise," she countered.

"No self-pleasuring." He kissed her slow and gentle. "No fingers." Another kiss. "No vibrators." He kissed her deeply as he massaged her breasts. "No touching these either."

He took a step away from her. "Can you make that promise?"

"I promise." She ran her gaze over his entire body, staring for several seconds at his impressive erection, before returning her eyes to meet his. "Same goes for you."

"You're a cool one, aren't you? Chill, as Brann would say." Logan moved closer to the door.

"I earned my handle of Ice-T," she noted.

He closed the distance between them once again and kissed her until she was breathing hard. "I prefer my tea hot."

He quickly walked out the door, closing it quietly so as not to wake the children.

Letting out a long slow breath, she decided that Saturday couldn't come soon enough.

CHAPTER SEVENTEEN

For Logan, Saturday was no different than any other day for him. He was up at the crack of dawn running on the beach, then swimming back to the house. As usual, the children were waiting for him on his deck.

"Uncle Logan, can we have pancakes this morning, please?" Anora asked as soon as he was within hearing distance.

It took him a minute to mentally check the contents of his pantry, to be sure he had all the ingredients, before he said, "We can do that." He then remembered that Teagan had made chocolate chip cookies the other day. "Do you think Aunt Teagan has any of those chocolate chips left? They're really good in pancakes."

Anora's eyes grew huge. "You put chocolate chips inside the pancakes?"

"You've never had them that way before?" He said as he stepped onto his deck.

"Never." Both children said at the same time.

"Mom never let us have much stuff with sugar in it," Brann explained. "Especially for breakfast. That's why we love it here with you. You buy chocolate cocoa puffs and let me eat them for breakfast."

"I never ate a toaster tart until we moved to North Carolina." Anora gave him a big smile. "And we get to pick what we eat here."

Brann added to the diatribe, "Yeah, Mom used to make us eat green beans and broccoli—"

"And spinach," Anora cut in and made a gagging noise.

"We used to have to eat a lot of chicken and rice." Brann stuck out his tongue in disgust. "I like going out to dinner. I get to eat hamburgers or whatever I want."

That confirmed it. He and Teagan were going to have a discussion about healthy food choices for children. They were obviously doing it wrong. Logan suddenly wondered what else they were doing wrong.

Mentally shrugging, he'd committed to making pancakes with chocolate chips, if there were any left. "Who wants to go check the pantry at Aunt Teagan's and see if she has any more chocolate chips?"

"I will." Brann shot off toward the other half of the duplex. As he ran through the house, Logan looked up at his duplex and wondered for the first time if the inside could be reconfigured? Maybe they would start with just one door that went between the two sides. He added that subject to his agenda for dinner that night with Teagan.

When Brann returned empty-handed, and with an unhappy face, he wondered what was wrong. "No chocolate chips?"

Brann pouted. "Aunt Teagan is—"

The door opened.

"Aunt Teagan is what?" She asked. "Awake?" She suggested. "Up and moving?" She bent slightly to look into his eyes. "Feeling better?"

"You said I couldn't have the chocolate chips." Brann crossed his arms over his chest and pouted.

She pulled the bag from behind her back. "You didn't tell me why you wanted them. Nor did you ask if you could take them. I might've had plans to use them in a desert this weekend."

Without moving his head, the boy's eyes met hers. "I'm sorry, Aunt Teagan, I didn't know."

"You didn't ask, either." She pulled up the stool next to him at the breakfast counter. "I didn't know if you were just going to take them and sit out on the deck and eat them all by yourself, or if you were going to feed the seagulls—please never do that. Human food isn't good for them. And chocolate chips aren't good for growing boys to eat for breakfast."

Anora, who had been standing by quietly watching the entire scene, jumped in to explain, "Uncle Logan sent him over there to get the bag if there were any left. We're going to put them in the pancakes this morning."

Teagan looked up at Logan as he prepared the dry ingredients. "Is this true?"

"Yep. I think Anora covered all the high points." He dropped the eggs into the bowl and started whipping. "Would you like to stay for breakfast? That is, if you like chocolate chip pancakes."

Teagan threw her arms around both children and pulled them in for a hug. "I do like chocolate chip pancakes." She looked from one child to the other. "Maybe he'll let us make happy faces with the chips."

Emojis? She wanted to use his pancakes to make emojis? What the hell. If it made the kids smile, he didn't care if they used them to spell out words.

Whenever Logan was off, whether it was Tuesday or

Sunday, they tried to do family-type activities, at least until Teagan had to return to work. Their current plan was for the children to complete one entire week of school before she started to work full time at the New River Naval Air Station.

Then life would grow exponentially more difficult.

Thankfully, that day, they were together and the sun was shining.

They built a castle out of the wet sand close to the water line. He and Teagan had been teaching the children about the tides. Since they'd never lived near or on a beach before, they had to learn about how the water covered most of the beach at high tide and how dangerous it could be for them if they didn't move closer to the house. Brann was getting the concept, but it just wasn't registering with Anora. Fortunately for them, it was low tide most of the afternoon those days. High tide happened around nine o'clock in the morning and after the children were in bed.

They played in the water for hours. Logan had been working with Brann on his strokes, trying to make him a stronger and faster swimmer. Anora was still a little young, or so Logan thought, to be swimming out in the ocean over her head.

He had arranged with Erin, the babysitter, to come by and spend some time casually with the children before she was thrown into the situation of caring for them alone for several hours. He had shared with her that he and Teagan were their godparents and had taken custody and guardianship of the children after their parents had been killed. He wanted her to be sensitive to the unusual situation.

A small group of teens, both boys and girls, approached from down the beach. They were laughing and tossing a football around, even among the girls who seemed as athletic as the boys. Their deep tans and surefootedness indicated they were locals or spent a lot of time on the beach. A tall brunette in a ponytail peeled off as they approached Logan, Teagan, and the kids.

"Hi, I'm Erin Hendrix." She had on tan shorts and a white tank top, but he could see a dark bathing suit underneath. "I'm hoping I have the right house. Teagan?" She held her hand out to shake.

"You're in the right place," Teagan said with a smile as they shook hands.

Erin turned her attention to him. "And you must be Lieutenant Colonel Jackson."

"Thanks for stopping by. I thought it might be easier for the kids to meet you first when we're here." He pointed to each child as he introduced them. "This is Brann and Anora."

Erin instantly dropped to the sand and engaged both children in a giant game of tic tac toe. Both he and Teagan sat back and watched their interaction.

"She's really good with them," Teagan whispered.

"She came highly recommended by one of my captains who lives a mile down the beach," Logan explained. "He used her to babysit his nieces and nephews when his family came to visit for a week. Luckily for us, Erin only lives five doors down. She just turned sixteen and is headed into her junior year at the local high school, so she'll be around for the next two years."

Two years. That suddenly seemed like a long time. Yet not long at all. They'd need to find another babysitter in two years. Anora would only be six so that meant they'd need to find babysitters for...how old were kids when they didn't need babysitters anymore?

Fuck.

There was so much he didn't know about raising children. Why the fuck had Gabe chosen him as godfather? Maybe he needed to start seeing the counselor Teagan took the kids to. Maybe he and Teagan needed to see her together, like couples' counseling. Another item for tonight's agenda.

"Colonel Jackson, Miss Williams." The mention of his name brought him out of his thoughts.

Teagan smiled up from her lounge chair at Erin. "Is everything okay?" He heard the slight tension in her voice, but Logan was sure no one else would have caught it. He'd come to know her slightest inflections.

"Yes, ma'am." Erin pointed down the beach where her friends had headed. "But Brann and Anora seem to be getting a little tired. They're acting a little hungry, too. Do you want me to make them some lunch?"

"No." Teagan slid from her chair. "I think they've had enough fun in the sun for now. Thank you so much for coming. We'll see you tonight."

Erin gave them a big smile and a wave. She hugged both children and promised to see them in a few hours before she jogged down the beach.

"Anora, Brann, let's go in and make lunch," Teagan called from the deck where they'd both gone when Erin took over kid-watch.

After lunch they all collapsed on the couch to enjoy the air conditioning and watch a Disney movie. Halfway through, Anora fell asleep, snuggled under blankets.

"This is a baby movie. Is it okay if I go play on my computer?" Brann asked.

"Do you want me to download more games?" Logan suggested.

"I need to learn to play the ones I have and get better." Brann looked tired as he dragged his way up the stairs.

"I think I'll go shower and start getting ready for tonight." Teagan stood and stretched, once again giving him a glimpse of that colorful belly button piercing. She glanced at Anora sound asleep on the couch. "She'll be fine. I'll let the video keep running in case she awakes."

"You kicking me out?" Logan stood.

She cocked her head to the side. "Yes."

Running her fingertips over his whiskers, she added, "I don't like whisker burn. It takes too long to heal, especially on skin in sensitive places."

"Are you telling me I'll get lucky tonight?" Oh, Christ, please say yes.

Her smile was salacious. "No. I'm telling you *I* might get lucky tonight." She stretched up and kissed him. Barely a touching of lips but he felt it throughout his entire body.

After she sauntered up the stairs—his gaze pinned to her perfect backside, sure she added more sway than usual—he let himself out quietly and all but ran to his side of the duplex.

Even though he and Teagan had been out to supper dozens of times together, Logan was nervous as he shaved for the second time that day. She was beyond special. He couldn't imagine his life with any other woman. He also couldn't imagine his life without her.

She was already in his life every day.

In every way...almost.

Like a wife...almost.

As a man, he wanted her in every way. As a highly sexual man, he could think of many ways he wanted her... Staring up at him with half-closed eyes as he drove into her, seconds before she came and screamed his name. On her hands and knees, looking back over her shoulder as he took her from behind. On her knees, his cock in her mouth, glancing up at him with those beautiful blue eyes.

She was his…almost.

He had never claimed a woman before through sex, but it seemed the only thing that was left for them to officially become a couple. He wanted them to be together, forever.

Logan loved the life he'd found with Teagan, Brann, and Anora. He wanted this to last forever. He loved all three of them.

In that moment, he'd just discovered the fact for himself. Sometime over the past two months, while they were playing house with the children, dealing with Marsha's murder, her real estate, moving everyone to his house, he'd fallen in love with the tenacious blonde with a heart so big she'd taken on two children…and him.

He had no doubt there'd be rough sailing, but they'd tackled everything thrown at them so far and come out on top. They could do this together, forever.

That night was the start of everything new. Or maybe it was just the next logical step. At least it was for him. He couldn't imagine a life without Teagan in it, even after the children were grown and gone.

That meant he wanted her in his bed. Tonight. Always.

Living at the beach meant dress was beyond casual for any restaurant. Shirts and shoes were required, but even those definitions were lax. As he slid into clean jeans that had faded with years of washings, he decided to go a hair above his usual polo shirt and grabbed a Colombia cool-tech shirt. It was a lightweight button-up that felt like silk on his body.

With one last glance in the mirror, Logan turned to head over on the well-worn path to Teagan's front door.

He glanced at the adjoining wall, trying to figure out where to put a connecting door. He'd call Tad, the contractor who had worked on the house before. Maybe he'd have an idea.

"Beautiful." It was all he could manage to say. Teagan was gorgeous in a light blue sundress that showed off her deepening tan and the tops of her perfect breasts. He hoped to be able to taste them and more in just a few hours. A white belt cinched around her waist that tucked in enough to highlight her curvy hips. The skirt dropped halfway down well-developed thighs.

Naked thighs.

Naked legs.

Bare feet inside strappy sandals. And her toenails were painted a light blue to match the dress.

As his gaze slowly came back up her outstanding body, he wondered what kind of panties she wore. Thong? Lacy? He didn't care if they were one hundred percent cotton and covered her from the bottom of her butt cheeks to her bellybutton. If he had his way, they wouldn't be on long enough for a second thought.

Her hair was down, his favorite way, although he'd never told her that. She'd dressed up, for him.

"You are absolutely the most beautiful woman I've seen in years." It sounded cheesy, even to his ears, but it was the truth.

"You clean up pretty good yourself, Marine." Her smile dazzled him all the way to his soul.

"I'm just a banged-up old jarhead, so fucking proud to be seen with you as my date tonight." Another truth that he doubted she'd believe. "Let me just go in and say goodnight to the kids, then we'll leave."

What should have taken two minutes became ten, but

they finally closed the door to two happy children and a competent babysitter.

Logan took her hand as they walked to his SUV. As soon as he'd started the car, the phone rang.

"It's Tony Alvarez. Is it okay if I take it?" This was her night and he wanted her to understand that short of a national disaster, she was his focus.

Ring.

"Answer the damn phone. He might have news." She sounded as excited about that possibility as he was.

After clicking the button on his steering wheel, he announced, "Hey, Tony. I have you on speaker with Teagan in the car."

"Wonderful." He hesitated. "Are the kids with you?"

"No. For once, it's an adults-only supper." Logan reached over and took Teagan's hand.

"I have a few updates I knew you'd be interested in. First, I wanted to let you know that Ashley Helms, Marsha's sister, was supposedly with friends at a private yoga retreat the whole weekend, including the day of the murder when she showed up at her sister's house. She held to that bullshit story even after we showed her the video. She claims that isn't her. *It must be someone else.*"

Tony released a long sigh. "The woman in the video looked strung out and haggard. The Ashley Helms we met with looked healthy, well-dressed, and surprisingly clean. She claims she's serious about changing her life and that rehab is working this time. Her counselor said the same thing."

"So, if that woman in the video isn't Ashley, then who is it?" Logan asked.

"I don't believe her for one minute," Teagan asserted. "She lied to Marsha over and over again. She'd get clean for a week, a month, and Marsha would get all excited that it worked, then in no time Ashley was hanging out with her dealer and getting high and begging Marsha for money."

"Well, that may be, but she was at the top of her game when we were there, which brings me to the bad news." Tony hesitated as though trying to pick his words carefully. "As soon as she's released from rehab, she and her new attorney are filing for custody of the kids."

"There's no way in hell she's going to get them." Teagan squeezed Logan's hand. Hard.

"She can try," Logan warned. "But we've had these wonderful children since the day their mother was murdered. Marsha wanted us to raise them and that's what we're going to do."

"Hey, ease off. I'm just the messenger." Tony claimed. "I'm on your side, remember?"

"I'm sorry, Tony." Teagan apologized. "I love these kids and won't let them go, especially not to her."

"I have a child," Tony said in a conciliatory tone. "I'd kill anyone who tried to take him away from me."

"Tony, you said you have other things to tell us as well." Logan stopped at a traffic light.

"Yeah, since the house is going up for sale, my men ripped out all the overrides on the security system. We don't want anyone else having access with its new owners."

"Thank you for doing that, Tony." Teagan said. "We've had a few lookers already but no offers yet."

"Lookers are good," Tony commented. "Hopefully you'll get an offer soon."

"Thanks," Logan offered. "Anything else for us?"

"You might want to give Matthew a call. He indicated that his computer specialist found something and was tracking its source but wanted to wait on the information." Tony sounded a little aggravated that Matt hadn't been more forthcoming. "That's all I have for you right now."

"Thanks so much for calling." Logan turned into the parking lot of one of the best restaurants on the island. "Please, keep us posted especially about Ashley."

"Will do. Enjoy your evening." Tony disconnected.

Logan pulled into a parking space and looked at Teagan. Something inside him screamed that he should call Matt.

"Can we call Matthew before we go in?" Teagan squeezed his hand once again. "I'd really like to know if he's found out anything."

Damn. The woman could read his mind. It was just another sign that they were connected, like an old married couple.

"Absolutely," he agreed as he hit their friend's number.

"Logan, glad you called." Matt's voice sounded serious.

"Teagan and I are sitting here in the car. You're on speaker. What have you learned?" Logan wanted him to be aware of the situation.

"Clarence, my computer geek, has found some buried files in the storage drives that Teagan sent to me." Logan slid a glance toward her. "If you didn't download the entire hard drive, there may be even more."

"I take it there's something important in those hidden files?" Teagan asked, a tinge of nerves sneaking into her question.

"Yeah. Like the entire transcript of our Syrian mission, with more words than Lizzie remembered."

Logan and Teagan exchanged a serious gaze.

"Pictures of the ammo dump, before, during, and after it was blown up. It looks as though there was a dedicated camera from one of the overhead satellites," Matthew continued.

Logan was starting to worry. "Brann now has that computer. We didn't wipe the drive, just downloaded his games. Is there any way he can get into those files?"

"He's seven, right?" Matt asked.

"Yes, and not a computer savant." She giggled. "He knows how to open and play games, that's it."

"Let's do this, Lizzie and I will be down there in two weeks. How about I bring a new hard drive loaded with games. We'll swap out drives and Brann will have lots more to play with," Matt suggested.

"Sounds like a plan." Logan liked the idea and had already been looking forward to spending time with Matt and Elizabeth again.

"We can't wait to see you guys," Teagan enthused. "The kids are really excited to show you around, which really means, show you how well they can swim."

"We can't wait to hang out on the beach all day and do nothing for an entire week. This'll be our first family vacation since our family-moon. Please tell me Lizzie and I have our own bedroom…without children."

Logan and Teagan laughed. They'd already agreed that all the kids would sleep over on Teagan's side and Matt and Elizabeth would take Logan's spare bedroom because it had a king-sized bed in it and a private bathroom that was shared by the other empty bedroom.

"Yes. We have everyone handled," Teagan announced. "See you very soon."

After they'd said goodbye to their friend, Logan held Teagan's hand until they sat down in the restaurant.

CHAPTER EIGHTEEN

Since the restaurant didn't take reservations, Teagan hoped it was their above average clothing that convinced the thirtysomething hostess to give them a table at the large windows overlooking the ocean. It might have been Logan's panty-melting smile and his deep sexy voice, though. Teagan hadn't missed the way the woman in the tight-fitting dress that hugged her every perfect curve and perky boobs had glanced at his left hand and smiled. She'd also caught the broadened smile after the young brunette had checked out Teagan's left hand.

No, bitch, we aren't married. Nor are we engaged. We're simply having an adult dinner alone while someone else watches our children.

Our children. Damn. That sounded like an old married couple. Or like two people amicably divorced. Their situation certainly wasn't the usual.

Logan pulled out the chair for her then glided it in once she was seated. He was such a gentleman. Teagan had thought that kind of manners had disappeared with the twentieth century. It was wonderful to be treated like a lady now and again.

"We have delicious fresh oysters on the half shell available tonight," the hostess handed Logan the leather-bound menu with a sultry smile. "Let me know if there's anything I can do for you." Without looking at Teagan, she laid the menu on the linen tablecloth next to her place setting.

"Do you like raw oysters?" Logan's gaze was heated and focused entirely on Teagan.

She matched his grin and shook her head. "No. I don't like them. I *love* them." She laid her hand on the table and he instantly reached out and took it in his. "What I really like about oysters is the dopamine boost I get about two hours after eating them."

He obviously understood that dopamine was one of the hormones that increased libido. "Then I'll be sure dinner doesn't run longer than an hour and a half." His eyes locked with hers. "We'll take a dozen as appetizers, please."

"I'll be sure to tell your waiter." The hostess disappeared from Teagan's peripheral vision.

"I'm glad you like raw oysters. A lot of women don't," Logan noted.

She couldn't withhold her giggle. "I'd think you would have learned by now that I'm not like most females. How many women do you know that have a master's in engineering and work on helicopter engines for a living?"

"Only you." He ran the rough pad of his thumb over the palm of her hand, sending tingles straight to her core. "You are unique in so many ways. I don't know anyone who would so readily agree to raise two children they weren't related to."

"I love Anora and Brann. I always have. From the day they were born." She wasn't ready to explain why it was so easy for her to step into a motherhood role. But she could tell him a few things. "I have plenty of room in my heart for children, especially those two."

A large platter of oysters was set in the middle of the table by a man dressed head to toe in black. After introducing himself, he took their orders with a practiced smile and cordially faded away.

Teagan's phone buzzed in her pocket. "This may be Erin," she explained as she pulled it out. Glancing at the screen, it showed nothing. "Damn. The call disappeared." Her phone was useless there in North Carolina. The company she had used in the DC area didn't have any local towers. "I don't even have a single signal bar."

"You want me to call her and make sure everything's okay?" Logan's voice was concerned.

"No. She has your phone number. I told her to call you if she couldn't get ahold of me." Teagan hated not being directly connected with the children.

Logan set his phone on the table. "Now, we can both set our minds at ease. Sure you don't want me to call her?"

"I'm sure." She tried to make her voice as convincing as possible. "I don't want to be *those* parents who have to phone home every ten minutes to check on the children."

"Tomorrow, let's go to the phone store and I'll get you added to my service plan." Logan picked up her cell phone and examined it. "How old is this thing?"

"I've had it a few years." Teagan had to think how long. Embarrassed, she had to admit, "Okay, it's at least five years old, maybe six."

Logan grinned. "I'd be surprised if they made this

model within the past ten years. I think it's time for an upgrade."

The condition of her bank account ran through her mind. Now that she was no longer using her personal money to purchase groceries for all four of them, and her mother's new memory care facility was considerably less than what she'd been paying in DC, she was in a better financial condition. "You're right. I need a new phone."

"What do you think about getting Brann one of those kid's watch phones?" Logan asked.

"He's only seven. Do you think he's responsible enough for a phone?" She loved her godson but sometimes he could be so immature, acting as babyish as Anora.

"I'm not talking about a regular cell phone, just one that he would wear like a watch." He went on to explain, "One of my captains just bought them for his seven-year-old twins. They live in base housing where the kids run from house to house on a regular basis. His wife got tired of calling all over the neighborhood to notify the boys that it was time to come home. From what Captain Donaldson said, they are God's gift to parents. The ones he purchased only have four phone numbers programmed in plus nine-one-one. They are waterproof and have GPS trackers."

The more Logan talked about them, the more excited Teagan became. "I agree. I'd love to be able to give Brann a little more freedom. When I can't find him in the house, most of the time he's at your place. But he has met a few of the children in the area. I've been hesitant to allow him to play at anyone else's house, so the boys usually hang out in Brann's bedroom or they play on one of the decks."

"So, you're okay with getting him a watch phone?" Logan confirmed.

"Yes. Definitely." Being able to track the children on her cell phone would be heavenly. "I think we should use the household account for that purchase since it's for the direct benefit of Brann."

"If we buy something for him, we need to get Anora something as well." Logan was right. They had made a point of trying to be equally fair with both children even though their age differences called for differing spending amounts.

"I think some inexpensive colorful bracelets will do the trick," Teagan suggested. "We'll just let her know that when she turns seven, she can have a watch phone then."

"Works for me. We'll give them to the children at the same time." Logan's gaze swept the now-empty platter. "You weren't kidding when you said you liked raw oysters."

Sometime during their conversation, they had demolished the appetizer. That's the way it was with Logan. Their discussions seemed to flow so easily.

Teagan had been holding back for days and couldn't wait any longer. "So, how was your date with Anora?"

His eyes shot to hers. "She didn't tell you?"

"I asked her about the food, and she said it was good. Nothing more than the one-word answer. I asked her about the waitress, and she said she was good. I asked her if she got any kind of special drink and she said yes, then promptly told me that her dates with Uncle Logan were special, just for the two of you."

Logan burst out laughing. "I guess you got schooled."

"Logan, don't be that way. I was worried. I was the one who convinced you to take her out on a date. How was it? How did she do? Did she mind her manners?" Teagan had lots more questions but hoped he'd answer at least one or two.

He wiped the corners of his mouth with the linen napkin and took a sip of his drink. "Everything Anora told you was correct. The food was good, but it always is at the Shrimp Shack and you know how much that little girl loves shrimp. Our waitress was excellent." The corners of his mouth kicked up. "Anora had to tell everyone that we were out on a date, starting with all the people in line around us."

Teagan's heart melted. He had given that little girl a memory that would last a lifetime, whether she consciously remembered it or not. That night, he had set her expectations for every man to follow.

"By the time we reached the hostess, everyone was in love with her." He shook his head. "I can't tell you how many women told her that her dress was pretty, she looked lovely that night, how much they liked her little shoes and frilly socks. By the time we were seated, she was acting like a princess."

Teagan's hand covered her mouth. She wasn't sure if she was going to laugh or cry.

"Teagan, are you all right?" Logan reached across the table and pulled her hand from her mouth and held it. "Tell me what's wrong."

"Absolutely nothing is wrong. Everything is completely right." How could she tell him? She had to, though. The heat transferring from his hand to hers and through her body gave her strength. "You know that I grew up without a father. When I was a little girl, I used to pretend that I had a daddy. In my fantasy world, I would get dressed up like a princess, and he'd take me out to lunch, or brunch, and if I was especially good, he'd take me out to supper somewhere fancy." She looked away to reign in her emotions. Pasting on a smile, she returned her gaze to Logan. Squeezing his hand, she confessed, "I'm vicariously living my childhood through Anora. You are the greatest daddy a little girl could ever have."

He cocked an eyebrow. "You haven't heard about the rest of our night. Anora is quite the little wing man."

"What?" Teagan's jaw dropped a fraction of an inch. "What the hell did she do?"

Logan grinned as though knowing the secret. "So, you know our little Anora. What happens every time within five minutes after ordering?"

"Oh, no." Teagan suddenly felt sorry for the handsome man across the table. Cringing, she asked, "She had to go potty?"

"Oh, yeah." He shook his head. "I wasn't about to let her go by herself, nor was I going to let her go into the men's room. That place has a rowdy pickup bar, but I was hoping we were there early enough so she wouldn't be exposed to that type of people."

Teagan gave his hand a little squeeze. She could only imagine how embarrassing the situation had been for him. "I'm so sorry. I never meant for you to be put into that position. You don't ever have to take her out by yourself again."

"No. I'll take her out again. I'll just have to be a little more conscientious of the establishment."

"So, what did you do?" Teagan asked, holding back a laugh.

"I took her by the hand and walked her to the ladies' room door and waited for her in the hall." He grinned, or maybe it was a grimace. "The door hadn't finished closing when *one of those* women walked by and asked me if I wanted her to help the little princess. I didn't want that bar babe anywhere near Anora so I told her that I was sure she could handle herself. Through the door, I heard her quizzing Anora, asking if I were her father. Our little girl told her no, I was her Uncle. The bitch pressed her harder and asked if I was married." Logan's grin showed two rows of bright white teeth. "Anora proceeded to tell her that no, I wasn't married, but she and her brother Bran and Aunt Teagan all lived together in my house. We were a family."

Teagan wanted to rush home and hug Anora. She also wanted to hug the man across the table. She knew the child's words had affected him as much as they had just touched her heart. They were all beginning to realize that yes, they were family, although uniquely unconventional.

Time slipped away as they chatted and devoured the perfectly pan-seared fish, tangy coleslaw and hush puppies. When the waiter returned, she was too stuffed to even think about dessert.

After paying the bill, Logan stood and made a show of looking at his watch. "One hour and thirty-eight minutes. Can I convince you to join me for a nightcap and maybe a movie for grown-ups back at my place?" He took her hand and started toward the door.

As soon as they were outside, and out of earshot of anyone else, he added, "I want you alone and in my arms when the dopamine kicks in."

"There you go again, reading my mind." No sooner had the words left her lips and Logan stopped in the shadow of his SUV.

"I don't want to rush you into anything." His fingertips touched her temples then slid into her hair, stopping when his palms cupped her cheeks. Logan's intense brown eyes stared down at her. "We can go home and watch a movie that doesn't involve cartoon characters or overly dramatic teenage actors."

"I don't want to watch any fucking movie." She leaned her whole body into his, rocking her hips against his impressive erection. "And considering we have been together every day for nearly three months, I don't think we're rushing anything. I'm a long way from a horny virgin. I know what I want and tonight, I want you. Inside me." Just to make sure he got the message, she pulled his head down until their lips met. She took control of the kiss but soon surrendered to him, opening her mouth and allowing him to run his tongue over hers.

"Hey, baby, if you're giving blowjobs here in the parking lot, can I be next?" Several loud male voices burst into laughter following the crude slurred question.

Teagan felt Logan's body tense. She glanced over, quickly assessing the four young men staggering through the parking lot. "A bunch of drunk frat boys. Let's get out of here."

Logan opened her door and she quickly stepped in. She watched to be sure Logan didn't do anything stupid, like take on four drunken idiots. She had no doubt he would win, but she wanted his ass in a bed, not in jail on assault charges.

"I'm sorry those boys insulted you." Logan said as he slid behind the wheel. "Any other time I would've taken pleasure in teaching them a little respect." He reached across the console and gently turned her face toward his. "But tonight is for us. I'm not going to let those inebriated assholes ruin it for us." He leaned over and gently kissed her lips.

It wasn't enough. She wanted more.

He must've seen the need in her eyes.

"If I kissed you again, we'd be arrested for indecent exposure because I wouldn't be able to stop until we were both boneless and sated." He started to lean in as though to kiss her again but then sat up straight and turned the key in the ignition. "I promise I'll give you everything you need as soon as we're back home."

On the short drive home, Teagan decided to warn the babysitter, fearing the children would see the headlights pull into the driveway and expect her home.

Teagan texted – Heading home now but going to hang out next door at Logan's.

Erin responded – No prob. Kids fell asleep right after bath bed and stories. Thanks for letting me use your Hulu!!!! Take your time.

– Thanks. I will.

Like a man on a mission, as soon as he turned off the engine, Logan was out of the SUV and opening the door on her side. He didn't wait for her to step down but grabbed her by the hips and slowly lowered her down his body.

There was no way she could miss his prominent erection.

"I can't hide how much I want you," he said before he pulled her against him and crashed his lips on hers.

It had been so long since a man had handled her so forcefully out of his own need. She didn't care. She wanted Logan more than she ever wanted a man in her whole life.

Regretfully, she backed off the kiss. It was so good, but she didn't want to give Erin a live sex lesson, in case the babysitter happened to look out a window. "Your bed. Now."

Without a word, Logan grabbed her hand and practically ran up the steps to his side of the duplex. He had his keys out before he reached the top and the door opened and closed behind them within seconds. He spun her around and shoved her against the wall, capturing her with his hands braced on either side of her shoulders.

Breathing heavily, he asked, "Are you sure?"

She let her actions be his answer. With one hand she pulled his head down to hers and bit his lower lip while she ran her fingers up his cock and gave it a slight squeeze.

"I'll bet I can be naked in the bed before you are." She ducked under his arm and dashed off toward the bedroom. Within three steps she had lifted the sundress over her head and let it fly to the floor uncaringly. Her bra was gone by the time she reached the steps.

She'd worn the blue lacy thong hoping he'd appreciate it, but when he grabbed the back string and ripped it off her, moisture pooled between her legs. This was the most erotic, and fun, foreplay she'd ever had.

When Teagan reached the second-floor landing, she didn't hear his footsteps behind her. She stopped and glanced back. Halfway down the stairs he stood shirtless, his jeans unbuttoned and unzipped, halfway down his narrow hips, displaying that distinct V in the dark line of hair that led from his bellybutton to under his boxer briefs. She could see the huge bulge fighting to get loose.

Logan stood perfectly still, his eyes closed, a scrap of blue lace against his nose.

She clicked a mental picture. She wanted to remember this, and everything else, about their first time together.

When he opened his eyes, they were filled with so much heat, longing, and desire. He moved faster than anyone she'd ever seen before, taking the steps two at a time.

She let out a high-pitched squeal and dashed toward

his bedroom. Just as she stepped through the door, he grabbed her behind her knees and across her back, picking her up and tossing her onto his bed. He followed her down, caging her between his hands and knees. Somewhere along the line, he'd lost the rest of his clothes.

She let out a giggle, feeling young and beautiful once again.

They were both breathing hard, not from the sprint but from anticipation.

"I'm sorry." Regret flashed in Logan's eyes. "I'm not going to last very long this first time." He dropped his head down to brush a kiss across her lips. "I promise I'll take more time next round."

She lifted her hands to his shoulders and rocked her hips so she could free her legs pinned between his calves. She worked her legs around his waist. "I'm not fragile. I need you hard and fast. It's been a long time for me."

"Fuck." He dropped his forehead to hers. "I knew it was going to be like that with us." He reached over and opened the drawer in the nightstand and pulled out a roll of condoms.

Teagan giggled. "I don't think we're going to be able to use all those tonight, but I like the way you think." She grabbed the roll from him and ripped off a packet, opening it with her teeth. She shoved him and he went willingly to his back. "Allow me."

The pearl on the tip of his cock indicating his readiness was more than she could resist. She leaned down and licked it up.

Logan bolted upright and grabbed her shoulders. "No. Not this time." He snatched the condom away from her and expertly rolled it down his length before he rolled her to her back. With the palms of his hands he gently spread her thighs.

He didn't move. Only stared.

With one finger he traced her wet folds, gently separating them, exposing her completely to him. He ran his finger the length between her channel and her clit then licked his wet finger clean. He closed his eyes as though savoring every drop. "I'm going to taste you, make you come with nothing but my mouth and fingers."

"You can do that next time, but right now I want you inside me." Because if he touched her one more time she was going to explode right then. "Please tell me you haven't forgotten what I asked for…hard and fast, remember?"

"Oh, I remember. I just want to make sure you're ready." He rubbed her juices over the tip before he positioned his cock at her entrance.

Teagan loved that feeling when a man first slid into her, filling her for the first time. Most men liked it, too, and Logan was no exception. A tense-filled bliss covered his face. It was agony and ecstasy all in one stroke.

When he didn't move for one breath, then two, she knew what he was doing. He was big and was letting her grow accustomed to his length and girth. After a second, she understood that he had more to give. She rocked up, taking him home.

Logan's body went completely stiff as he sucked in a ragged breath.

Good. She'd surprised him.

"Christ, Teagan," he said on a long exhale. "You're perfect."

"Not hardly." She smacked his bare ass. "This looks much better if you move."

As ordered, Logan withdrew almost completely before slamming back into her.

"Yes," she huffed out. "Again."

"Fucking perfect." He repeated his act, pulling out almost completely before shoving back in.

She met him stroke for stroke by lifting her hips. Within minutes she was close, and by the strain on his face, she could tell he was too.

"Come for me, T. Take us both," he ordered through clenched teeth.

"Almost there," she panted out.

Logan bent and took one of her nipples into his mouth, sucking hard.

Holy fuck. Teagan had never felt the connection between her breasts and her clit before. His teeth scraped across her nipple and she exploded. Her whole body shook with its release. Just as dark bliss closed in around her, Logan's body arched and he drove deeply into her, holding the position as his arms and shoulders quivered.

Teagan rose from the depths of ecstasy as a butterfly flitted over her face. Opening her eyes, Logan completely filled her vision.

"Next time will be better," he promised and lightly touched his lips to her chin.

"I don't see how it could be." Teagan was no virgin, but she had never had sex that intense before in her life. "You wore me out."

Logan brushed a few strands of hair back from her face and curled them around her ear. "Take a power nap." He kissed her softly and pulled the covers over her shoulders. "We'll try this again when you're rejuvenated."

She awoke with an aching clit, arching her back as

Logan sucked on her breast and kneaded the other one with his hand.

"Your breasts are perfect," he claimed when she opened her eyes.

He needed to know the truth, and now. "No, actually they aren't."

CHAPTER NINETEEN

Logan had never met a woman who thought her breasts were perfect. He'd had surgically enhanced ones in his hands, and his mouth. He'd once dated a woman who'd had breast reduction surgery. Personally, he considered that a shame. He was undeniably a breast man. Sure, he could admire a woman's perfect ass. Long shapely legs were always nice. But show him a pair of rounded breasts and he was instantly hard. Let him caress the soft skin and weigh their fullness, and he'd drip in anticipation.

Breasts did it for him every fucking time.

He loved their different shapes. Large, small, round, long, it didn't matter to him. He enjoyed them all. He was also fascinated with nipples. Some women had large dark areolas and nipples smaller than a pea. Other women had small circles barely darker than their own skin. He'd once slept with a frog hog who had extremely long nipples.

Teagan's breasts were perfect. There was no other word for them. They filled his large hands but didn't look huge on her petite frame. Her aerola was a peachy-pink color, several shades darker than her naturally ivory skin. He loved the way they wrinkled, and her nipple hardened instantly when he touched them. She was so responsive.

"In my unquestionably male opinion, which from now on is the only one that counts, these are perfect." He cupped them in both hands then kissed each nipple. To his delight, they pebbled immediately.

Teagan rolled away and sat up, her back against his headboard, and wouldn't look at him. "Don't get used to them. I might not have them for long." She swallowed hard. "I...I...I'm thinking about having them removed."

He couldn't control the way his body jerked back. "Why the fuck would you do that?" He glared at her. Was she fucking crazy?

Her eyes glistened in the subdued bedroom light.

Fuck. Now he'd gone and done it. He'd upset her. He hated when women cried. Especially when he didn't understand why.

She inhaled a deep breath, visibly gathering her resolve. "I carry the breast cancer gene."

He didn't know anything about breast cancer, but he knew that any kind of cancer was terrible. "Does that mean that you're going to get breast cancer?"

She shrugged. "Most women in the United States have about a twelve percent risk of developing breast cancer. Recent studies show that because I have mutations in both breast cancer genes, I'm at about a seventy-two percent risk."

Fuck. That was nearly a seventy-five percent chance that she would get breast cancer. "Are you sure?"

Her eyebrows pinched together. "About the exact numbers? I try to stay current—"

"No." He closed the distance between them. "Are you

sure that you carry that gene? If it's DNA, then it's hereditary. Does your mother have it?"

"Yes, it's hereditary but I don't know if my mother carries the gene or not." She glanced away, then back at him. "Mom was always closed-mouthed about anything family health related. She's never told me who my father was. Given her current state of mind, I don't think I'll ever find out. She doesn't even recognize me when I walk in the room to visit her. Sometimes she'll talk to me as though I'm a child. Her body is healthy, at least for now, but her mind..."

At the moment, Logan didn't give a shit about her mother. He was much more concerned with Teagan and her cancer revelation. "I'm sorry about your mother." He put his arm around her and pulled her tight against his body. "She's in a safe place, now, where they seem to be taking good care of her."

Teagan nodded. "I like this new place so much better than where she was back in DC. They really treat her with respect, even though she tells them the same story over and over again."

"T, I don't want to talk about your mom right now, I want to talk about you." Logan turned his head and kissed her temple. "You said you were sure you have this cancer gene."

She nodded but said nothing.

"How long have you known?" He pressed.

When she didn't answer right away, he knew she needed more time. They needed more time. He hoped that one day she would trust him enough to tell him all her secrets.

She let out a long breath, then finally spoke. "When I got promoted to Lieutenant, they discovered a lump during my annual exam. They biopsied it and thankfully it was benign. They were able to give me the DNA test which confirmed that I carried the gene. Actually, both my BRCA one and two are mutated. That puts me at an even higher risk."

Okay. This he could deal with. Assure that there is a problem. Next step, possible resolutions. "What can be done to increase your chances?"

"I go for a screening twice a year. One time I'll get a digital mammogram and the next an MRI." She forced a grin that didn't reach her eyes, then she cupped her bare breasts. "These babies get groped a lot. I also do my monthly self-exam."

"I can help with that," Logan tried to tease.

"No, you can't." She stared at him with heat in her eyes. "When you touch me, you're so gentle. It ignites every nerve in my body which screams it wants sex, immediately." Teagan blinked and her blue eyes were cold. "When the doctors and technicians touch me, there is nothing sensual about it. They're looking for lumps that don't belong there. They're repositioning my breast for the best possible picture to catch even the smallest clump of cells mutating. When you touch me, you bring me pleasure. When they touch me, it's a necessary ordeal."

Logan ran the tips of his fingers from her forehead to her chin. "I don't want to bring you anything but pleasure." He touched his lips to hers briefly. He needed to know more. So much more. He intended to research those BRCA genes, but he had a perfect source in his arms. "Other than continual checking, isn't there something else that can be done?"

She rolled her lips between her teeth and rapidly nodded. "I can have a double total mastectomy." She grabbed her breasts once again. "The surgeon takes out everything and replaces it with fake boobs."

He hesitated, but then had to ask. "How much does that decrease your risk?"

Her smile was genuine when she answered, "Between ninety and ninety-five percent."

"What the hell are you waiting for?" He twisted so he could look at her complete face. "Teagan, let's get this scheduled. From the little you told me, the longer you delay the surgery, the greater the chance the cancer will appear."

"I couldn't. My insurance company in DC considered it elective surgery." She turned her head away from him. "Between the cost for mom's memory care nursing home, living in DC, and all the testing on the new CH-53 King Stallion helicopter for the Marine Corps, I couldn't afford it or the time off work. I'd been saving up all my vacation time, then Marsha was murdered." She threw her hand toward the other side of the duplex. "I'm now mother to two small children. Are you going to take care of them while I'm in the hospital for a week and help out during the six weeks of recovery?"

"Fuck, yes. They're my kids too, you know. You are not in this alone." He would do anything, and everything, she needed. "Have you seen a...breast...specialist down here yet?" He had no idea what kind of doctor she needed, but dammit, he'd find the best one within two hundred miles. He didn't care what it cost. He would find a way to pay for her surgery if he had to. First, though, he would go head to head with the insurance company.

"No, not yet. I was going to look more seriously after the kids went back to school. They needed me here, establishing a new normal for them." She shook her head.

"Brann and Anora have been through so much lately. I'm afraid seeing me sick would devastate them."

"We could talk to their grief counselor about that." He leaned in and gave her a soft, tender kiss. "We should also talk to her about how to tell the children about us."

"Is there an *us*?" He could see the multiple questions in her eyes.

"Fuck, yes, there is an us." If Logan had his way, there always would be, but he didn't think Teagan was ready to hear that just yet. Glancing at the clock, he calculated there was enough time to hear her call his name as she came at least twice more.

He started his kisses at her chin and worked his way down her throat before paying particular attention to each breast. With nips and kisses he made his way over her flat stomach to the apex of her thighs. He liked that she spread wide for him. He spread her lips with his thumbs, then kissed her swollen clit before running his tongue through her folds as she writhed and bucked under him. He slid two fingers inside her hot wet channel, pumping them in and out as he sucked on her clit.

"Logan, I can't hold back much longer." She begged, "I want you, not your fingers."

He glanced up her body, stopping only briefly to say the single word, "Nope." He flicked her clit with the tip of his tongue and her hips raised six inches off the bed. Logan grinned. "Let yourself go."

Fingers shoving in and out, he alternated between sucking and flicking her bundle of nerves.

"Logan." She cried out his name as her entire body shook its release.

Christ. He almost lost it just listening to her come.

He grabbed another condom from the nightstand and

rolled it on, sliding inside of her while her muscles still convulsed.

Teagan's eyes flew open.

"One more time," he ordered.

Panting for breath, she managed to say, "I can't."

Holding himself up with one arm, he used the pad of his thumb to rub her overstimulated clitoris with each stroke. "Sure you can." Within a minute, he could feel her muscles tense once again. When she came the second time, he was only two strokes behind her. His entire body went rigid. Buried deep inside her, he let her spasming inner muscles milk him dry. With just enough brainpower before he blacked out, he rolled to one side, pulling her with him. He wasn't ready to lose their intimate connection.

Logan could never let her go. Teagan was his.

The alarm on his phone chimed all too soon. It was time for Teagan to return to her half of the house. He'd programmed in enough time for her to shower, but she insisted on gathering her clothes and returning a few minutes earlier than they'd promised the babysitter.

Logan slid on the jeans he'd worn out to dinner, not bothering with underwear. He snagged one of his polo shirts rather than fussing with all those buttons.

Retracing her steps, unabashedly naked, she went up and down the steps twice, more slowly the second time.

Grinning, he reached into his pocket and pulled out the scrap of lace, dangling it from a single finger. He could still smell her arousal. "Looking for this?"

She frowned up at him from the bottom of the stairs with fists planted on her tanned hips. "You owe me a new pair of panties. Those were expensive."

He fingered the soft lace as he slowly descended the stairs. "I'll gladly replace them. From now on, though, you don't need to bother wearing any when I'm around." He sat down on a step near the bottom and pulled her to him. He wanted one more taste.

Burying his nose in her trimmed golden curls, he used his thumbs to open her wet folds. He licked a circle around her clitoris before he latched on and sucked.

She moaned. "Logan, I really have to go." She stepped back. Heat blazing in her darkened blue eyes, a slow sensual smile crossed her face as she looked down at him. "Promise me, though, that we'll pick up right here next time. I've never had sex on the staircase."

"Absolutely." He'd have sex anywhere and everywhere she wanted. He stood and had her in his arms within a single step. When he kissed her, he hoped she could taste herself on him. It was his new favorite flavor.

His cell phone buzzed, interrupting them. It was the five-minute warning. Teagan needed to get next door and Logan was going to see to it that Erin got home safely.

He looked at the wall that connected, and separated, the two halves. "I'm going to talk to a contractor about putting a door right there." He pointed to a blank spot on the wall. "Then we won't have to go outside to get to the other home."

She laughed. "Just put a door between our bedrooms and call it good." Teagan grabbed her bra from the floor and quickly put it on. Still walking toward the door, she slipped the pretty blue sundress over her head. Peering into the mirror at the entrance, she combed her fingers through her mussed hair. Showing up with sex hair the first time Erin babysat for them probably would not be a good thing.

On the short walk to her side, Logan thought about the cancer gene and the beautiful, giving woman next to him. "That's why you never had children, isn't it?"

She nodded. "I wouldn't want to curse any daughter of mine with this gene."

"Is that why you've never had a serious relationship?" Logan had so many questions.

"I was engaged when they did the DNA test," she quietly confessed as she slowed their pace. "Greg said he really wanted kids and broke off the engagement. We were in the same squadron, so seeing him move on was really hard. When mom got sick and I was nearing the end of my contract, leaving the Navy was an easy decision."

"What a dick." Logan wondered if the man had ever even loved her. He didn't care if she was sick. He would be there for her. Through thick and thin.

"Yeah." Teagan sounded defeated.

Somehow, he had to convince her what a gorgeous woman she was, with or without breasts, worthy of love even though she didn't want to have children of her own.

As they walked up the steps to the house where their children slept, he realized their current situation was for her. "Did Marsha know about your condition?"

"Of course." Teagan smiled. "She was my rock, and I was hers. She went to almost every appointment with me, from the beginning. And I helped her whenever I could. When taking care of two small children, while Gabe traveled, became too much, she'd call me and ask if I wanted to play mom for a few hours, or even a day. I love Brann and Anora as though they were my own."

"I love them too, you know." Logan held open the door and followed Teagan inside. He also loved her, but knew she wasn't ready to hear those words.

CHAPTER TWENTY

The man behind the large mahogany desk was shocked at the familiar ringtone. "I'm sorry, senator, I have an emergency call coming in. Would you like to continue this conversation over drinks later this afternoon at the club?" He hoped the man would say yes. The private gentleman's club they both belonged to would give him even more secrets to use against the elected official.

He could also take advantage of the facility's private rooms. He'd been under so much stress lately and knew the powerful release he could get from the hands and mouth of Mistress Tigress would go a long way. Maybe he'd even fuck her tonight.

The man on the other end of the line agreed quickly.

"Perfect, then I'll see you at eight." He quickly opened the locked drawer and pressed the button to bolt his doors and engage the sound encryption before he answered the secure satellite phone. "Uncle. Is there a problem?" His uncle knew damn well what time and date it was, and that he would be at work. Calling him there was becoming dangerous as they moved toward their ultimate goal.

"You tell me, Abd al Rashid." His uncle sounded angry. "My sources say there are hidden files in a computer that you failed to retrieve. Partial copies are right there in your own building. You'd better hope they don't have enough to lead them to you, and you had better make sure there is absolutely nothing tangible that connects you to me. Double your security methods."

Half a world away, the man let out a heavy sigh. "Even though you are of my blood, we are all disposable soldiers in Allah's army. Let me know as soon as you have secured and destroyed those files."

The line went dead.

The man stared at the tight grain in his mahogany desk.

Who the fuck did his uncle have inside the CIA? Where the hell were those files? Who within the organization had found them?

As soon as he asked himself the last question, he knew the answer. Matthew Saint Clare. He was becoming a bigger threat every day. He allowed himself time to consider sending the special agent back through reprogramming but discarded the idea when he remembered that Saint Clare had remarried Elizabeth. She would instantly realize something was amiss, as one of the original members of the mission, and may put the fragments together. She was a very smart woman, a threat in her own right. She had been onto his uncle, Nassar al-Jamil, for years.

His own men had checked the computer they had found in Gabriel's apartment. It contained very little, only personal bills. Tax shit. Nothing of interest.

It was his own fault. He had ordered his men not to take anything that might be missed. He would not punish them for following orders precisely. Besides, they were his best protégés. They were moving quickly through the ranks at the secret camp in Pennsylvania. They had a future with his organization.

The first thing he needed to do was seek and destroy the copies currently in the hands of the CIA. Then he needed to retrieve that laptop. If Matthew Saint Clare had recently gotten possession of information, then the laptop was active, which meant its location was traceable.

He picked up the phone and called his personal geek on sub level two. Within moments, he had the location of the computer and a bit of bad news. The copies they had in-house were just that, copies. Worse, there were two copies created.

Gabe's old computer was now filled with games for young children. Unfortunately, the computer had been disconnected from the Internet too soon so his computer genius could not delve deeper into the hard drive. He was, though, able to determine that two copies of the hidden files had been created.

The man rocked back in his leather executive chair. He concluded that the laptop was now being used by Gabriel's children. If he were a gambling man, he'd bet the Marine special operator had made two copies of the hard drive and shared one with his friend Matthew Sinclair. Logically, he would keep the second copy in a safe at his house in North Carolina.

He knew exactly who he'd send to retrieve the computer and backup files. It would be good practice for his men, pitting their covert skills against those of Lieutenant Colonel Jackson. It would also be an excellent test of their creativity. This was a real-life situation, and a real-time test.

He picked up the encrypted phone and issued orders.

Glancing at the clock, he thought he'd head to the club. He had plenty of time to take advantage of the services of Mistress Tigress before he had to meet with the senator. He was definitely going to fuck her.

He chuckled. It was his doctor's orders.

He was following his doctor's orders.

CHAPTER TWENTY-ONE

"Aunt Teagan, I'm hungry," Anora whined for the thirtieth time that hour, her shoulders dramatically slumping and looking up at her with those big blue puppy eyes.

"Anora," Teagan was beyond calling the little girl any term of endearment. The child was pushing her last raw nerve. "Do you remember what I told you less than two minutes ago?"

"Yes," the four-year-old mumbled dejectedly. "I should have eaten all my breakfast. This isn't a restaurant. Lunch will be served at noon like usual." She looked up at the clock. "How many more minutes until noon?"

"Two less minutes than the last time you asked." Teagan stirred the pot of macaroni. She'd become very adept at making mac and cheese, but the noodles would only cook so fast. She hated that yellow shit with fake cheese that came in a box, so she was using the recipe that Elizabeth had shared. Setting the pasta scoop down, she picked up the wooden spoon to stir the thickening mixture of real cheese and whole milk. With her friend's help, she was getting the hang of this motherhood deal.

In her next private conversation with Elizabeth, though, she was going to find out the secret to sex. It had been two weeks since her date with Logan and they had only been able to successfully have sex once, and Brann had almost caught them. They needed another fucking date, emphasis on the word 'fucking.'

Sure, Logan had been around constantly before their amazing date, but now that they'd had sex, she seemed to want it all the time. So did he. Just the other night, as they snuggled on her huge couch under blankets watching a children's movie, he'd captured her breasts in both hands and had her so worked up she was panting. Brann had asked her if she was okay. Completely embarrassed, she hopped off the couch and retreated to the kitchen where she downed an entire glass of ice water in an attempt to cool off.

Last week they had waited until the children had fallen asleep...or so they'd thought. Thank God they'd locked the door to her bedroom. Logan had her clit in his mouth, working her perfectly with his tongue and fingers. Just as she was about to come, Brann knocked on the door, asking if she was having a nightmare. She lied to the boy for the first time and told him it was a show on television. It was the truth, though, when she'd added that she'd be sure to keep the volume down from that point on. She was surprised that he didn't hear her and Logan giggling like teenagers.

When did parents find time to have sex with children in the house? Maybe it would get easier once the kids went to school, but that was still three weeks away. There was no way in hell she and Logan would find a moment alone together during the next week. They'd have a house full of company.

The thought of the Saint Clares visiting for a week was both wonderful and terrifying at the same time. The four children played extremely well together, and Teagan was looking forward to spending time with Elizabeth. Matthew had blended seamlessly into their group. Thankfully, Logan seemed to enjoy his company, even though there was a ten-year age difference.

She and Logan had worked out the logistics for everyone. All the children would stay in her side of the duplex and Matthew and Elizabeth would take Logan's guestroom which had a king size bed and an attached bathroom.

Teagan opened the refrigerator and grabbed the almost empty gallon of milk to pour some for Anora and Brann. She quickly added milk to her growing grocery list. She would definitely need two more gallons. Scanning her list while stirring the sauce, she made the executive decision to double up on everything.

Quickly assembling the children's lunch, she called out, "Brann. Time for lunch."

The boy pounded down the stairs and shot to his stool at the breakfast counter. "Aunt Teagan, I can't find my computer. Did Uncle Logan already take it?"

"Why would Uncle Logan have it?" Between preparing for company, and in a constantly aroused state every time Logan was around, had she missed something?

"Unc—" the boy started to talk with a mouthful of food.

"You know better than that," Teagan warned.

Brann chewed and swallowed then chased it with a gulp of milk. "Uncle Matt is bringing me a new hard drive filled with games. I guess Dad's old hard drive has some work stuff still on it."

"Now I remember." Teagan thought about the flash drives containing the backup copy that were still upstairs in the loft. She probably should have locked them all in the safe in her master bedroom with her gun. Since she'd left the Navy, she'd only considered operational security where it concerned her job. She hadn't given those drives a second thought after shipping a copy to Matthew. She should probably send them back with him. She had no reason to keep them.

The phone buzzed in her back pocket. She could only hope it was Logan informing her that he didn't have to work late that night after all and would be home for supper.

Glancing at the caller ID, ice cold fear shot through her veins.

"Hello." She braced for the worst.

"Good morning, is this Teagan Williams?" The efficient female voice asked.

"Yes." Teagan's throat grew tight. Her mother hadn't been well since she'd been transported from the DC facility to the new one in North Carolina. She, and the new nurses, had feared that she had caught a virus somewhere along the way.

"This is Anna Fritz. I'm the nurse today for your mother's unit. She woke up very agitated this morning and has been calling for you. Is there any way you can come in and see her today? Otherwise, we're going to have to sedate her."

"She's calling for me?" Her mother's periods of lucidity had become nearly nonexistent in the past year. Most of the time she didn't even know who Teagan was.

"Yes, ma'am. She's been calling for her daughter.

Actually, screaming. She wants to see you," the nurse explained.

Teagan looked at her watch. It was only eleven thirty. She had so many things yet to do that day, but if her mother needed her, she would go. If she didn't have the children with her, she could move twice as fast. "Let me call my babysitter and I'll call you right back."

"Thank you. Can we tell your mother you're on the way?" The nurse suggested.

"Yes. If I can't get a sitter, then I'll bring the children with me."

"Our guests love children, so they're always welcome. We'll see you soon."

Teagan quickly called Erin who was at her door within a minute. "Hi, Ms. Williams. I'm glad you called. I've missed these two." She scooted into the house and made a beeline for the children sitting at the breakfast counter, hugging them both as they squealed with joy.

"Erin, you're back," Brann said with a huge smile on his face. He shot his arm out, nearly punching her in the face. "See what I got? It's not a watch. It's a phone." His little eyebrows pinched together. "But it does have the time, so I guess it is a watch, too."

She held her watch to show him. "Mine just tells the time. Yours is really cool."

"Erin, can we have a tea party?" Anora begged.

"Give me one minute to talk to your aunt and I'll be right back. You guys finish your lunch so we can play." Erin trotted back to Teagan as she collected her purse and keys. "I see they had their lunch. Is it okay if we just play in the sand? I'll keep them far away from the water." Her eyes lit up. "Did you hear? We're going to have a spring tide this evening that's going to be really high. My dad said they are predicting it might be one of the highest in twenty years, not counting tidal surges because of hurricanes."

"What time is high tide?" Teagan put her hand on the doorknob.

"It should reach its peak around six o'clock," Erin announced.

"Oh. No problem. I should be back home before then." Teagan started to step through the door then turned back to Erin. "We have friends coming in tonight, but they may show up early. If they do, have them call me. The kids will be fine with their aunt and uncle. I'll pay you when I get home."

Erin giggled. "It's okay. I know where you live. If they show up, I'll stop by tomorrow."

"That would be wonderful." One less thing for Teagan to worry about that day. Elizabeth had mentioned when they talked yesterday that Matthew was going to try to get off work early to avoid the DC traffic. Mentally she added another pack of chicken to her grocery list in case they made it there before supper.

Four hours later, Teagan was emotionally exhausted as she pulled into the large parking lot of the chain grocery store. When she'd arrived at the memory care facility, she could hear her mother screaming from the foyer.

As she approached the nurses' station, a tall woman with dark curly hair slid around the corner.

"Are you Ms. Williams?"

Teagan hadn't been there enough times to memorize the names of all the nurses and aides. "I am."

"Thank God you're here. We were just about to sedate her." They walked side-by-side towards her mother's room. "Thanks for coming so quickly. By the way, I'm Anna."

"Mom, I'm here," Teagan called out as she stepped into

the room. She was shocked to see that her mother had been restrained with padded leather cuffs.

"We were afraid she was going to hurt herself, or someone else." Anna slid her a glance. "She took a swing at the nursing assistants who were trying to help her."

"Who are you?" Her mother yelled. "I told them I wanted my daughter. Where's my little girl? I want my baby."

Teagan approached the bed and placed her hand on her mother's forearm. "Mom, I'm here. It's me, Teagan. I grew up." It was all she could think to say if her mother was picturing her as a child. She continued to try for over an hour to calm her mother down.

They were finally able to convince her to take a pill, which she promptly threw up. It took another two hours for them to get ahold of the doctor to prescribe an injection. She agreed with the nurses to speak to the doctor early next week to include in her standing orders that if the situation repeated, they could give her another injection. Another nurse suggested that this may have been caused by the medication they were giving her. Teagan would have to talk to the doctor about that as well.

As she walked toward the store, tears flooded her eyes with the realization that her mother was truly gone. That woman back at the long-term care facility was no longer the wonderful, caring mother who had raised her. The physical shell of that woman may not be with her long. She'd done the best she could for her mother ever since she'd been diagnosed with rapidly progressing Alzheimer's.

Now, Teagan had to be a good mother to Brann and Anora, trying her very best to replace Marsha, who she seemed to miss more that day than she had in the past two months.

Her mother, the children, week-long visitors, and her relationship with Logan, weighed heavily on her thoughts and heart.

Somehow, she managed to complete her grocery shopping, filling every square inch of her cart. When she saw the total, she almost had a heart attack. She'd never bought that much in her life. Thankfully, she and Logan had agreed that the house account would pay for everything for their friends' visit because it had been encouraged by the children's psychologist.

As she pushed the overburdened cart toward her car and popped the trunk, she hadn't been aware of the two men approaching her until they were blocking her between her car and the van next to it.

"Are you Teagan Williams?" The taller man closest to her trunk asked.

Sizing him up quickly, she could easily see that he was military. That was nothing new. There were at least fifty thousand Marines stationed at Camp Lejeune and New River Air Station, plus at least that many retirees. Although he wore civilian clothes, jeans and a tightfitting, drab-green T-shirt, he looked like any other Marine on a Friday afternoon.

"I am," she tentatively answered and started loading her SUV with groceries. "How do you know my name?" She had been to the office at MCAS New River where she would begin work in four weeks testing the Marine Corps' new CH-53 King Stallion helicopters. She'd met so many men that day, there was no way she could remember all their names.

The men moved in closer. She was still able to put the

bags into her car, but they were just a little too close for comfort. Her fight or flight instinct was kicking hard at her manners which demanded she be polite.

Covertly, she scanned the parking lot. She could push the cart into one man and swing a bag filled with canned goods at the other then sprint toward the store, screaming and yelling.

"You have something our boss wants," claimed the man on her left.

"And we have something you want." The man on her right shoved his cell phone in front of her face. A selfie of Brann and Anora filled the screen...with Ashley Helms sitting between them, smiling like a Cheshire cat.

Teagan's knees almost gave out.

She couldn't breathe.

The bag of cans dropped into the back of her car with a thunk.

"What did you do with Erin?" Teagan hated that her voice shook.

"That pretty little thing?" The man with his cell phone smiled, making chills run down Teagan's spine. "As soon as Ashley showed up and introduced herself as the children's aunt, she smiled as though she was expected and left."

Teagan was relieved that Erin wasn't going to get sucked into the situation. At least she was safe. She didn't think that Ashley would hurt Brann and Anora, but the involvement of these two men added a whole new dimension. They could hurt any one of them, or all of them, and probably would.

They hadn't disguised themselves. She knew exactly what they looked like and could easily identify them again. They were probably going to kill her. Before they did, though, she had to be sure Brann and Anora were safe.

"What makes your boss think I have something he wants?" Re-fortifying her nerves, she continued to unload the cart. Plan A was still the possibility. As soon as she was safe she could call Logan and he would find the children… or die trying.

The man with the cell phone punched a few buttons then thrusted it back in her face. "You're live with the kids. Say hello."

"Say hi to *Aunt* Teagan," Ashley said with a big smile, practically spitting out the word aunt. "We all know she's not your real aunt. I am," she sneered.

Teagan couldn't keep her eyes off the two little faces she'd come to love. They look scared.

"Are you coming home soon, Aunt Teagan?" Brann asked hopefully.

"I'll get there just as soon as I can." She hoped she could keep that promise. "You are such a brave little boy, Brann. You take care of your little sister. Will you do that for me?" He had no idea she meant for him to care for his sister…forever. Teagan was pretty sure this was the last time she'd ever see them.

Brann nodded and reached across Ashley to hold his sister's hand.

The man turned the phone toward himself. "Ten minutes. You know what to do."

"Of course, I know what I'm suppo—" He cut Ashley off by hanging up and stuffed the phone back into his pocket.

Brann and Anora scared, in the clutches of Ashley, was not the last picture of them she wanted to hold in her memory, but their looks of desperation helped transform her fear into anger. She had to figure out a way out of this. She learned in SERE school—Survival, Evasion, Resistance, and Escape, one of the many adjunct classes taught during flight training—when captured, make them see you as a human.

"Help me out here, men. Who's your boss? Maybe then I can figure out what I have that he may want." Her immediate thought went to her testing of the CH–53 King Stallion. She'd been on that project since leaving the Navy. Could these men be spies? Does some other country want to know the specs on the helicopter? It didn't make sense.

"You don't need to know his name," the taller man said gruffly. "We know what you have and you're going to give it to us." He picked up the last several bags and tossed them into the back of the SUV. "Get in and drive." He grabbed her by the bicep and jerked her toward the driver's door.

By the time she slid behind the wheel, the other man was in the passenger seat, a gun in his lap, pointed at her.

Yes. They would definitely kill her, she could see it in his eyes.

She turned the key and started the vehicle. "Where am I supposed to go?"

"Where do you think, bitch? To wherever you hid Gabriel Davis's computer and the backup copies." The man's smile was anything but comforting. "We thought that Marine officer next door had them. He doesn't have shit."

"But he does get to fuck you." His hand touched her bare knee and started creeping up her thigh under her sundress. She'd started wearing them since moving to North Carolina because they were so comfortable and easy to slip on and off. She now wished she'd worn slacks, but in the coastal heat, they were just too hot.

She smacked his hand away. "Don't touch me," she growled.

"Oh, you're a feisty one." His smile broadened. "So, you like it rough."

Oh, shit. Did they intend to rape her before they kill her?

Concentrate! You need a plan. At the moment you are holding all the cards.

She shifted the car into reverse. "Everything you want is at my house."

His cell phone seemed to appear out of nowhere. "She says they're at her house."

"We already searched there," claimed the voice on the other end.

"I know. I was there searching, too. Maybe you missed it," the man in the shotgun seat accused.

Okay. So, they had searched her house, probably while all four of them were out to supper. That would have been three days ago. They could've searched Logan's house at any time since he's gone to work all day. Her traveling companion's lewd suggestion indicated they had been watching the house for at least the last two weeks. She wasn't sure how those deductions helped her formulate a plan, but at least they had her concentrating on something other than the gun pointed at her.

She was heading home. At least that would put her closer to Brann and Anora.

If they had searched her side of the duplex while they were out to supper, then that explained why they couldn't find the laptop. Brann would've had it in the car. Inwardly she laughed at them. The backups were still in the loft, mixed in with several flash, SD, and even a few micro SD drives in a plastic box labeled NEW. During the move, her box labeled FULL had been broken so she'd combined the two. She knew which ones they were looking for, but they certainly couldn't tell the difference. Talk about hiding in plain sight.

As for the computer, she wasn't sure where it was at the moment, remembering Brann's complaint just before she left the house. She was glad these thugs hadn't found it, though.

As she thought more about it, she remembered taking the children out to pick up supper last night. Pretending to adjust the rearview mirror, she checked the back seat, mentally shaking her head when she realized what they wanted was less than three feet away. There was no way in hell she was going to tell her abductors. Nor would she give them the backup drives.

She'd figure out another way. She had to.

As soon as she had put the car in park, she flew out the door and up the steps. "Brann. Anora." She called their names in desperation. The video had shown them sitting on the couch.

They were gone. She could feel the emptiness of the house.

As her kidnappers followed her in, yelling at her, she turned to them and punched her fists to her hips. "Where the hell are my kids?"

"They're safe, with their aunt." The man raised the gun to her chest. "Get the computer and the backups. Now." He ordered.

"I want to talk to the children before I get it for you." She was going to hold her ground. "I want to know they're safe." And alive.

The same man as before punched at his phone before he said, "Want to talk to kids." He held it out to her.

She sighed and held back the tears as she forced a smile. "I'm home, now. Hopefully your Aunt Ashley will bring you home soon." She could tell by the background that they were about two blocks down the beach at their favorite ice cream shop. She swallowed hard. As the man grabbed for the phone, she called out, "I love you both."

The second man stepped into her personal space. "You've seen the brats. Where the fuck is the computer and drives?"

She decided to go with the truth. "They're in the loft." She turned and headed up the steps to the second floor. Without looking back, she climbed the spiral staircase.

It was a tight fit with the three of them, especially given the size of the men, in the small space with the slanted ceilings. She grabbed a plastic box and stirred the drives with the tip of her finger. She extracted a microSD drive, one that she knew was empty.

"Here." She handed the closest man the tiny chip.

Movement in her peripheral vision caught attention. Since they lived almost at the end of the road, people didn't often drive down their way. She instantly recognized the black SUV. Logan was almost home.

CHAPTER TWENTY-TWO

"Thanks for letting me tap into your vacation with Elizabeth and Matthew." Micah stared out the side window at the beach, smiling. "I really needed a break."

"No problem. The more the merrier." Logan knew what his good friend hadn't said was that he needed to reconnect with people who understood the life of an active duty special operator. Their whole field had changed in the past five years and neither he nor Micah believed it was for the better. Thankfully, General Lyon, commanding officer of USSOCOM, didn't either.

As Logan approached his home, he once again felt the excitement of seeing his family. He loved coming home to Teagan, Brann, and Anora. They were his. He was going to have to figure out a way to spend more alone time with Teagan. What they had started two weeks ago had become torturous to continue. He wanted to make slow love to her, showing her physically exactly how much she meant to him. Emotionally, he would be there for her, too.

She'd finally gotten an appointment with one of the top surgeons at Duke University. Logan hadn't been happy that it wouldn't be for another five weeks. They were still discussing options as to whether to take the children or see if they could find someone to babysit overnight. Erin was wonderful for a few hours at a time, but she was only sixteen.

"This is such a great place that you have here," Micah noted.

Logan's gaze swept over the duplex. Movement in Teagan's loft caught his attention. There seemed to be a lot of people up there. He wondered if Matthew had been able to get off early. Perhaps their friends were already there, and she was showing them around. When the bodies moved, the hair on the back of his neck stood straight up. There were two men in the loft with Teagan.

Micah instantly read his body language and looked to the loft. "I don't like the way this feels."

"Right there with you." Logan made a spur of the moment decision and drove by his house slowly.

"Pennsylvania plates," Micah announced. "Do you recognize that van?"

"No." Logan pulled into a driveway several doors down. He reached to his side and pulled his gun out of his holster, checking it before shoving it back in.

The base had been put on high alert nearly a week ago. Since his battalion dealt with the highest-level information, he had increased security measures to include keeping the gate to their exclusive area closed and guarded as well as all officers carrying weapons.

If someone was inside Teagan's house, threatening her to get to him, this wasn't going to end well for the intruders. "I'll go to my house, master bedroom, jump deck to deck and sneak in through her bedroom. You take the front door."

Fuck. Logan wished he had some kind of communication unit with him.

Micah pulled out a pair of earbuds. "You have some?"

"No," he said with disgust. An idea dawned and he opened the back door. The kids were always plugged in, so Teagan kept extra pairs around all the time. He checked the multiple pockets in the thingy that hung over the back of the front seats, so the children had everything they needed within reach when they traveled.

Seeing what he was doing, Micah did the same on Anora's side. Grinning across the back seat, his friend dangled pink earbuds from his fingertips.

Logan wanted to roll his eyes, but it was better than nothing. He wiggled his fingers and Micah tossed them. After plugging them into his phone, and running the cord up his back, he called Micah to test it. They worked.

Logan dashed along the dunes, noting the tide seemed to be coming in faster and higher than normal. He remembered his training officer mentioning they had to reschedule a swim due to the rip tides caused by a higher than usual spring tide. He was glad the children were nowhere near the beach.

As Logan approached his home, he crawled to the far side of one dune. Nearly crawling on the ground, he soundlessly made his way to his door. On silent feet – he moved to his bedroom, out the sliding door and leaped like a monkey from balcony to balcony. Ten seconds later, he was standing with his back against the wall next to her bedroom door.

"In position," Logan spoke in a low tone into the sparkly pink microphone hanging from his ear.

"Hall closet," Micah replied. "Downstairs clear."

"This doesn't look like the computer we saw in DC. It's all girly and glittery," a gruff voice scoffed.

"I made it mine." Teagan's voice may have been convincing to the other men, but he heard a tinge of fear. He also knew that it was her computer. Is that what they were after? "I gave you what you want. Now you need to call Ashley and tell her to bring my children back home."

Ashley? Who the hell…Ashley Helms? Was Marsha's sister involved in this?

"We need to make sure this is the right computer and backup drives." Anger wove through this second man's voice. "Downstairs, bitch."

"Stairs," Logan said under his breath.

He heard Teagan's soft steps followed by two distinct sets of pounding boots. Through the crack of the door, he watched Teagan walk across the second floor landing to the stairs leading to the main floor. Two men followed her. He waited to be sure he didn't hear any more footsteps before silently stepping out of the room.

Both men carried guns pointed at Teagan.

Anger burst through Logan. He came up silently behind the last man in line and wrapped his arm around the man's neck. It was thicker than any he'd come across before. Snapping it was out of the question. He pulled tight and attempted to choke him out but the man stiffened his neck and lowered his chin. The guy pulled his gun hand up to shoot, but Logan kicked it from his hand.

Logan saw the second man turn around to help his friend.

Micah emerged from nowhere, grabbing the second guy and dragging him down the steps.

"Run!" Micah screamed.

"No fucking way." Teagan scrambled past Micah and his

tango, to the steps where she grabbed the fallen gun. She kicked the first man square in the crotch then took a perfect shooting stance, pointing the gun at his balls. "Freeze, fucker."

The man continued to writhe, and she shot him in the knee.

He howled in pain.

"Lie still or with the next shot you'll lose your precious dick. I should shoot it off just because you touched me," she threatened.

Logan's gaze lifted to the bravest woman in the world. "He touched you?" Anger tightened his grip around the struggling man's neck. He lowered his head so his mouth was next to the man's ear. "I should kill you for that alone."

"Don't. We need them to get back Brann and Anora." When she glanced over her shoulder at Micah, Logan looked down the stairs at his friend. His tango was trussed with zip ties, blood dripping from his crooked nose as his eyes swelled.

"If you two are done playing with your bad guy, what do you need to do to get the kids back home?" Micah kept at the man on the floor. "And what the fuck are we going to do with these two?"

Teagan strode over to Micah's tango. "What were you supposed to do after you retrieved the computer and backups? Did you ever intend on bringing the children back home?"

He curled his upper lip, exposing bloody teeth. "I'm not telling you a fucking thing, bitch."

"Why don't you use his phone and call Ashley?" Logan suggested. "She should answer since it's coming from his number. See if she'll just bring the children home. If she refuses, show her that we have her friends."

"Excellent idea." Teagan had the man's phone out of his pocket and hit the redial. She put it on speaker.

"Is it over?" Ashley's voice was anxious. "Are they both dead?"

They heard young voices crying in the background. The sound shot straight to Logan's heart. Those were his children and that bitch had made them cry.

"Ashley, yes, it's over. We have taken the two men into custody." She glanced up at Logan and held his gaze. "If you bring the children back to us, right now, we won't press kidnapping charges against you."

Logan knew the love of his life was lying.

"Fuck you, bitch. These are my children, now. They promised me that I would keep the children and all their money." The woman sounded crazy. Logan could barely hear her voice over the crashing waves. She must be right next to the ocean. But where? She must be on foot. There was nowhere to get a vehicle that close because of the dunes.

A tear ran down Teagan's cheek and Logan wanted to kiss it away. He couldn't. He was still holding the tango.

"Ashley, do the right thing. Bring Brann and Anora back to the house. Their home. This is where they belong."

"They belong with me, their real aunt. They're mine now and you can't have them." The line went dead.

"Let's try this one more time. New question. Where did Ashley park her car?"

"I'm not telling you anything." The man spat blood onto the hardwood floor.

She ran her gaze the length of his bound body. "What do you think, my Navy SEAL friend, shoulder?"

At the mention of Navy SEAL, the man's eyes grew wide.

"Knee?" Teagan continued her verbal torment. She squatted down and placed the gun barrel next to his head. "Maybe I should just kill him, and we can take our chances. Ashley had them at the ice cream shop down the beach. Topsail Island isn't that big. You ready to talk, yet?"

"Fuck you."

"No, thanks." She dramatically pulled up her arm and stared at her watch. "I've got all the time in the world, but your friend over there is bleeding out."

Logan watched her eyes light up as she stared at her wrist. "We don't need them." She stood. Pulling out her cell phone, she started tapping the screen. With a huge smile she turned to Logan. "I've got them. Well, at least I know where Brann is and I'm hoping they're still all together." She headed toward the door.

"Whoa. Ice-T." Logan called out. "You need to wait for us."

"What are we going to do with these two?" Micah asked and booted the man at his feet.

"I don't want to call the cops, or an ambulance, until the kids are home safe with us." The man in Logan's arms went totally limp. He took his pulse. He still had one, so he was still alive. "Micah, do you have some more of those zip ties?"

A minute later, tango number one had his hands tied behind his back. Logan felt sorry for him and bandaged his knee using one of his field first aid kits.

Headlights flashed across the living room.

"Someone just pulled in," Teagan and Logan said at the same time.

"You think someone heard gunshots and reported it?" Teagan sounded a little worried.

"No flashing lights, so I doubt it's the local cops." Micah moved toward a window facing the street and peered through the crack. "It's Elizabeth and Matthew."

Teagan turned toward Logan. "I'll have Elizabeth take the kids next door to your house. Maybe Matthew can help with this mess. We need to go get the kids." She dashed out the door.

"Micah, help me get this asshole off the steps. I'll never get the blood out of this carpet." Logan ran his gaze down the steps. He'd have to replace the carpet anyway after he fixed the bullet hole.

His friend took the stairs two at a time and past him. "Grabbing a shower curtain."

Just as they were setting the man on the foyer tile, Matthew strode in. He looked at the two constrained men. "Good work. You've just captured two terrorists."

"How the hell can you tell that?" Logan said as he let go of his corner of the shower curtain.

"They were looking for Gabe's computer. Gabe worked for the CIA. They must have been looking for national secrets." His fake grin dropped. "I don't give a shit if they are really terrorists or not. These fuckers kidnapped my friend Teagan, but there's no way in hell I'm going to turn them over to the FBI. These assholes are mine. I have some people on the way right now to clean up this mess. Now, let's get the kids."

Teagan stepped through the door, cell phone in hand. "They're twelve houses down on the beach side, and have been stationary for the past two minutes."

Logan looked out the back door toward the ocean. The surf was really high. It was lapping between the dunes in front of their home. Although the children could swim, this tide was extremely strong with several rips. They could be carried out to sea in less than a minute.

"Micah and I will take the beachside. Teagan, you sneak along next to the houses. Matthew, you stay here and deal with this." Using the same communication method as before, Logan called Micah's cell phone. He then conferenced in Teagan, tossing her a pair of earbuds from the coffee table. Last, he added Matthew to the call.

Logan strode over to Teagan and placed his palm on her cheek. She was magnificent. Fierce. Determined. And his. He leaned down and whispered in her ear. "I love you." Pulling back slightly, he gave her a quick kiss on the lips. "Let's go get our children."

He turned to step away, heading for the deck off the back of the house. Teagan grabbed his bicep and whirled him around. She stuffed her gun in her belt and cupped his face in both hands. "Be careful out there. She's crazy." She leaned up and kissed him, soft then harder. When she broke the kiss, she remained a breath away from his lips.

"I love you, too." Stepping back, her gaze bounced between all three men. "I'm ready, now." She walked past them and out the door.

Logan and Micah were on the beach within thirty seconds. He had the GPS app open on his phone and could see the small blue dot about four hundred feet ahead. Teagan's pink dot was one hundred feet to his right and moving in tandem with him. They had to hug the dunes, often running several feet up the side to avoid the water, afraid their splashing would warn her. Surprise was always best.

"I'm just passing the yellow duplex," she whispered into the phone, but he heard her perfectly.

When they were about thirty feet away, Logan had an idea. "Ice-T, hold your position. Let's give her another chance to surrender."

Logan indicated for Micah to climb over the top of the dune and check things out. As soon as his friend disappeared around the side, Logan called out, "Ashley. Ashley Helms. Walk out with your hands in the air and we won't press charges. We just want the children returned."

"You can't have them. They're mine." Logan could barely hear the words. The wind was carrying them away.

"I see them." Teagan's voice was excited. "They are about halfway up the inside of a dune that's surrounded by water. This GPS is good, but it's not precise. Micah, move down to more dunes. Logan, you can move a little further down. There's no way she can see you. I'm moving in closer. Going silent."

"No. Teagan. Stay where you are." Logan was afraid she would move into their line of fire. She was trained. She knew what she was doing. He had to trust her and her skills.

"Ashley Helms, we have you surrounded. Walk toward the ocean with your hands in the air."

"She's headed your way," Micah announced. "I have her in my sights. Ice-T, you can move in and retrieve your children."

"I don't see her, yet." With his gun raised, Logan was scanning the dunes. He heard splashing and zeroed in on the spot. "Got her."

The woman walking into view was a replica of the one on the video from the day Marsha was murdered. Haggard, thin to almost emaciation. She looked tired and worn.

Logan was concerned that she did not have her hands in

the air. In the shadows of the dune, he couldn't tell if she had anything in her hands.

"Ashley."

She lifted her head when he called her name.

"Hands in the air above your head," he ordered.

"I've got the kids. We're heading back to the house the way I came." Teagan's pronouncement sent waves of joy through Logan. The children were safe. Teagan was safe.

Ashley hadn't moved her hands, but she was walking toward the ocean, sloshing through water up to her knees.

"Hands in the air, Ashley."

She shot up her left hand and flipped him the bird. "Fuck you."

She kept going into deeper water rather than turning toward him.

"Ashley, you can see me now. Walk towards me." What the hell was the woman doing?

"Fuck you. You're going to shoot me. They're going to shoot me. I'm going to drown in the ocean. No matter what, I'm going to die." She stopped in water nearly to her waist, swells touching her shoulders, and turned to face him. "I have nothing left to live for."

"Ashley, walk over here right now and surrender. I'm not going to shoot you." Logan did not want to shoot this woman. She was crazy. She needed help.

"That bitch, Teagan, stole my life. I was Marsha's sister and sisters are supposed to be close. But, no, Marsha chose her over me. I should've had custody of the children, but, no, Marsha chose Teagan." She pounded her chest and declared, "I should've been in charge of all that money, not her. But Marsha chose her."

Logan was so glad that Teagan was not there to listen to this insane tirade.

A wave nearly knocked Ashley down. She stumbled forward but continued, "My parents always loved Marsha more. All I ever wanted was the same thing that she had; a husband, a nice house, two kids, and a great career. Oh, and lots of friends."

In the distance, Logan could see Micah had circled around behind Ashley, but was staying out of her line of sight, and his line of fire.

"Ashley. Walk over here so we can talk about this," Logan suggested.

"I'm done talking about my sister. And I'm done talking about me. I'm not going back to rehab, ever. It doesn't matter anymore." Her gaze wandered down the beach. "They didn't get what they wanted so they're going to kill me, anyway." She raised her other hand.

Gun.

How the hell had they missed a gun?

She pointed the weapon at Logan.

He pulled the trigger at the same time as Micah.

CHAPTER TWENTY-THREE

At the sound of gunfire, Teagan's heart stopped.

She'd heard every word through her earbuds. When Micah and Logan started talking, she let out a long sigh of relief. Neither had been hurt.

"Let's keep moving, kids. Our house is only down a few more." She hoped her voice was reassuring. Ever since climbing up the dune and hugging her children, neither had let go of her.

Crossing the tidal water had given her a scare. The additional weight of carrying Anora made her sink down nearly to her knees in the water-soaked sand between the dunes, but she had righted herself and trudged through.

She'd chosen to dash between two houses and bring the children back on the paved road, as far away from the scene taking place in the rising ocean.

"We're going to stay at Uncle Logan's tonight," she announced as she steered them to the far stairway and his door. "Guess who's already here?"

"Liza and Austin?" Brann answered through chattering

teeth. Teagan knew it wasn't just because he had gotten wet in the cool ocean water, he was in shock.

As soon as she opened the door, Elizabeth ran toward her. "You're all right," she said giving her a big hug. "Let's get these kids out of the wet clothes."

"Clothes," Matthew said through her earbud. "I'm on it. Cleanup crew ETA six minutes."

"We have a third body for them," Micah announced. "We'll bring her to you."

"I can't find the fucking gun." Logan sounded angry. "She had one. I saw it."

"I saw it, too. It was a clean shoot." Micah sounded calmer than Logan. "We were justified."

"Fuck. I'll call some of my men to bring dive equipment and we'll find it." More resolved, he added, "I think we have an underwater metal detector in the equipment locker. I'll get the master sergeant to bring it."

"Good plan," Micah agreed. "I've got this, let's go."

"Here, Teagan." Elizabeth wrapped a blanket around her shoulders, bringing her attention away from the chatter in her ear. "Do you want to go next door and change?" she said aloud, then pulled her in for a hug. "You can bring back night clothes for the children," she whispered directly into her ear.

Teagan could do that. "Why don't you strip the children of their clothes and pop them into the bathtub for me." She kneeled down to be at Brann and Anora's level. "I'm just going to run next door and grab your nighty and your Batman pjs. I'll be right back."

"Why can't we go with you?" Anora asked as she clutched Teagan's neck.

"Because you are going to get warmed up in the

bathtub upstairs." She hugged the little girl who meant more to her than her own life. "I'll be back in a flash."

Brann took his sister's hand and led her toward the steps. "It'll be okay. Aunt Teagan is back. Uncle Logan and Uncle Micah will make sure that Aunt Ashley can't ever take us away again."

As though for reassurance, Anora turned and looked at Teagan.

"That's right, sweetie. I'll be back before you're done in the tub." Teagan waited until the children had turned the corner at the top of the stairs before she trotted over to her side of the duplex.

"Matthew, it's me, Teagan." She closed the door behind her and nearly tripped over the two men on the shower curtain in the foyer. Both were out cold. The bandage Logan had applied to the knee she'd shot was soaked with blood. One cheek and eye were beginning to swell. The other man's nose was off-center and both eyes were already turning black and blue.

She skirted around them and sprinted up the stairs, avoiding the bloodstained carpet.

"Matt, where are you?" She yelled as she darted into her bedroom.

"I'm in Brann's room," he replied.

Quickly lifting the sundress over her head, she tossed it into the hamper and peeled out of her underwear.

"Matt, grab the Batman pajamas under his pillow and a change of clothes for tomorrow." She changed into comfortable shorts and a T-shirt.

"Already in the bag," her friend called from the room across the hall.

Chilled, she threw on her favorite pair of sweats.

"Shorts or jeans for Anora for tomorrow?" Matthew had obviously moved on to the little girl's room.

"Better throw in both. You know how the girls are when they get together." As an afterthought she added, "Did you grab a pair of gym shoes or sandals for Brann? His are soaked."

"Already in the bag."

As Teagan stepped out of her bedroom, Matthew emerged from Anora's room holding a small suitcase.

"Cleanup crew will be here in less than two minutes. They prefer to work in private so you might want to get a move on," her friend suggested.

"Color me gone." She grabbed the bag from his hand and trotted down the stairs. Just as she was about to leave by the front, the sliding door toward the beach opened. Micah staggered in with Ashley's body in a fireman's carry, Logan right behind him.

The minute she saw her lover, she dropped the suitcase and ran to him, throwing her arms around his neck. He was soaked head to foot.

"You're home." The kiss she gave him was filled with thankfulness and joy mixed with a boatload of relief. She vaguely heard the front door open across the room.

With one hand, Logan picked up the small suitcase, and with the other, maneuvered her out onto the deck, closing the door behind them.

"The kids?" He asked as he broke the kiss.

"Bathtub," was all she could manage to get out.

He glanced to the sliding doors and watched. "You need to leave." Returning his gaze to her, he added, "I'll be there as soon as I can." He gave her a peck on the lips. "Our children need you." After handing her the suitcase, he spun her around and smacked her butt. "Ice-T, you were incredible."

"You were pretty bad ass yourself, Marine." She didn't look back as she trotted down the steps, then cut through the stilts that held up their home. She didn't want to know what the cleanup crew did. That day, that night, would be more than enough to generate nightmares for the rest of her life.

Thirty minutes later, Anora was on one side of her and Brann on the other, snuggled under a soft-as-mink blanket. In their favorite pajamas, warmed by the bath, they had finally stopped shaking.

Elizabeth had taken her children up to the king-sized bed for stories, giving them some privacy. Their friends showing up had been a true godsend.

The children hadn't said much; one-word answers when asked a direct question was the extent of their conversation. Teagan didn't know where to start, so she remained silent, holding them. The child psychologist said that the children would talk when they were ready. But this was a completely different circumstance. Maybe they needed a little encouragement.

"I'm sorry about what happened today." Teagan regretted the events from the bottom of her heart. "I'm sorry I had to leave you and go take care of Nana."

"That's okay. We understand. Nana is old." Brann patted her leg. "She doesn't have anybody else but you, and us. Is her tummy still sick? Did she eat something bad?"

Teagan loved this little boy. He had such a generous heart. After everything he'd been through that day, he was concerned about her mother. "She was just really upset, and they had to give her a shot."

"I'm not upset anymore," Anora announced. "I don't need a shot."

She hugged both children. "It's all right to still be upset. I'm still upset. I was so scared when I got home and found out your Aunt Ashley had taken you out for ice cream."

"I didn't want to go with Aunt Ashley, but Erin said that since she got here, we were supposed to stay with her and do what she said." Brann's words cut through Teagan. Those instructions were meant for Elizabeth.

"You're not mad at Erin, are you?" Teagan looked from one child to another. "She did exactly as I asked. It wasn't her fault that Aunt Ashley showed up before Aunt Elizabeth."

Neither child said anything.

"Look at me," Teagan demanded. Both turned their eyes upward to meet hers. "This was not Erin's fault. You like her as a babysitter, right?" When they both nodded their heads, Teagan continued, "We like her too. How about a promise that aunt Ashley will never come back here, again? Would that make things better?" Teagan had just made the executive decision not to tell the children that their Aunt Ashley was dead. They had experienced enough death in the last few months.

Both children nodded vigorously.

"Never?" Brann asked.

"Never. I promise." Teagan kissed both children on the forehead. They sighed in unison.

The front door opened and both Logan and Micah walked in.

Brann and Anora bolted from the couch and ran to Logan. They were both crying. He kneeled down and spread out his arms. The children buried their small faces in his neck and bawled.

Micah quietly slipped up the steps.

"You kids trying to make me even more wet than I already am?" Logan joked.

Teagan's heart liquefied into a puddle of love. She loved those children. She also loved the man holding them.

He picked up one child in each arm and brought them to the couch, sitting them beside her and tucking them into the blanket. "Will you keep my spot warm for me while I run upstairs and shower and change into my jammies?"

Logan returned five minutes later in a pair of sweatpants and a T-shirt. He crawled under the blanket next to Teagan and pulled both children onto his lap. "Now, what is with all the tears?"

"Aunt Ashley said you were going to...die." Anora leapt onto Teagan, throwing her small arms around her neck. "She said the bad men were going to kill you, too, if we weren't good and did exactly as she said."

"That fucking bitch," Logan said just above a whisper.

"We were really good. Really, really good." Tears streaked down Anora's rounded cheeks.

"Yeah, Anora didn't even cry very much when Aunt Ashley slapped her face for sassing." Brann told them.

"I..." Gasp. "I..." Gasp. "I don't know what sassy is." Hiccup. "I sorry I sassy to Aunt Ashley." Anora rubbed her cheek.

"Oh, sweetie, you're not sassy." Teagan held the small, trembling body to her chest. "You'll never see Aunt Ashley again."

"Absolutely never," agreed Logan.

"We're going to live with you and Aunt Teagan forever, right?" Brann stared into Logan's face.

"Right. Forever." Logan nodded. "But right now, I'm looking at two very sleepy little children. Their friends, Austin and Liza, are already asleep upstairs. How about we all sleep in my bed tonight? Even Aunt Teagan. Deal?"

Both children nodded eagerly. When his eyes met hers, she smiled in approval.

"Let's get these kids into bed and see if the adults would like to join us for drinks back down here." Loving Logan's suggestion, Teagan stood with a half-asleep Anora and headed upstairs.

By the time they had tucked in their two children, their guests had already made themselves at home downstairs in the living room.

Teagan took a sip of wine and savored the flavor as it washed over her tongue and down her throat. "How soon will we be able to move back in next door?"

"Late tomorrow," Matthew replied.

Damn. Those cleaners worked fast.

She settled into the soft leather couch and Logan put his arm around her shoulders. "You're going to have hardwood steps when you get back over there."

"So, do we know who the fuck those assholes were?" Micah sat down in the overstuffed chair, swirling his twelve-year-old scotch.

"Not exactly." Matthew took a sip and set his glass on the coffee table. "The plates on the van parked downstairs in the driveway, which will be gone by morning, were traced to a private compound in Pennsylvania. Homeland Security has been watching the place for over two years. They're pretty sure it's a military training camp for an extreme Muslim cell. Well-funded."

He sipped his drink and looked each person in the eye. "One of the names Homeland keeps hearing is Nassar al-Jamil."

The quiet gasp sounded almost deafening in the large living space.

"You're fucking shitting me." Micah set his glass down on the table with a thunk.

Matthew shook his head. "They rattled off a few other names, but as soon as I heard that one, I knew. It just felt right."

"It seems like everything that happens comes back around to him," Elizabeth noted. "I've been analyzing chatter from his group for over ten years. Now that Iran has given him space to establish his New Islamic State, we can't keep up with the translations."

"Do you think all this is centered around those gold bars?" Teagan couldn't keep the connection out of her mind. She shook her head. "So many deaths," she whispered.

"According to Tony Alvarez, money is one of the biggest motivators for murder." Matt took a swig. "Ten million dollars is a lot of motivation."

"Speaking of Tony, I settled his bill but told him we might need him again, now that he's familiar with our situation," Logan said. "He said he was really sorry he couldn't find out who killed Marsha."

"On that subject," Teagan interjected, "did the Fairfax cops ever reclassify Marsha's death as murder?"

"I got an email on that just before I left," Matt smiled. "Her autopsy showed no gunshot residue on either hand. The medical examiner changed it to murder."

Whoops of joy went up around the room and quieted

just as quickly when they thought about the children upstairs sleeping.

"So, was that Ashley on the video? Could she have killed Marsha?" Teagan shook her head. "Before she tried to shoot Logan, tonight, I would've said the woman wasn't capable of murder. Now, I'm not so sure."

"Clarence, my computer geek, compared the video of Tony Alvarez's meeting with Ashley at the rehab facility with the security video taken by Marsha's neighbors. He gave me some kind of accuracy percentage, but he's pretty damn sure it's the same woman."

"How can one woman look so different?" Elizabeth sipped her wine. She was so pretty, naturally. She could wear minimal makeup and still look beautiful.

"Simple. Drugs." Matthew hugged his wife. "When Ashley was high, she didn't give a fuck what she looked like. The only thing an addict cares about is where she's going to get money for the next fix. Ashley Helms would do anything for money when she needed drugs, including kidnapping her niece and nephew."

"So, her alibi was bullshit." Micah picked up his drink and held it.

Matthew chuckled. "According to the rehab center, that's where she is right now, enjoying a physical and mental cleansing at a private yoga retreat that doesn't give out its member's names."

"I take it yoga is rehab code for hooking up with your dealer?" Logan lifted Teagan's chin, so she was looking directly into his eyes. "You are never going to take yoga."

Teagan stretched up and kissed his lips. "I love doing yoga and I'm not going to stop." Then she added, "I've never done drugs, and I'm not going to start."

"I'll accept that." He kissed her nose before turning his

attention to Matthew. "Are you going to use the yoga retreat to cover…" Logan tilted his head toward the other side of the duplex.

"Fuck, no, we're not going to hide her drug addiction." Matt scowled. "Officially, Ashley Helms was hit twice in a drive-by gang shooting while trying to buy drugs. Her body will be sent home to her parents and they can deal with her one last time." Almost as an afterthought, he asked, "Have Marsha's parents ever called to arrange seeing their grandchildren?"

Teagan and Logan looked at each other. Simultaneously, they shook their heads.

"I made sure they had my phone number before they left on their RV trip up the East coast." Teagan looked at Logan expectantly.

"I don't give a flying fuck if they ever show up. As far as I'm concerned, the farther we can keep our children from that family, the better." She had to agree with Logan.

"If Ashley didn't kill Marsha, then who did? The guy in the baseball hat on the video?" Micah had a point.

"We haven't had any luck identifying that man. He was damn good. Hell, Clarence can't even be sure of the man's skin color."

Somebody killed Teagan's best friend and she would do everything within her power to see that person come to justice. "Do you think it was one of the thugs who kidnapped me?"

Matthew shrugged. "I have no idea. Both those men will be interrogated by the best. We'll have to wait and see if one of them talks."

Elizabeth yawned. "It's been a long day, and an emotional night. I'm heading to bed." She stood and reached out her hand for Matthew. "Are you coming?"

Matt stood. "Not with a bed filled with our children. Liza thinks she's a starfish and takes up half the bed, and Austin is a hot box, throwing all the covers onto whoever has the misfortune to sleep beside him." He pulled his wife to him and kissed her, hard and fast, ignoring everyone else in the room. When he broke the kiss, he turned to Logan and Teagan. "All the kids are moving to your side as soon as the cleaners are done. We have a baby to make."

Logan gave her a little hug. He leaned in close enough so only she could hear. "No babies. Our two are more than we can handle."

"Absolutely." She turned her head to whisper in his ear. "But we can still have sex. Lots and lots of sex."

Logan stood, pushing her to her feet. "To bed, woman. We have traumatized children who need cuddling."

CHAPTER TWENTY-FOUR

The man was not surprised when the unique ring tone on his secure satellite phone sounded at ten o'clock at night. It was six thirty in the morning in Iran. He pulled into an empty Christian church parking lot, the irony not missed.

"Good morning, Uncle."

Had the Caliphate for the New Islamic State already heard about the incident in North Carolina? "You tell me. Has it been a good day?"

Well, whoever his uncle had working for him in the CIA was well-connected.

"I believe so," he said with a smile.

"How can this be? Your men failed to retrieve both the computer and the data. Then they allowed themselves to be captured." His furious voice boomed across the planet.

"Everything has worked out well, Uncle. The captured men are on their way right this moment to the jail cells in my building. The hard drive from Gabriel Davis's computer is accompanying them as well as all backup copies. By morning, my time, I'll be able to put my hands on everything. I have been assured that a computer virus will be released in the CIA system tomorrow afternoon targeting anything dealing with your gold, that Syrian mission eleven years ago, and a few other items I've deemed necessary to delete."

"Your computer man can do that?" He sounded worried. Yes, his geek could do a lot more than wipe out specific files.

"Not only can he, he's already uploaded the virus. It'll trigger the millisecond anyone tries to access the information from the microSD drives." He felt smug as he leaned back into the white leather of his expensive sports car.

"What of the men? Will they talk?"

What a worrier his uncle had become. He looked up at the lighted cross in front of the church. His uncle should have more faith…in him.

"Dead men don't speak."

"It seems you have the current situation handled."

"I do. Our plans are firm. Everything will begin on the date we agreed upon. Glory will be ours, Uncle."

"Allah be with you and give you strength."

The line went dead.

He let out a long slow breath. The tension in his shoulders was almost unbearable. He needed a release.

Pulling out of the church parking lot, he headed to the private club.

Teagan lay naked, completely satisfied in Logan's arms. They were in his bed, this time completely alone.

Matt and Elizabeth had taken all four children out to lunch and a movie. It had been four days since the children had been kidnapped but Teagan would have nightmares forever about those hours they had spent with Ashley Helms.

Her friends worried about her reaction. Yes, she too had been kidnapped, but she was handling it. She had far too many things to do to worry about those few hours she'd spent with her captors. The children would be starting at a new school in two weeks. She would be heading back to work for the first time in months. She had an appointment to meet with a surgeon at Duke University and a video chat with one of the world's leading geneticists.

And then there was her mother. She had another episode a few days after the first. The doctors were doing what they could, but they couldn't stop the progression of the Alzheimer's. Teagan had already come to terms with her mother's mind. That was already gone. Eventually, the disease would take her mother's body. All she could do at this point was make her comfortable, and the new facility seemed to be accomplishing that task.

Logan tucked a stray strand of hair behind her ear. "I can practically hear those brain cells of yours. What are you thinking about so intently?"

She sighed. "My life. It's so complicated, but it is what it is. I just keep plugging along, doing the best I can."

"That's what I love about you." He placed a gentle kiss on her lips. "No matter what life throws at you, you're up for it." He shifted and leaned against the headboard pulling her up with him. "I know we said we weren't going to talk about it right away, but I need to tell you something that happened to me during all that shit that went down with Ashley and the two mercenaries."

Teagan rolled so half of her body was laying on top of

Logan. "What is it?" She ran her fingertips through his salt and pepper chest hair.

"I don't want to wait any longer." His words came out quickly.

"Okay, you can tell me." She was ready to listen.

"No. That's what I wanted to tell you. I don't want to wait any longer." He rolled to face her. "Life is too short. I have a very dangerous job. Well, it *was* a lot more dangerous than it is now, but it's still dangerous, just in a different way."

"Logan, what are you trying to say?" She wasn't really following him.

"I love you. I want to marry you. I want us to adopt Brann and Anora. I want us to live in one house, not two sides of the same building. I want to be with you, in sickness and in health, like the vows state. I want you. Forever. And I want the kids forever."

"Was that a marriage proposal?" She really needed to clarify that point. There were a lot of reasons why she had decided not to get married.

"Yes. Do I need to repeat it?"

"No. But before I give you an answer, I just want to be clear about the fact that I will never give birth." She hated the thought of losing him over this, but she was absolutely firm about this one point. "I refuse to take the chance of passing on these mutated genes. I would never curse a child simply through genetics."

"I understand and I'm good with that." His response seemed too quick.

"Are you telling me, that you would be okay without children of your own? Of your blood and DNA?" She had to be completely sure that he wouldn't change his mind. Ever.

He twisted so he was facing her. "I don't need my sperm to create more kids. I'm perfectly happy loving the two children we already have." He circled his hand in the air. "This is what I've always wanted. A loving wife, two adorable children, a great house on the beach. That's a perfect life. Well, it will be if you agree to be my wife."

"I think you need to ask me, not just give me a list of what you want." She knew she was being difficult.

"Teagan, I love you with all my heart. I can't imagine my life without you…and the kids. I promise to always love you, for better or for worse, in sickness and in health, till death do us part. Would you do me the honor of marrying me?"

"Yes." She kissed him with all the love she had inside. "I know you'll keep your promise to love us forever."

The End.

You have reached the end of *A Promise Never Forgotten,* but not the end of the series. Continue reading for a sample of *A Moment Never Forgotten*, Book #3 and the conclusion to the trilogy.
Micah finds love where he least expects it. Everyone must work together to reveal, and stop, "the man" behind the mahogany desk, and all the murderers.
Micah's story that picks up a few months after the above chapter.

CHAPTER 1 - A MOMENT NEVER FORGOTTEN

A cold December gust slapped Navy Captain Micah Reid across the face as he followed the Caisson Platoon through Arlington National Cemetery. The hard metallic klomp of steel shoes on the black horses pulling the highly polished carriage with the flag-draped casket through the arch of leafless gray trees under a sky of bruised clouds epitomized the day.

The somber processional followed Petty Officer First Class Mark Schaefer to his final resting place.

The Navy had lost a good man.

The SEALs had lost a good man.

Micah had lost a good man on one of his many teams. As Commanding Officer of Naval Special Warfare Group Two, he oversaw more than seven thousand active duty and civilian men and women. He usually didn't attend funerals unless they were for an officer or very senior enlisted in his chain of command.

Schaefer was an exception.

Micah had been in the Operations Center at the United States Special Operations Command Operational Center when "Ram", the squad's point man and breacher, had been killed. The small team had been ambushed. What was supposed to have been a clean meet-and-greet with a local asset had turned into a clusterfuck. The twenty-six-year-old, on the fast track through promotions, had entered the supposedly empty home designated by the CIA contact. Seconds later the building exploded.

Watching the op live via satellite brought back too many memories of Micah's only failed mission. Eleven years ago, his coed joint task force team had been ordered to blow up a munitions dump in Syria. A charge had detonated early before his friend, Mason Sinclair, could get out. Army Special Forces had lost a good man that night. His teammate, and good friend, Elizabeth, had lost her new husband.

Thoughts of her, now pregnant and married to the director of the CIA's covert Special Operations Group, reminded him that he was to have supper with her and Matthew Saint Clare in a few hours. He was going to need a stiff drink after this funeral.

Micah's mind wandered to the similarities between the death of Mark Schaefer and his friend Mason. Both had been killed because of bad CIA intelligence. Both had been blown to smithereens in what should have been a simple operation. Both had been in SpecOps for years and knew the dangers.

Not for the first time, Micah wondered how he had been so lucky as to have survived over two dozen missions and to have lived such a dangerous life for forty-four years. Even as a child, he'd been a bit of a daredevil.

He hadn't been nearly so lucky in love, whatever the hell that really was. He certainly didn't know. He'd never been in love. Lust. Oh, yeah. At least a hundred times a year. Even more when he was younger. As a hotshot SEAL when he'd pinned on that single silver bar for lieutenant junior grade, he thought his dick ought to be bronzed for all the women he'd fucked.

He'd been making up for the four years at the United States Naval Academy where he'd concentrated more on his studies and physical fitness rather than his female classmates. There were a few girls, but none lasted beyond the second date. He didn't have time for their silly notions of a relationship. He had a silent goal and knew that his brain and body had to be in top shape at graduation.

During his plebe summer, when asked which military occupational specialty he hoped for, he had proudly announced he wanted to become a SEAL. Big mistake. Everyone had ridden his ass that entire hot humid summer.

He had learned a valuable lesson, though, that would follow him the rest of his naval career...keep your mouth shut. Over the next four years, he never told another single person that he desired to become a SEAL. No. He was *going* to become a SEAL. His roommates had no idea. Neither did the three women he had dated during those days. No one knew until Service Selection Day near the end of his senior year when it was announced that he got his first choice, SEAL.

Graduation week Micah had stood in front of the altar of the famous Naval Academy Chapel as best man while both his roommates said *I do*, then as a groomsman for a dozen other friends who tied the knot. Willing bridesmaids had warmed his bed every night until he left for Coronado, California where he discovered base bunnies loved fucking SEALs.

He never had a long-term girlfriend. Over the years, a

few women had moved in with him, always her idea, never at his request. Coming home to a hot meal and a hot woman was wonderful, but he'd come to the realization about ten years ago that he truly wasn't comfortable around women. He never knew what to talk about with them, or what to do when he had that rare day off. Most of the women who followed him home didn't share his interests. He loved history and read nonfiction constantly. They leafed through fashion magazines and celebrity rags.

Everything was fine as long as they were in bed. He would make sure she was satisfied before he took his own pleasure. The problem was when the woman was living in his apartment, or his house, he couldn't tell her it was time for her to go. He certainly wasn't going to leave. It was his home.

Several got upset when he left them sleeping and went into the living room to watch a ballgame or just read the latest historical biography. None of them ever understood that he needed space, quiet time alone, away from her unspoken demands for attention. And why was he a magnet for the clingy ones?

In retrospect, he was thankful they seldom lasted long. That was probably his fault. When he was sent out on a mission, he rarely remembered to call his female roommate-with-benefits and let her know he was leaving. He could never tell her where he was going or how long he would be gone. Operational security was sacred. He was all about the mission, always. He had to be. Lives depended on him.

But there was no way he could have saved either Mason Sinclair or Petty Officer First Class Mark Schaefer.

The caisson came to a stop at the orders of the platoon leader. The pallbearers lined each side and through the solemn ceremony that Micah had seen far too many times, Schaefer's fellow SEALs slid the casket off the carriage. He knew those men were cold. They had opted not to wear the all-weather coat over the Navy blue crackerjack uniform so they would have easier access to their Trident.

Every SEAL attending the ceremony converged in two straight lines from the caisson to the gravesite. Micah stepped in last alongside Commander Evan Hubbard, Commanding Officer of Team Two, and across from Lieutenant Knox, Schaefer's Platoon Officer in Charge. By the look on the young officer's face, he'd been close to Schaefer. Unfortunately, Micah was very familiar with the younger man's gut-wrenching pain.

The pallbearers stepped slowly through the sentinel of SEALs. Each pulled off his precious Trident pin and pressed it into the lid of the coffin before offering Petty Officer Schaefer a personal salute. Although Micah's was the last in the line of shiny gold pins, the pallbearers would add theirs after folding of the flag, just before it was presented to his wife along with the bullet casings from the twenty-one-gun salute.

"The Schaefer family would like to thank all of you for attending," the minister announced as soon as the benediction prayer was completed. "The family will have a private gathering at their home later this evening. May God be with you all and keep you safe."

The chorus of "amen" was swept away on the frigid breeze.

Micah's feet were chilly. He hated the shiny corfam shoes that were part of his dress blue uniform. Cold emanated from the earth and seeped through the leather soles and thin patent leather uppers. He was more a boots-on-the-ground comfortable camouflage officer than spit and polished office dweeb.

"Sir, are you staying in D.C. for the night or heading back to Virginia Beach?" Commander Evan Hubbard asked him in a low tone as they walked through the neatly trimmed grass back toward the paved road.

"I'm staying up here for the weekend with old friends." He grimaced. "I'm taking a few days for house-hunting."

"We're all hoping you can help us out from your new desk at the Pentagon." Evan scanned the crowd then lowered his voice even more. "It seems like we're losing more men every day under these new *directives*." He spat out the last word. "If this shit keeps up, next thing we know we're going to have to send the bad guys a letter telling them what day and time we'll be invading their base of operations then give them a call the day before to remind them. Fucking politicians sticking their nose into war. I especially hate the ones who have never served and have no real concept of what we are faced with every day."

"You're preaching to the choir." Micah was thankful his feet were moving and warming up. "You know I'll do whatever I can."

"Mom." Someone called from off to their right.

"Thanks for coming, Momma Barker." A second man said over the first.

"Hey, Mom Barker, we really appreciate you coming." Sailor number three spoke loudly.

All the deep voices and the sea of enlisted blue uniforms taking turns hugging an unseen woman caught the attention of both senior Navy officers. Lieutenant Knox caught up to them, then broadly smiled at the scrum of his platoon.

"Sirs, would you mind taking just a moment to come

over and meet Mom Barker? She would be thrilled to meet you both." The lieutenant gestured toward the woman just ahead and to the left. As though to explain, he continued, "She adopted the entire platoon when Mak became Bravo Squad Leader. We get a care package from her almost every week. That lady can bake."

One glance at each other and a slight nod was all it took for Micah and Evan to change directions. On their approach, the blue uniforms parted, and Lieutenant Knox swept in.

After a brief hug, the lieutenant stepped back from the pretty woman in her mid-forties genuinely smiling as her gaze swept all the men in their twenties surrounding her. "Mom Barker, I'd like you to meet Commander Hubbard and Captain Reid. Sirs, I'd like you to meet one of the most supportive SEAL mothers, Berit Barker."

Micah couldn't place her, but he knew he'd met the tall woman with a distinct professional air once before. She'd probably attended one of the social functions the teams occasionally held. Her heart-shaped face surrounded by dark brown hair with its God-given silver strands was so familiar. When blue-gray eyes that matched the winter sky met his, he was sure they'd met.

"Nice to meet you, Commander Hubbard." She shook Evan's hand first since he was closer. "I'm sorry it was under such sad circumstances." She sniffed and rolled in her lips as though biting back the tears. "I'm going to miss Ram."

"Yes, ma'am." Evan dropped his large left hand over both of theirs. "We're all going to miss him."

As her eyes tracked to Micah, they widened. The corners of her mouth quirked up. "Captain Reid, it's nice to see you again." She slid her right hand out from between Evans' and extended it toward him.

At his obvious lack of recognition, Berit continued, "It seems like just yesterday we laid Senior Special Agent Gabriel Davis to rest."

Click.

Berit Barker. They met briefly at Gabe's memorial service. Micah still wasn't sure how he felt about his former friend. She'd helped Marsha Davis with the arrangements for her estranged husband's funeral. Micah figured she was the CIA version of the military's Casualty Assistance Officer. Her boss, Joseph Lambert, had mentioned that she would be helping Marsha over the next year. Obviously, that didn't happen.

Her gloved hand slid into his.

She stepped in closer and lowered her voice. "I was sorry to hear that Marsha was killed the next day. It's my understanding that the Fairfax police believe she interrupted a home invasion and was shot by the armed robber. Have they caught the man yet?"

That was such a bull-shit story they had filed. All four members of the original Syrian mission believed it was much more than that. Someone had shot Marsha with Gabriel's gun then staged the area to look like a suicide. With the help of Matthew, and a private detective they'd hired, they had finally convinced the police to change the cause of death to homicide.

At Berit's expectant look, Micah bit back the derogatory retort he almost blurted. Instead, he managed to answer, "Her murder remains unsolved. They're supposedly still looking for the man caught on video by several neighbors' security systems, but I don't think they're looking very hard."

"I'm sorry to hear that." Berit seemed to be an unusual combination of casual and professional. He knew few female flag officers who maintained the same kind of bearing. "I've been working with Teagan Williams, I mean, Jackson, establishing education funds for Gabriel's children through a foundation we have. I'm also handling the confusing payout of his life insurance due to the unusual circumstances."

Visions of young Brann and little Anora playing in the sand at Topsail Island beach in their wedding clothes popped into his mind. His good friends, Logan and Teagan, had become husband and wife in an oceanside wedding in early September. Once again, Micah had been a groomsman in the small ceremony.

He grinned. "I don't imagine insurance companies often see the godparents taking on the responsibility of raising two small orphans." His grin grew into a smile. "Did you know they're trying to adopt Anora and Brann?"

When Berit smiled her whole face lit up. It struck him that she was pretty in a way that only older women could be. There was also intelligence learned from life experiences—that couldn't be hidden. "Teagan told me that. I'm so happy for all of them, but especially the children. Kids need parents." Her gaze wandered over to the pallbearers before returning to meet his eyes. "The next time you see Teagan, please tell her I said *hi*."

"She's coming up tomorrow, along with Logan, and of course the children. She has to handle some of the probate issues." Micah wasn't sure why he was explaining all this to Berit.

"Commander Hubbard, sir, permission to hug my mom." The anxious SEAL saluted Evan.

"Permission granted." His friend of several years, and

SEAL Team Two's Commanding Officer, smiled as the heavily bearded man in his mid-twenties threw his arms around Berit Barker and lifted her off the ground. She lost one of her black low-heeled pumps but didn't seem to care. The joy on her face said everything. She loved this young man.

"The petty officer we just buried was on Mak's team," Evan said in a low voice meant for only Micah. "He should still be in the hospital in Germany, but he and two of the less-injured men, insisted on accompanying the body back. They may be able to ship back the others next week."

When the young sailor finally set his mother back on the ground, Evan called to him. "Mak, have you ever met Captain Reid?"

"No, sir." He performed a perfect about-face and strode the three paces to face Micah. He came to attention and snapped a salute. "Petty Officer First Class Makensey Barker, sir."

Micah returned the salute and the man in his mid-twenties lowered his right hand. If he hadn't been carefully watching, he would have missed the slight wince. "What are your injuries?"

He heard Berit's gasp but didn't take his eyes off the man in front of him.

"Two broken ribs, flying debris grazed my right shoulder, and I'm still thirty-five percent deaf in both ears." He squared his shoulders imperceptibly. "Nothing major. I'm good to go, sir."

Micah nodded once. Those injuries were all to be expected given the explosion he had watched via satellite. He was confident that Evan would keep the squad stateside for at least six weeks while the men recuperated. Christmas stateside was a possibility in between training exercises. Slots would have to be filled with FNGs straight out of BUD/s. Deciding where the Fucking New Guys would best fit in was no longer Micah's job. He trusted Evan to rebuild Mak's squad. In a matter of weeks personnel issues at Naval Special Warfare Group Two would no longer be his concern. He had orders to the Pentagon.

"No, you're not *good to go* anywhere except to the hospital." Berit's declaration kept Micah's brain from wandering into his future. She spun around and got into his face. "You are going to order my son, and the rest of his squad, to report tomorrow morning to Walter Reed Medical Center where they will undergo extensive testing to determine the precise extent of their injuries. None of them are fit for duty until their bones are completely healed."

Petty Officer Barker looked ready to panic while Evan was visibly fighting to withhold a snicker.

"Sir, permission to remove my mother. And please forgive her. She's used to ordering people around over at Langley." His shoulders raised a fraction of an inch. "She's kind of a big deal over there."

"Permission denied." Micah had never seen a woman defend a SEAL. He wasn't sure he'd ever seen the mothering instinct displayed before in his life. He was both impressed and amused.

Micah's mother had died when he was five and his father never remarried, so he had never seen a mother in action. It had always been just the two of them in the house on the shores of Lake Erie.

There were only two hundred seventy-two people who could give him orders and all except the President of the

United States wore stars on their shoulders. Yet, this woman had just given him a direct order.

Through his peripheral vision, Micah could see all the eyes of the young sailors staring at him. He held her gaze. "Thank you, Ms. Barker, for your *suggestion*." He purposely emphasized the last word. "I'm sure Commander Hubbard will take it under consideration…next week."

He lifted his head, his gaze sweeping over all the young faces in Navy dress blue uniforms around him. He understood their emotions and knew they needed a break. "Gentlemen, since tomorrow is Friday, and I believe we have all been through enough today, liberty is granted until oh eight hundred Monday."

"Ten hut," Mak called out.

Everyone wearing a uniform came to attention, even Micah.

"Sir, on behalf of the men, I would like to thank you." Mak raised his hand in salute and all the SEALs followed.

"Sir, thank you, sir," they said in unison.

Micah and Evan saluted back. "Enjoy your weekend, and for Christ's sake, stay out of trouble. SEALs have been getting enough bad press lately. Dismissed."

Cheers resounded as fists pumped into the air.

"I'll meet you all back at Mom's house." Mak's voice carried as they all but ran to their cars.

"It looks as though I need to stop by the grocery store on my way home. Best I be going." Her smile was that of a proud mother.

"Commander Hubbard, it was a pleasure meeting you." Berit had moved back into her warm yet professional persona.

"The pleasure was all mine." Evan grabbed her hand and enveloped it in both of his, giving her his lady-killer smile that under other circumstances was almost a guarantee to get him laid. He was between wives, again, but Micah thought the man had more class than to troll for women at a funeral. On the other hand, there was something special about Berit Barker.

She returned a congenial smile. "Until next time."

When she retrieved her hand, she thrust it toward Micah. "Captain Reid, it was nice to see you again. Perhaps next time we meet it will be under more positive circumstances."

He shook her hand in the professional manner it was offered. "We can only hope."

Micah and Evan started walking in the opposite direction where military drivers waited with official vehicles, secretly armored to protect two of the most sought-after Navy SEALs on the East Coast.

"She's something else, isn't she?" Evan commented. "For a few minutes there, I'd forgotten who she really is, besides being Mak's mother."

"What the fuck are you talking about?" Micah's mind had been desperately hoping that his driver had the heat on. Ever since he'd experienced light frostbite on a mission years ago in North Korea, his toes were extremely sensitive to the cold.

"Berit Barker," Evan said as though Micah should have known.

"What about her?" Then he remembered his conversation with her and decided he should explain his connection to her. "Ms. Barker handled the funeral arrangements for an old friend of mine who used to be the Director of Special Activities at the CIA. She's some kind of Casualty Assistance Officer for them."

"No, she's not." Evan stopped and turned to face him.

"Berit Barker is the Deputy Director for Support for the entire CIA. At her new job, she's poached more than a dozen of our best SEALs in just the past year. She was an in-country handler for years, one of the first female station chiefs in Africa. She wanted Mak to go to high school in the USA, so she came home and has been in clandestine services ever since. Rumor has it that Joseph Lambert is getting ready to retire and she'll step into his job as the number five person in the whole CIA. If scuttlebutt is right, she's being groomed as the first female Chief Operating Officer, as in the civil servant who actually runs the CIA."

"Holy fuck," Micah said on an exhale. She was one hell of a woman. If given the opportunity, he'd enjoy getting to know her better.

This concludes the sample of *A Moment Never Forgotten*. To buy the rest of the book, check here for the format you prefer... https://kalyncooper.com/a-moment-never-forgotten

ALSO BY KALYN COOPER

BLACK SWAN SERIES

Military active duty women secretly trained in Special Operations and the men who dare to capture the heart of a Woman Warrior.

Unconventional Beginnings Prequel (Black Swan novella #0.5)

He's dead. But they can't allow it to affect her. She's too important.

Download FREE https://dl.bookfunnel.com/uec4utb66d

Unrelenting Love: Lady Hawk (Katlin) & Alex (Black Swan novel #1)

Women in special operations? Never… Until he sleeps with the most lethal woman in the world.

Noel's Puppy Power: Bailey & Tanner (A Sweet Christmas Black Swan novella #1.5)

He's better at communicating with animals than women, but as an amputee she knows firsthand it's the internal scars that can be most difficult to heal.

Uncaged Love: Harper & Rafe (Black Swan novel #2)

The jungle isn't the only thing that's hot while escaping from a Colombian cartel.

Unexpected Love: Lady Eagle (Grace) & Griffin (Black Swan novel #3)

He never believed in love, but he never expected to find her.

Challenging Love: Katlin & Alex (A Black Swan novella #3.5)

A new relationship can be fragile when outsiders are determined to challenge that love.

Unguarded Love: Lady Harrier (Nita) & Daniel (Black Swan novel #4)

She couldn't lose another sick baby…then he brought her his dying daughter.

Choosing Love: Grace & Griffin (A Black Swan novella #4.5)

Hard choices have to be made when parents interfere in a growing relationship.

Unbeatable Love: Lady Falcon (Tori) & Marcus (Black Swan novel #5)

Scarred outside and in, why would his beautiful friend ever want more with him?

GUARDIAN ELITE SERIES

Former special operators, these men work for Guardian Security (from the Black Swan Series) protecting families in their homes and executives on the road, but they can't always protect their hearts.

Double Jeopardy (Novella #1 Guardian Elite series crossover with Hildie McQueen's Indulgences series)

Guarding a billionaire and his wife isn't easy when you can't keep your eyes off your bikini wearing, gun carrying partner who is lethal in stilettos.

Justice for Gwen (Novella #2 Guardian Elite series crossover with Susan Stoker's Special Forces World)

She's not what she seems. Neither is he. But the terrorist threat is real. So is the desire that smolders between them.

Rescuing Melina (Novella #3 Guardian Elite series crossover with Susan Stoker's Special Forces World)

When Jacin awoke stateside, he remembered nothing about his escape from the Colombian cartel or his torture. He was sure of only one thing, his love of Melina, his handler. When she disappears, neither bruises nor the CIA will keep him from rescuing her.

Snow SEAL (Novella #4 Guardian Elite series crossover with Elle James Brotherhood Protectors World)

Terrorists want her…but so does he. The chase isn't the only thing that heats up when the flint of the former SEAL strikes against the steel of the woman warrior.

Securing Willow (Novella #5 Guardian Elite series crossover with Susan Stoker's Special Forces World)

Guarding her wasn't his job, but he couldn't let her die…even before she stole his heart. When he discovers the temptingly beautiful foreign service officer is being threatened, his protective instincts take over.

SEAL in a Storm (Novel #5 is part of the Suspense Sisters new wave of connected books, Silver SEALs featuring a seasoned hero and heroine, second chances, and edge of your seat suspense.)

With a hurricane bearing down on the tiny island, they only have days to find and rescue ten kidnapped young girls and their chaperones…and keep their hands off each other.

CANCUN SERIES

Follow the Girard family —along with their friends, former SEALs and active duty female Navy pilots— as they hunt Mayan antiquities, terrorists and Mexican cartels in what most would call paradise. Tropical nights aren't the only thing HOT in Cancun.

Christmas in Cancun (Cancun Series Book #1)

Can the former SEAL keep his libido in check and his family safe when the quest for ancient Mayan idols turns murderous?

Conquered in Cancun (Cancun Series Novella #1.5)

A helicopter pilot's second chance at love walks into a Cancun nightclub, but she's a jet fighter pilot with reinforced walls around her heart.

Captivated in Cancun (Cancun Series Book #2)

His job is tracking down terrorists so he's not interested in a family. She wants him short-term, then needs him when their worlds collide.

Claimed by a SEAL (Cancun Series crossover Novella #2.5 with Cat Johnson's Hot SEALs)

How far will the Homeland Security agent go to assure mission success when forced undercover for a second time with an irresistible SEAL?

Never Series

The mission brought the five of them together, disaster nearly tore them apart, a mystery and killer reunited them forever.

A Love Never Forgotten (Never Series novel #1)

Dreams or nightmares. Truth or lies. He can't tell them apart. Then he discovers the woman who has haunted his dreams is real. Is she his future? Or his past?

A Promise Never Forgotten (Never Series novel #2)

As a Marine Lieutenant Colonel, he could take on any mission and succeed. Raising his two godchildren…with her…just might kill him.

A Moment Never Forgotten (Never Series novel #3)

The moment he realized she was in serious danger…he couldn't protect her.

ABOUT THE AUTHOR

KaLyn Cooper is a USA Today Bestselling author whose romances blend fact and fiction with blazing heat and heart-pounding suspense. Life as a military wife has shown KaLyn the world, and thirty years in PR taught her that fact can be stranger than fiction. She leaves it up to the reader to separate truth from imagination. She, her husband, and Little Bear (Alaskan Malamute) live in Tennessee on a micro-plantation filled with gardens, cattle, and quail. When she's not writing, she's at the shooting range or paddling on the river.

For the latest on works in progress and future releases, check out KaLyn Cooper's website www.KaLynCooper.com http://www.kalyncooper.com/

Follow KaLyn Cooper on Facebook for promotions and giveaways https://www. facebook.com/KaLynCooper1Author/

Sign up for exclusive promotions and special offers only available in KaLyn's newsletter https://kalyncooper.com/ kalyn-cooper-newsletter facebook.com/kalyn.cooper.52

twitter.com/KaLynCooperbooks

instagram.com/kalyncooper

bookbub.com/authors/kalyn-cooper